The Guardians

Loving Eyes Are Watching

Richard Williams

authorHOUSE®

AuthorHouse™
1663 Liberty Drive, Suite 200
Bloomington, IN 47403
www.authorhouse.com
Phone: 1-800-839-8640

First published by AuthorHouse 9/29/2008

ISBN: 978-1-4343-7663-3 (sc)

Library of Congress Control Number: 2008903827

Printed in the United States of America
Bloomington, Indiana

This book is printed on acid-free paper.

Chapter One

Reflection

It was on a cold, gray, autumn day when we saw the dark blue Lincoln SUV driving up the long driveway. It was coming to take us to our new house. We were leaving the home where we had been so very happy with our mistress, Sally. Current events had us heading to a new place. Our future did not hold the promise of the same amount of happiness we had known living with Sally. She had passed away, and her brother, Bill, was coming to take us to live with him. He had promised Sally while she was sick, he would take care of us. He assured her we would have a safe home, and that he would not give us away. We were both so terribly sad over the death of Sally. We had lived with her for years and our lives had grown so intertwined. You see, Sally knew our secret, and had kept it for all those years.

* * * * *

Sally Thomas was the kind of person who would make one feel comfortable the moment she entered the room. At least, that's how she always made me feel. She loved us, and the years we shared together were some of the most wonderful years of my life. We knew she was very sick, and like everyone in the family, we came to hate the very sound of the word *cancer*. But, I'm getting ahead of myself. Let me take you back to the beginning.

* * * * *

We first saw Sally one warm, spring afternoon when she walked into the door of the screened-in porch at Mrs. Louis Browne's home. Sally had light red hair and the bluest eyes you have ever seen. She had a wide, friendly, wonderful smile. She was tall, however, one shoe was built up because her right leg was two inches shorter than her left leg. Sally came, hoping to adopt only a little male puppy, but Mrs. Browne told her we were a pair, DJ and me, and that we had to go together. She told Sally how DJ had been seriously injured when he was very young. No one, not even the vet, thought he was going to live. But, he's a fighter, and he did pull through. The situation left him scarred for the rest of his life. Not scarred as one might think, with something visibly noticeable. The scar was inside and would cause him pain and insecurity for many years. That's why we were a pair. Mrs. Browne knew we would be good for each other, and that his injury had not, nor would not, matter to me. I loved the silly little puppy. I wanted to stay with him and probably some inner female, nurturing instinct, made me want to take care of him. After Sally heard about DJ's injury, she reached down and picked him up and held him close to her.

"I understand how you feel little man," she said. "Don't you fret, you will be safe with me."

I just stood there waiting to see if, indeed, Mrs. Browne was going to let DJ go without me. That's when Sally looked down at me. She knelt down, put her arm around me. "Don't worry Maggie, you're going too," she stated while looking into my eyes with great compassion. "we're going to have a good home together."

* * * * *

At that time we thought Sally was going to be our caretaker for the rest of our lives. You see, Mrs. Browne knew about our special gifts and she always said to us, "God will send the one who needs you two the most to my doorsteps."

After the papers were filled out and Sally paid for our adoption, she loaded us up into the cage in her Toyota to take us home with her. We were both a little nervous and also happy. We, at last, were going to have a permanent home.

* * * * *

Sally talked all the way home about the house where we were going to live. Her boyfriend, Steve, had just asked her to marry him. She was giddy about everything it seemed. It really looked as if we were going to have a really easy 'assignment', and just have a nice life where everything was going to be simple and wonderful. I remember looking over at DJ, and seeing a far away look in his eyes.

Later on that evening after Sally had settled into bed, and we were in our cage in the laundry room, I asked DJ, "What's the matter with you, Bud? This looks like a wonderful set up for us."

With the same far away look in his eyes that he had this afternoon, he said, "Maggie, don't be fooled into thinking everything is going to be a bed of roses. We're here for a reason, and that reason just hasn't come to light yet. I am certain Sally is going to need us down the road."

I laughed at him and replied, "Silly boy," but in all honesty, I was the one being silly. Little did we realize how, not far into our future, everything in Sally's world was going to turn upside down. DJ was right, we were there for a reason, and Sally's need would be almost overwhelming.

* * * * *

We had only been there a short while when everything in Sally's world seemed to crumble. Steve had been traveling a lot with his job, and had not been around. It was still a surprise when he phoned to end their relationship because he had found someone else and had fallen in love with her. I remember how hard Sally cried that night and how hurt she was. The pain which settled in her heart was going to cause her so much trouble. Sally began to change. She started staying out late every night, drinking and partying. It seemed she ended almost every evening by bringing some new guy home with her. Inevitably, the morning after, she would say "I don't know why I let him stay over last night. It seems no one will love me for who I really am. I'm just not like everyone else."

I so wanted to tell her she was wrong, but we were bound by an oath never to reveal our secret to anyone. All we could do was sit back and watch as Sally headed down her road of self-destruction. Oh, we showed her all the love we could, but she wasn't seeing anything but her own hurt and disappointment with life. There were times when she would walk in, then, immediately head right back out the door, as if by keeping on the go she would forget the hurt she had experienced.

* * * * *

Every night DJ and I would pray while she was out, always asking for angels to watch over her. This mad race went on for over a year. Sally lost weight and her health began to deteriorate, yet she just kept on running from all the pain she didn't want to face. I remember one night while we were praying, DJ, looked over at me with such sadness in his eyes. He said "Maggie, if something doesn't happen soon, I fear we will lose Sally."

"You must never say anything like that again," I chided. But, deep down inside I knew he was right.

Sally was becoming more depressed, and we often heard her mumbling about not wanting to live anymore. In the early stages of the depression, Sally would snuggle both of us with her on the sofa and say, "I've got you two. I'll just be happy with that." However, soon the phone would ring, and off she would go with a new guy, hoping this time it would end differently.

* * * * *

That's how it happened, the night Sally found out about our secret. She came home crying again. This time she was completely out of control. She was yelling at us, "I wish I had never gotten you, then I could just do whatever I wanted to."

She swore under her breath as she rummaged through the medicine cabinet in search for something. "Yes, here it is," we heard her say. With bottle in hand, Sally went into her bedroom and sat down on the bed. Both of us jumped up onto the bed and sat near her. That's when we discovered she had a large bottle of sleeping pills. She just sat there looking at the bottle of pills talking to herself.

"No one loves me. I don't care whether I live or die, and obviously no one else does either. I might as well take these and die and just be done with it all. I'll just sleep away," she mumbled, almost in a whisper.

She opened the bottle and before she took any of the pills, she just looked up to heaven and said, "God, if you're up there, then why don't you care about me?"

As she reached for the glass of water she had placed on the bedside table, I broke my oath. "Sally," I said loudly. " He does care about you, very much in fact."

A startled, fearful look appeared on her face. She looked up, as if a voice was coming from heaven, then all around the room. Meekly she asked, "Who said that?" Then with fear and trembling she asked again, "Who's in my room?"

"I am," I said, "and I am here to tell you that God ***does*** love you."

She turned suddenly and looked at me. "Maggie?" she questioned, "Did you say that?"

"Yes, I did, and I have wanted to tell you for the longest time how wrong you are about no one loving you," I replied emphatically.

I heard DJ behind me, "Maggie, no! We're not supposed to tell anyone our secret!"

" I'm not going to let her hurt herself, DJ. I'm not! I don't care about oaths or anything like that right now. Sally needs us, and that's why we here in the first place. You know that," I snapped back.

With that Sally dropped the bottle of pills, threw her hands over her face and cried, "I'm losing my mind, I have been drinking so much... I think my dogs are talking." I walked across the bed, laid my head on her shoulder and said, "No love, you're not losing your mind. You have just lost sight of what true love is all about, that's all."

"But how can you talk, and what love are you talking about anyway?" she almost wailed.

" How we can talk, is as old as time itself, but as to love, it's God's love that you're looking for Sally. It's his love that will fill your heart with peace and that will take all the hurt and pain away," I continued.

* * * * *

DJ moved closer to us on the bed. "Oh Maggie! What a mess you've gotten us into with your big mouth!" he yipped.

"Would you have just stood there and let her take those pills?" I asked with what was probably an air of condescension.

He held his head down for a moment, then replied quietly," No, But Maggie what about our oath?"

Sally looked confused while asking, "What oath? Why are you just now talking to me? Why?"

That's when I just giggled a little, replying, "Well, we have really had to discipline ourselves to keep our mouths shut."

Sally had such a strange look on her face as she looked at us. "Did you just giggle Maggie?"

" Why yes, I guess I did," I answered, then I giggled again.

"Oh, don't pay her any mind about that Sally," said DJ "She's always giggling about something when you're not at home."

Sally looked at me quizzically. "What *is* this love you're talking about? I'm not understanding what you're trying to tell me."

"Why, God's love Sally," I gently stated. "He's the one who has done so much for you, even though you are totally unaware of it. He's the one who has been trying to reach you in the midst of your pain."

Sally was crying again, and at first, I had to admit, I didn't know if she was crying because we were talking to her or if she was beginning to grasp some truth about God's love.

* * * * *

"Well, if He loves me so much, then why did He allow all this crap to happen to me?" she questioned with anger.

I moved around where I could look into her face, and did just that for the longest time. I wasn't sure just how much I should tell Sally, but then I knew it didn't matter anymore, because she already knew more than she was supposed to anyway. Just as I started to speak, DJ spoke up and said, "Sally, if God was behind all the trouble that's happening to you, why did He send His Son to die for you and why did He plan to have us here right now, when you were going to need us the most?"

" Oh Sally," I said as I placed my head on her arm, "you've looked for the wrong kind of love, and it has left you empty inside. Don't you understand that's why you feel as if no one could ever love you, when in truth, you've been running from the very love your heart has been looking for?"

"No, I don't understand. You tell me, how do ***I*** find this love? I've looked everywhere, and still can't find anyone to truly love me."

" Love, true love, Sally, will never be found in a boyfriend, but only in the love of God's Son."

"Yes, that's right," DJ agreed. "That's the only place you will ever find true love."

Sally looked so confused, she threw her hands over her face again. She just shook her head sobbing, " I must be out of my mind, dogs don't talk.... I must be out of my mind, dogs don't talk....I must be out of my mind, dogs don't talk."

Taking my head off her arm, I explained, "We are guardians, my dear, not dogs."

"Well, we are dogs," DJ butted in, "but not like the kind of dogs you're use to. We're here for one purpose and one purpose only."

" What! What purpose?" Sally said almost yelling it at us.

"To show mankind the love of the Creator. You have heard of guardian angels. We are not supposed to tell anyone. However, we have been instructed by God to tell our owners if we must. Our responsibility, is then, to tell about God's wonderful love, He has sent to you through His Son," I quickly responded.

* * * * *

"Oh, God!" she wailed. "That is just stories from childhood, like nursery rhymes. Besides, I've been so bad, why would God love me now?"

"His love, Sally, isn't dependent on how good you are," I told her. "It is given to all humans because He is so loving and good. All you have to do is to open your heart to Him right now, Sally. God so wants to fill the void in your heart with His cleansing love."

DJ and I just sat there as we watched Sally fall to her knees on the floor beside the bed and began to cry. The agonizing sobs went on for a long time. We knew it was a cleansing of her soul. Finally, she raised up, reached for a tissue on the bedside table, blew her nose, and sat there looking out into space. Then the sobbing began again. There was a glow on her face. We knew this time the sobs were for joy-- the pure joy of finding what you've been searching for.

We sat up all that night talking and answering all Sally's questions about us, but she had to promise us she would never tell a soul about us.

* * * * *

At that point in our relationships with her, we entered into a time of so much happiness, which I convinced myself, would go on forever. Sally changed. She had found herself. She was happier, and she was taking better care of herself again. Plus, she would read to us every night. I liked the book of Ruth, but DJ liked the book of Acts.

One night as Sally was reading to us, DJ spoke up, "Boy, if I had lived back then, my assignment would have been to travel with Paul."

I upset him when I laughed at him the night he told us. He got up to jump off the bed and leave the room, but Sally caught him and pulled him close to her, and whispered in his ear, "I can see you doing just that DJ, and what a fine helper you would have been to Paul.".

DJ put his head back on her and with love in his eyes, licked her on the side of the face. "Thank you, I love you, Sally," he responded quietly.

Tears filled her eyes, as she held him close. She then reached out to pull me close, as well. "I love you two more than you could ever know. You truly are my guardians. Just think, without you, I might not be here right now." We both sat by Sally, one on each side of her as she continued to read to us. I don't know how long Sally read, but by morning, we had all fallen asleep. Yes, there was peace back then, and we both thought it would never end.

* * * * *

Sally found a good church home, and she would get tapes of the Sunday morning services for us to listen to, and oh, it was so good to join in with the people as they sang. DJ has such a fine voice, and with Sally joining us, we had the best time in worship. Those days were our happiest days with Sally. She had put the past behind her and was now living her life to the fullest. Why, she even helped me and DJ through one of our few misunderstandings.

It happened one day, quite by mistake, but you know how things can happen. One minute you're laughing and then the next minute everybody is upset with each other. Well, it was like that. Sally made the comment she wished we had been able to have had puppies, because she just knew they would have been so pretty. Without thinking how it might affect DJ, I said mystically, "Oh, yes, they would have been so pretty, I know."

Before it was out of my mouth, DJ turned around and just stared at me. He was so upset, I could tell, and then he just yelled, "I never asked you to stay with me, nor did I ask you to give up that life to be with me!"

He jumped down and ran into another room before we could say anything to him. It hurt me so for DJ to yell at me. I started to go to him to try to explain that I didn't mean it as he had taken it, but Sally stopped me. "Let me talk with him," she ordered, "you stay here. I'll see if I can cool him down a bit."

Sally got up to walk into the dining room where he was, but DJ had hidden behind a chair. Sally came back where I was and told me it was best if we just left him alone for now. Oh, my heart was hurting so badly. I needed DJ to understand how I really felt about him. I didn't want this day to end like this. No one could get close to him the rest of the day or that night. He didn't come and sleep by me as usual, but stayed behind the chair in the dining room by himself. It was our first real fight, and it was killing me that he had misunderstood what I meant. DJ didn't eat the next day, and when Sally went to work, he stayed behind the chair. He wouldn't talk to me or even look at me. I spent most of that day in the other room just crying over my love, and how I had hurt him.

* * * * *

This went on for about three days. DJ staying behind the chair. He didn't even come out while Sally was at home, and during the day, he only came out to drink some water and go outside through the dog door. One day he stayed outside under a tree most of the day. I went out there to talk with him, but as soon as he heard me coming, he got up and went back inside. Now, DJ was normally the kind of fellow who, if he got upset over anything, would get over it really soon. I mean, I have seen him mad one minute, then the next, he would be licking Sally right in the face. This pouting was so unlike him. However, I knew he was hurt, and I tried to make allowance for him. Those three days were the loneliest three days of my life. By the third day, I was getting past the point of hurting over him and I was starting to get a little out done with him myself. It was then that Sally stepped in to help us out. When she came home on the third day, she went straight to the chair where DJ had been hiding, and got down on her knees and reached in and pulled him out.

"Let me alone!" he cried.

It was no use, Sally wasn't listening to anything he said. When she pulled him out she just held him close to her and would not let him go. He yelled and fussed, but all to no avail.

"DJ, you're going to talk to me or we will sit here in the floor for the rest of our lives," Sally pleaded.

"Fine," he quipped. "I have nothing better to do anyway."

With that, she turned him around and made him look her right in the eyes. "D.J., how could you say that after what both of you did for me? Why, if it hadn't been for you and Maggie, I might be dead right now, or out with some man whose name I couldn't even remember. Where's the guardianship you both talked about? You certainly can't do your job pouting behind a dining room chair," she scolded.

DJ's head went down. "But Maggie didn't have to stay with me! She would have been better off without me, you said so. And she wanted babies. You heard her say that!"

"Now you wait just a minute little fellow, I've never said that. What I said was *if*, and you hear me, when I say, *if*, you two could have had puppies, they would have been very pretty and special, at least to me."

I walked to where they were sitting, and I said, "DJ, I'm here because I want to be here. I fell in love with you when we were just little pups, and I could never love anyone else. How could you ever think I would want to be anywhere else?"

He wouldn't look at me, but he said in a low voice, "But you would have been better off with some other guardian."

"Oh no I wouldn't, because I love you. When you were at the hospital, I hardly slept and I told Mrs. Browne then, if you did come back home, I did not want to be paired with anyone else," I simply explained.

"Why Maggie? Why would you feel that way about me? We were just pups?" a deeply confused look appeared on DJ's face.

" Even so you silly little boy, I knew I loved you even back then. I knew we were going to work together for the rest of our lives."

DJ's eyes showed the sorrow he felt. He was still looking down when he said, "I'm so sorry I yelled at you Maggie, and you too, Sally."

Sally was still holding DJ, so she just held him up closer and kissed him on the side of his face. "Oh DJ, how could you ever think you were not loved? Please never do this again. We both need you, and Maggie has cried herself to sleep for three nights."

I sat down next to Sally. She put DJ down on the floor by me, then got up to leave the room.

"Where are you going?" I asked.

"Well," Sally said, "I know when two lovers need to be alone, and this is one of those times. You have to talk and I can see that I am not needed anymore." With that, Sally started walking out of the room.

DJ ran to her, "Forgive me, Sally, for the way I acted." And as he looked at me he said, "Maggie forgive me, I'm so sorry for hurting you."

Sally sat down once again and pulled us close to her side. "Tonight, I have seen what true forgiveness really is. You see, DJ, you're still teaching me by the way you live. I guess that is what God wants from me as well. To show my little world what Christianity truly is by the way I live, and not just by the words I speak."

"Yes," DJ spoke up, "that's exactly how God wants all of His creation to act--- by showing His love through our actions, as well as our words. I guess I just forgot that for a time. Even we have to be on our guard against the enemy. He will try to turn even guardians from their true path to one of self-centeredness, if we are not careful."

Chapter Two

Sally's Illness

As trees and cities flew by the window of the SUV, I wondered how long it would take to arrive at our new house. There were so many questions and fears. I sat up and looked out the window. It was a bright day with the leaves falling from the trees. Sally loved this time of year the most, I think. I remember the first time she became ill. It was during the time of month that women have, but this time the bleeding didn't stop. After a week, Sally went to see her doctor. He had her take some tests. That's when they found the cancer. Oh, they put her right in the hospital and cut it right out. She was told she would not be able to have children. She was so young. She was very depressed when she first came home from the hospital. Her brother, Bill, came and stayed a few days with her. He wouldn't let us get close to her. I wondered if he blamed us for her cancer.

At night, when Bill went upstairs to bed, Sally would open her bedroom door and in we would go. I remember the first night how she cried quietly, lest Bill would hear her and come back downstairs. Sally held us close to her and just kissed our face again and again. Then she just held us and cried some more. I understood the pain she was going through, for even though I chose to stay with DJ, I had to give up the idea of having babies in my life as well. Sally reached down and held my face in her hands and asked."Oh Maggie, will the pain ever go away?"

"Oh, love," I said, "in time it will go away and you will see what wonderful things God has in store for you. Besides, when you marry, you could always adopt a child; you've made a wonderful parent for us."

DJ looked around and said, "Maggie have you forgotten that we are the guardians and Sally is our charge?" Then he looked into Sally's face, softened and said, "But truthfully, Sally, you have made us a wonderful home and I wouldn't want to live anywhere else."

Shaking my head, I said, "DJ, you forget that,----- oh, what's the use, you're a boy and you will never understand how girls feel."

His eyes flamed up a little, then, Sally reached over and pulled us both close to her side. "I'm tired now, let's just lie down and go to sleep." With that, she kissed us both and whispered something in DJ's ear. His little cocky self just turned and gave me one of those looks he can give, and then he lay down to go to sleep.

I scooted over by him, and in a low voice said, "Tomorrow you're going to tell me what Sally said to you."

"Huh, I've already forgotten--- now go to sleep, Maggie." He knew just how to get under my skin, and he was good at it when he wanted to be.

Sally just reached over and patted me on the head and said, "Maggie, some things are meant only for those to whom they are spoken. I love you both, now please let's get some sleep, I'm so tired."

* * * * *

The next morning Sally's brother, Bill, was in a cheerful mood, until he saw us in Sally's room. "Get Out!!" he yelled at us.

When Sally raised up to speak to Bill about the way he was treating us, he just waved his hand and said, "You don't need those dogs in here with you right now. Shouldn't they be outside or something?"

Sally spoke with a very quiet voice, but it was firm. "Bill, they're my dogs and if I want them in my room it's my business."

He just stood and looked at Sally. He had never seen her like this before about anything. She was actually standing up to him, and she was sick on top of it. "Ok, ok, they're your dogs, but they aren't going to sleep in *my* room."

With that Sally started laughing. "Now what's so funny?" he asked.

"You!" Sally said, "Bill, they don't like you right now because of the way you have been treating them, so why would they want to sleep in your room?"

"Oh that's crazy. How do you know they don't like me?"

"Well, they told me so," Sally just laughed which made her brother so mad that he just walked out of her room, and we walked right back in.

* * * * *

The next few weeks with Bill there were the most uncomfortable weeks I think I have ever spent anywhere. And just to think, here we are riding in his car to go and live in his house. Here I am getting ahead of myself again.

After Bill left to go back home, things returned to normal, or as much as they could with Sally being so sick. There was always someone coming over to bring her some food from the church. DJ liked it when they brought chicken. One day, one of the church ladies, Mrs.

Catherine Clark, brought a lot of chicken. You should have seen how DJ was following her around the house. He was certainly hoping she would drop some on the floor.

"DJ," Sally said to him, "will you get out of the way and let Mrs. Clark get through the living room?"

Of course, as soon as she was out of sight, DJ started to beg Sally for some chicken. "I'm so hungry! Couldn't we just eat a little right now?"

"You little boy you. If I gave you all of it you would eat until you were sick," she answered.

I think it embarrassed him a little, because he hung his head down and said "I really do like chicken, Sally."

I could see in Sally's eyes he had won the battle. "Come here," she said as she held out her arms. As DJ went over to Sally, she reached down and patted him on the head, then she gave us both some chicken. I must confess, I like it as much as DJ, but why beg when you know he is going to get you some in the end. I mean two beggars-- come on-- besides, I could never out do DJ when it comes to begging.

Sally finally did get somewhat better and even went back to work, but she was never her old self, or at least that's how it seemed to me.

* * * * *

The months following Sally's time in the hospital we didn't get to go outside as much as usual. With the arrival of warmer weather, we started sitting in the backyard once more. I always liked Sally's backyard. She had a high wooden fence which allowed us freedom to run and play. If we kept our voices down, we could even talk with Sally outside. Sally loved to cook outside, and DJ loved it too. I mean if you think he would beg in the house, you should have seen his outside act. There were times I had to tell Sally if she kept on feeding him, he was going to get sick. During her recovery time, Sally would never go to church on Sunday night. I think going in the morning took more out of her than she let show. Plus, after working all week, well, there were times DJ and I were both worried about her and even talked with her about staying home a little more. "No," Sally said, "you two taught me how important it is to worship God, and fellowship with other believers. Now that I am better, how can I stay home on Sunday mornings? She was right of course; it was just our love for her speaking.

* * * * *

Some months later, Sally started dating a man she met at church. He was a nice man, and he really did like both of us, so we were hopeful this was going to be something very positive in her life. Who knew whether or not this might be the man Sally was going to spend the rest of her life with. She was very self-conscious, because of her right leg being shorter than her left, but Frank Nichols never seemed to notice Sally's legs being different in length. I remember one night, Frank was over for dinner and the two of them just sat around and laughed and talked for hours. It was good to see Sally doing so well again. Frank would even pick DJ up and hold him in his arms. DJ liked it very much. Then one day Bill came to see how Sally was doing. He had been drinking. When Sally started talking about Frank, Bill just cut her off.

"How could you like him? He's all into church and that religious stuff. Do you think he hasn't noticed your leg?" he questioned through thick tongue.

It made my blood boil when Bill insulted Sally, mainly because it made her cry. Sally walked across the room, then she turned around and said, "Bill, you have no idea what you are talking about. I learned, after wasting a lot of time doing just exactly what you are doing, primarily hating myself and searching for someone to love me, God is real and I accepted Him as Lord of my life one night and I have been happier than I have ever been in my life. I have peace, Bill, real peace. Believe me, that is something considering what I have been through with my 'wonderful' cancer," she both admonished her brother as well as confessing her faith to him.

He backed up and gave her a look of pure disgust, "How could you, after everything that happened to me?" By now, his voice was getting louder. He was angry and before Sally could say anything to him, he just started backing away from her. Bill held his hands up, "Don't say anything to me, I don't want to hear it from you. Just remember this, Frank, ole boy, will never forget your leg, and yes, one day he will walk away from you when he has gotten what he wanted, just like all the other men is your crazy life!"

I heard the door slam shut as he left, but Sally was just standing there, as if she was unable to move. I saw the tears running down her face as she just sat down on the floor stunned. It had been a long time since I had seen Sally cry like that, and it hurt DJ and me that Bill would be so ruthless to his own sister.

DJ bounded over to Sally and licked her face, catching the salty tears on his tongue. "Sally," he comforted, "don't cry; everything is going to be all right and in the end. Who knows, maybe one day Bill will be sitting right by you in church."

"Oh you sweet, silly little boy," Sally reached out and held him close to her and kissed the side of his face. "My brother Bill hates God and he blames God for the death of his wife and daughter," she explained.

I walked over and leaned against her. "Sally, why does Bill blame God for that?" Her quick reply dismissed the question. "Not now, Maggie, not now. I'm tired so let's get up and go get some ice cream and hot coffee."

My eyes lit up, "May we have some ice cream too?" I was hoping for a yes. "Of course you can, but now, Maggie, DJ doesn't eat as fast as you, so you can't help him eat his tonight." The answer was almost a command.

"Oh, I won't, I promise," I replied as I bounced around in circles.

DJ was laughing at me and was jumping around too. We both loved ice cream, and Sally would always give us some whenever she ate it. Looking back, it was good that the night ended on a good note for Sally. We sat and ate our ice cream, Sally laughed at both of us for getting ice cream all over our faces.

* * * * *

Later that night while Sally slept, we went into another room for our time of worship. It was an old custom going back to the beginning of time. It was while we were worshipping that DJ, stopped and looked over at me. "Maggie, we need to really pray for Bill every night."

"Why? I mean, looked how he hurt Sally tonight," I showed my lack of concern for her mean brother.

"I know love, he was mean and hateful to Sally, but that was the pain talking. His life is filled with so much pain and anger right now, it is all flowing out of him. He needs our prayers," DJ petitioned understandingly.

"Well, you pray for him and I will pray for Sally," I replied without sympathy for Bill. "I just can't pray for him tonight."

DJ just put his nose right up to mine and spoke so softly, "Maggie, don't walk down the path I almost went down, love. Let it go, remember, forgiveness is always the best way."

"You're right, I know," my voice was shaking with emotion as I remembered how hateful his voice sounded as he yelled at Sally, "but I don't think I will ever be able to trust him."

"Well, if we can forgive him for now, at least it's a start. We can worry about the trusting part later down the road," DJ was insistent.

" Yes, let's do that," thinking to myself I would never see that road, however, you know providence has a way of changing our paths.

* * * * *

Frank kept coming around more and more. When Sally was too tired to go back to church on Sunday night, he would come over and they would watch TV together. A lot of the times they would watch Christian TV. Some of the preachers I liked, but some I didn't care for much. At night during our worship time, DJ and I would discuss some of the preaching we had heard. One night DJ was laughing about one preacher, who seemed more worried about people sending their money to him than teaching his audience anything.

"Did you see the way that fellow kept giving his mailing address? Man, it was flashing on and off. He never said anything about the love of God, or how much God cares for the individual. He forgot to even mention about God's Son coming into the world to die for mankind. The enemy can really get people so sidetracked if they're not careful, Maggie."

"Sure, that's why we also have to be careful in whatever we think and do. If we are sidetracked, then who will be there in times of pain to show folks love. DJ, it doesn't seem there are enough guardians to go around does it?"

"No, but isn't that why the church is here? We just help fill in the cracks, Maggie. That's our job. We stand in the gap when there aren't any believers around, which is why we are not suppose to ever tell anyone about our ability to talk?" DJ was pensive.

"DJ, I had to tell Sally that night, you know I did," I defended myself.

"I know and I would have done the same thing myself, even though, at the time, I thought I wouldn't. I've thought a lot about it and really there was no other way to stop Sally from taking her own life that night. Maggie, you did a very brave thing."

Oh, how it made me feel so good when DJ complimented me and made me feel I had done something well.

Chapter Three

A False Hope

It had been over a year now since Sally had her operation and she was seemingly more like herself every day. DJ and I were so hopeful she was never going to get sick again. Frank was also coming over more and more, even to the point we had to be very careful and not talk with Sally too much, lest he walk up and hear us in the house. It was a small inconvenience, when you looked at how happy Sally had become with Frank in her life. They were even starting to talk about maybe one day getting married. Now let me just state for the record, her brother Bill was so wrong about Frank. Frank was a believer too, and he wasn't out to get anything from Sally. All he wanted to do was to show her his love. For that, DJ and I were thankful. We weren't even bothered when Bill 'ole boy,' showed back up one day. At least this time he hadn't been drinking and he was even nice to Sally.

The doorbell rang, which of course, set DJ to barking, and when Sally opened the door and we both saw who it was, DJ just stopped barking and stared at the door. I walked up to see what could make

DJ act so strangely. I almost spoke out loud when I saw Bill. I mean, who did he think he was, coming back here after the way he had talked to Sally? I waited for her to slam the door in his face, but instead she stepped back and opened it wide for him to come in.

Before Bill could say anything, Sally reached out and threw her arms around his neck and exclaimed, "Bill! How good to see you! I have missed you. I love you so much, my brother."

Now I was shocked as Bill broke down and began to cry. "Oh, Sally, I'm so sorry for what I said to you. I'm ashamed of being so hateful. Know I am happy for you and I am sorry I hurt you."

" Oh Bill, I know and I am glad you came over today, because I was planning to drive down to see you later this month. I couldn't stand this thing between us any longer." They just held each other and cried. I have to admit, I saw a side of Bill I didn't believe existed, and now, here he was proving me wrong.

DJ just stood back and watched the whole thing, I thought maybe he was making sure Bill didn't act up again, but later that night he told me he always liked seeing people forgive one another. "Love is the most powerful force in the world, Maggie," he stated. Anyway, Bill came in and they sat down for a long talk, and when he finally left Sally was so happy that she just danced around the living room. It was then I noticed how Sally seemed to lose all of her strength, just all of a sudden like, ---and Sally just sat down on the floor right where she was.

"Are you all right?" I asked her as I ran over to her, with DJ right behind me. "Yes, I'm all right. Ya'll are the biggest little worriers I have ever seen,". Sally picked DJ up and held him in her lap.

I just sat down and looked at her. She had a sallow color and she looked more tired than usual. Something was wrong, I could sense it, but no one was seemingly seeing it except me. Was she keeping something from us? Did she know more than she was letting onto us about? I wondered.

* * * * *

Over the next few days Sally seemed to be all right and when we questioned her about her condition, all we got from Sally was the same old song about how we were worrying way too much over nothing. One day Sally came home from work and before she got into the house good, Frank called to see if she wanted to go out and get something to eat. Now, none of this was strange, but it was Sally's answer which alarmed me.

"No, Frank, not tonight. I'm just tired from today. It was a really rough day at the office. No, I'm ok, just a little tired that's all."

When Sally hung up the phone, I walked over to her and asked her, "Is everything alright with you, Sally?"

"Now Maggie, don't you start in on me too, you heard me tell Frank the only thing wrong with me tonight is; I am tired."

"Yes, Sally, I heard what you told Frank. But, I also heard you talking on your cell phone as you were coming into the house, and you told that person today was a light day at the office. So, which was it?" I drilled.

"Oh Maggie," Sally's voice showed she was getting agitated with me. "You should know better than to listen in on other people's phone conversations."

"I wasn't listening in on your conversation. Can I help it that I hear better than people? Besides, you didn't answer my question."

As Sally jumped up, her chair fell backwards on the floor. DJ came running to see what was happening.

"What's happening?" he asked.

"Oh, I don't know, just ask Maggie, she seems to know everything around here," Sally replied angrily. With that she went to her room and slammed the door.

"Maggie, what did you say to make Sally so upset?" DJ now was questioning me.

"You don't even know what you're talking about? Just go and leave me alone right now!" I snapped and walked out of the kitchen toward the spare bedroom.

Poor DJ just stood there trying to take it all in and make sense of it all. How could he, when I didn't even understand it myself. That night I learned something about DJ which I didn't know or maybe just hadn't seen. I was sitting in the spare bedroom where he and I went each night to worship and pray. Finally, DJ followed me into the room.

"Maggie, this is going to be hard for you to take, but Sally has been sick again for some time now."

"What? How do you know that? Did she tell you something and you have been keeping it from me?" I snapped at him again.

"No, Sally did not tell me anything. About three weeks ago, I sensed Sally was sick again. I wanted to be wrong. I didn't have the heart to tell you then. Since you have guessed it, I might as well tell you now," DJ replied in a soft, sad voice.

"But, Sally hasn't been to a doctor, so how do you… I mean, what makes you so sure your right?"

"Maggie, it's something the Creator puts within us. You know, the ability to sense things when they're not right. Sally hasn't been to a doctor yet, because she is afraid to go back. Let's give her more support and love right now."

" Well, why haven't I seen it before now?" before he could answer, I asked with deep concern. "She is going to get better isn't she, DJ?"

His response was that far away look he gets. It made me worry even more. We both slept outside Sally's bedroom door that night. She never opened it all night. There was a time I knew I heard her crying, but DJ said we needed to let her have her space. So we just waited. The next morning as the door opened, I could see Sally had not slept much either. I looked up at her while DJ slept on the floor. Sally held her head down and started crying again. It was a soft cry, but she still cried.

"Maggie I am so sorry for the way I treated you and DJ last night. I can't believe I left ya'll here on this hard floor all night, " she sobbed.

"Oh, that's ok," DJ said as he lifted his head from the floor, but please let's not make a habit out of it will you?" DJ starting chuckling and then he broke out into full laughter. Well, since laughter is contagious, I started laughing and soon Sally was laughing right along with us.

"Come on in here and let's go back to bed, I called in sick an hour ago," she coaxed as she climbed between her covers.

"You called in sick?" I asked.

"Maggie, I haven't slept all night and neither have you, so let's stop with the inquisition for right now and go back to sleep, shall we?" was her reply.

As I lay on the bed, I watched DJ sleep. Sally was sleeping, too, but it was a fitful sleep. Soon, I went to sleep as well, wondering what was going to happen next.

* * * * *

I woke up later when I heard Sally talking on the phone to someone at the doctor's office. "Yes," I heard her answer. "I can make it in tomorrow. No, I am sure it most likely is nothing, but I will feel better if I get checked out to make sure. What are the symptoms? Well, I have been really tired lately and I haven't had much of an appetite either. Come in an hour earlier fasting? Yes I can. Yes, I know you won't know anything until you get the test results. Ok, I will see you tomorrow."

I laid my head back down so Sally wouldn't know I had heard her conversation. I also discovered DJ can fake really well. He had been listening all the time, he had kept his eyes shut. How do I know? When Sally got up to go to the bathroom, he opened his eyes and watched her leave the room.

"DJ, I said to him in a real low voice, you have been listening all this time!" "Maggie, love, I'm not deaf and besides, I at least know when to say something and when to keep my mouth shut," he chided.

"Well, I couldn't hear what time her appointment is going to be in the morning," I ignored his snide remark.

"Early, Maggie. Which is not a good sign, because, that means the doctor thinks something is wrong. Also, he moved her appointment up. Be still now, here she comes, pretend you're asleep," he ordered.

* * * * *

Sally didn't say much to us as she got ready to go in for her doctor's appointment the following day, but we could both tell she was nervous. Consequently, we were even more nervous waiting for her to come home. I think DJ jumped a dozen times or more at every sound he thought he heard, and I have to admit, I jumped a time or two, myself. It was late in the day when Sally finally came home. She looked so tired and worn out that we just sat back and didn't ask her anything. We just welcomed her with licks. Finally, Sally asked, "Do you two want to know what the doctor said?"

"Of course we do! We didn't want to push you to talk about it until you felt like telling us," we replied in unison.

"Oh, ya'll are so sweet." Then she starting crying, "How I am going to miss you two. I love you both so much."

DJ looked at me and then let out such a sigh, and with that, he put his head down between his front legs on the floor and started crying. I know what you think---dogs don't cry, but we do, just not like humans, but we cry, nevertheless. I was crying, too, by this time. I tried to think of something to say to Sally, but nothing came to my mind. All we could do at that moment was to share in her sorrow and cry along with her. In life there are times when you can do nothing else.

After a while Sally finally got control of herself again and told us, "It's back, and it is too widely spread to treat."

DJ, bless his little heart, walked up to her and asked "How much time do they think we have left together?"

Sally's eyes were so red by now, and as she started crying again, she said, "Somewhere around six to eight months, maybe more, but not over a year."

"Well," DJ said, "then we will stay right by your side the whole time. Sally, please don't send us away. Let us stay with you until the end. We love you more then we have words to express. We could not bear to be separated from you."

Again, Sally reached out and pulled us both up close to her, "I won't. I couldn't send you away. I am going to need your strength now more than ever. I went by to talk with my boss, and we have very good insurance. So, as of right now I am on medical leave, with full pay. My boss said what the insurance company didn't pay, our company would. At least, I won't have to worry about paying my bills."

"He is a good man, Sally, and we are going to pray for him tonight, aren't we, Maggie?"

"Yes," I answered in an almost whisper. And with great difficulty, I turned to Sally. "I don't want to lose you, where will we go after you're gone?" Not waiting for an answer, I just got up in a hurry and ran out of the room.

"She'll be ok, Sally," DJ comforted her. "It's hard on all of us right now, but she is right about one thing ,Sally."

"What's that DJ?"

"We do love you, Sally, and our life will never be the same when you're gone; for you have touched our lives as much as we have touched yours."

As Sally got up, she said to DJ, "Let's go fix something to eat. The doctor told me I would stay healthier longer, if I ate something every day and took better care of myself." As they walked into the kitchen Sally said, "DJ, do you think you and Maggie could stand eating a steak tonight?"

* * * * *

Over the next few weeks Sally stayed at home most of the days and nights, but I did notice that Frank never did come by anymore, so one day I asked "Sally, is Frank working out of town?"

"No, he isn't going to be coming around anymore, Maggie, so let's not talk about it anymore, ok?

"But why? I mean ya'll enjoyed each other's company so much,---" but I didn't finish my sentence because I could see from her expression any further discussion would only hurt Sally again.

"Look," she said, "the day I went to the doctor and he told me the cancer was back, I broke it off with Frank. Now, don't look at me that way, Maggie. His first wife died from cancer and I didn't want to put him through it again."

"Is that what you told him?" I inquired.

"Not exactly, end of subject," she quickly quipped.

There was nothing I could say. Sally was being the person she had become-- the one who put others before herself. But some how I knew

I would have to find a way to let Frank know the real reason why Sally broke it off with him.

* * * * *

One night Bill showed back up again, but this time Sally did all the talking. He just sat there as if the air had been knocked out of him. Bill finally stopped Sally from talking and said, "Sis, I have some money put away and we will get the best doctors money can buy."

"I wish it were that easy, Bill, but you haven't been listening to me. The cancer has spread too far now, there is nothing *anyone* can do. However, I do have one favor to ask of you."

"Whatever it is, you know I will do it Sally. You don't have to ask," he replied somberly.

"Yes I do, because I want you to promise me you will take care of DJ and Maggie for me. Don't throw them away or give them to someone else. They're all you will ever have left of me. Bill, I can't tell you how much they mean to me. I trust, one day you will understand. Correct that, I know you will," she spoke with great emotion.

"Understand what, Sally? They're just dogs," he was almost impatient.

"Oh no, Bill, they are far more than just dogs, far more, and they can show you more love than you could ever imagine."

"Whatever you say, Sally, I promise I will take care of them for you," he was patronizing.

"As long as they both live, Bill, that's the deal. You have to give me your word, because I know you would never go back on your word, not even when I'm gone," she was emphatic.

With that, Bill broke down and started crying again. They both just held each other and cried. Later that night, while we were having our time of worship and prayer, I asked DJ, "What do you think about Sally making Bill promise to take care of us?"

"Well, Sally said she knows he will need us more than many others; who knows what might happen in his life? Maggie, we have to look on the bright side of it."

" I don't want to. I want to stay with Sally. We are, love. Bill isn't going to take us to live with him until after Sally is gone."

That night was a sad one for me and I think for DJ as well, we both knew our lives were going to change very soon. Is that how it was going to be for us, one change after another? This new master we were to watch over, and hopefully guide to an understanding of God's love, was going to be challenging.

Chapter Four

Our Last Days With Sally

The months rolled by much too soon for me. It seemed every day Sally was getting weaker. One day as I was thinking about Frank and how much he could help to comfort Sally, I had an idea about how to reach him, but, I needed DJ's help.

"You want to do what and contact whom? Just where did you get this idea, Maggie?" was his initial reaction to my idea.

"Well if you must know, it came to me the other night during our time of worship," I answered.

"How do you think you could ever pull it off?" he responded doubtfully.

"You leave that to me. You just keep Sally outside long enough tomorrow for me to make the call," I requested.

So, the next morning finding Sally felt a little better, DJ asked, "Sally, wouldn't you like to go out into the backyard to drink your coffee?"

"Yes, that's a good idea. I could use the fresh air and it's not too cool. Maggie, are you coming too?" Sally answered.

"Oh yes, just give me a little time and I will come out. Ya'll go on, I'll be right out."

As soon as they closed the door behind them, I jumped up on the chair, picked the phone up with my mouth and set it down so I could talk into it. Thankfully, Sally still had Frank's number on the speed dial, so all I had to do was to push the right number on the phone. As it rang, I tried to think just how I was going to word this, but then I heard Franks voice on the other line.

"Sally is that you?" Frank asked, seeing her number on the caller ID.

Before I knew what I was saying, I changed my voice to sound like one of Sally's friends at work."

"No, this is Rose, and please don't tell Sally I called you. She is outside and I have to get out there really soon or she might come back in," I answered.

Frank asked with great concern in his voice, "What's up, why are you calling me?"

"Frank, I have to tell you why Sally broke it off with you,--- the real reason. Her cancer is back. It is so wide spread there is nothing the doctor's can do for her, and to keep from hurting you, she hurt herself by breaking up with you so suddenly," I explained to him.

Frank didn't say anything at first, then he asked, "How is Sally now?"

"Not much time left I'm afraid, so if you want to spend time with her you had better make up your mind soon. I have to go," and with that I put the phone back down to turn around and see DJ, standing there.

"If you talk much longer, Sally is going to come in here and catch you. Besides you never told me you could disguise your voice," DJ said.

"It's just a small gift I have, nothing to brag about, really."

DJ looked at me with that little gleam in his eyes, "My dear, you are something to brag about."

Oh, how I just loved it when he would tell me things like that. It made my head spin as we walked back outside,

Sally was sitting in the morning sun and at first you didn't notice how sick she really was. I was so hoping everything would work out with Frank. Later in the day the door bell rang and of course DJ went barking to it as if he were the headmaster of the house. As Sally opened the door, an expression of total shock appeared on her face. There stood Frank, he was dressed real nice, but you could tell he had been crying.

"You know," he said, "I think what hurts the most is the fact you didn't believe I loved you enough to go through this with you, Sally."

Tears began to stream down Sally's face. "It's not that at all, Frank. I knew how much losing your first wife hurt you and I didn't want to be the cause of hurting you that way again."

"I'm just glad your friend, Rose, called me while she was here this morning to tell me the truth," said Frank as he wrapped his arms around Sally.

Oh no! Now it hit the fan for sure. DJ and I both started walking back into the back of the house when Sally called out to us, "Where are ya'll going?"

Then she addressed Frank, "Rose called you did she, well, I will have to thank her later myself."

"Please don't be mad at your friend, Sally. She didn't want you to know she had called. I believe she did it out of love for you, that's all," Frank pleaded.

Sally started laughing, "You're right Frank, you're so right about that. Well, come on in and let's go sit down."

As they passed by DJ and me, Sally reached down and kissed me on the top of my head and whispered, "Thank you, Rose." DJ had to run outside to keep from laughing out loud right there.

* * * * *

We didn't go back inside because we knew they needed time alone to talk. "Sally, why didn't you let me know? You knew how much I loved you and cared about you."

"I know Frank, but at the time I honestly thought I was doing the best thing for you. I have missed you so much, and I have thought about calling you more times then I can remember. I just never had the nerve to call after I had hurt you. I thought breaking up with you would not hurt you as badly as your sitting by my bedside watching me die." "Marry me Sally, right now, today, marry me."

"No, I can't, and it's not because I don't love you, but because I do. I don't have much time left, so let's just spend it together without fighting and enjoy each other's company. I get tired very easily these days and sometimes I have to go to bed early."

"Sally, may I move into the room upstairs? I will be here if you need someone to call the doctor or to take you to the hospital?"

"That would be asking way too much of you, Frank."

"You didn't ask. I offered out of my love for you. Besides, I'm not taking no for an answer. Let me go home and pack up some things and I will be back within the hour." We stood there as Frank walked out the door.

"After he was gone, Sally turned around and said, "Now, young lady, we have to talk before Frank gets back here."

"Oh no," said DJ, "this is one of those girl talks, so, I will leave you two alone." "Oh no you won't. I have this sneaking suspicion you had a hand in this as well. So out with it, whose bright idea was it to call Frank?" Sally pretended anger.

"I hate to admit to this," DJ said, "but it was Maggie's."

"Well thank you very much DJ, it didn't take long to get that out of you did it?"

I said to DJ defensively.

"Well, I was outside with Sally, so just please tell me who else could have made that call?" DJ asked feigning innocence.

"Ok, all I want to know is, how did you sound like Rose?" Sally asked curiously.

I looked up into Sally's eyes trying so hard to see if she was mad or just wanting to know more about us. "I have this gift, which allows me to sound like other people. Not every one of us has this gift, but some do," I was still defensive.

"So, Mr. DJ, when were you going to tell me about this gift of Maggie's?" Sally turned and looked sternly at him.

"Oh now, wait just a minute there, Sally. I didn't know Maggie had the gift until I walked into the room and heard her talking to Frank. She never told me anything about it either," DJ wasn't going to accept any responsibility.

"Maggie, how could you keep that a secret from DJ all this time?" again, Sally's face was filled with curiosity.

"My mother told me there were some gifts we were to keep secret until the time was right to use them, and only then were we to let our guardians know about our gift."

"I can see that if I….." then Sally stopped what she was saying. Tears filled her eyes, and she said to us, "I'll never know everything about you two will I?"

"You know more now than anyone is suppose to," DJ told her "and some gifts don't manifest until we are older, so, we might not even know all the gifts we will ultimately have. I surely wish you were going to stay with us, so we could experience it together. Sally, you are going to a wonderful place where there will never again be sickness or death, and just think about all the beauty you will see. Just remember us please, and how much we are going to miss you and how much we love you."

We all had one more good cry before Frank arrived back at Sally's house. At least now, there was someone else to help look after her.

* * * * *

With each passing day, it seemed Sally was getting weaker. Frank was kind enough to allow us into her room most of the day. Sally told him we meant the world to her and she didn't want us being kept out of her room. At night, after Frank went to sleep, we would quietly walk into Sally's room and if she was awake, we would visit with her. We knew it was going to be the last times we had together, so we tried to make the best of it.

One night right before the end, Sally asked us, "Would you two do me a favor?" DJ and I both replied in unison, "Anything you want"

"Then, please stay with my brother, Bill. I mean, don't run away and try to find your way back to Mrs. Browne's house, ok? I know he's going to be hard to live with, but you have to promise me you will stay with him" DJ and I both looked at each other, wondering how Sally could have known we had talked about doing just that. "Oh," Sally continued on, "I see that look. One thing I have learned from you two, is how to play like you're asleep when you're not. I heard you discussing the other night, how, if everything didn't go ok at Bill's ya'll could try and find you way back to Mrs. Browne's house. Please promise me that you won't do that, you're my only hope for my brother."

I didn't know how DJ felt, and I wouldn't look at him either, but I spoke up, "As far as I am concerned, if that is your wish, Sally, I will stay with Bill, not matter what." DJ walked up to Sally and reached out and licked her ever so softly on the side of the face. It was as if he was afraid he might hurt her. "I'm in too, Sally, no matter what happens. We'll stay with Bill."

Neither of us knew to what depth that promise was going to take us, nor what we would have to walk through to keep our promise to Sally. But love has a way of binding you to someone, even after they are gone from this world to be in the Master's kingdom. We did learn one important thing that night. We weren't going to whisper in Sally's room anymore while we thought she was asleep.

* * * * *

Three days before Sally left this world, her brother Bill came and was staying in the house along with Frank, which meant we were not able to have our time visiting with Sally anymore. Either Bill or Frank was with her every minute of the day and night. The day Sally died, her color was so bad, and her breathing was very difficult. It seemed every breath was so hard for her to take. We were in the corner of the room, when Sally started calling for us. Bill tried to reason with her, however she was insistent in seeing us one last time. So, Bill and Frank put us both on the bed and told Sally we were there by her side. My heart hurts, even now, as I tell this. Even though I knew she would be better off, it was the suffering she was going through, which hurt me most. We could see the pain in her eyes as she looked at us. I thought for a minute DJ was going to start crying, but he was able to hold himself together.

"Oh how much I am going to miss you two. I wish we could sing together those old songs you taught me, just one last time." I couldn't believe she was saying this right in front of Bill and Frank, but we both just sat there looking at Sally as if we didn't have a clue what she was saying to us. "Ya'll are the ones who reached me in my darkest moment and I will always love you for that." Bill it seemed was growing tired of Sally talking to us, and I heard him whisper to Frank, it must be the drugs they were giving her, and with that, they picked us up and put us back on the floor.

"Now go sit over there," Bill pointed us back to the corner. We did just that. Frank couldn't seem to stop talking about what Sally had said to us, and he asked Bill, if he understood any of it.

"Frank, get real, Sally's not herself right now, it's the drugs talking. Look at her now she is sound asleep already," Bill remarked.

But they were wrong, for Sally was between two worlds now, more in the other one than this one, and it was just a matter of time before she finally crossed over. I heard her take a deep breath and then she was gone. It happened so quickly, it took even DJ and me by surprise. Bill stepped over to her bedside, reached out and touched her arm, then he just fell down by the side of her bed and started crying. Frank stood there shocked at first, then his tears flowed freely as well. We just walked out of the room for now. Our time of sorrow would have to come later, when there wasn't anyone around. All we knew was, Sally was no longer going to be our mistress, and we would never again be her guardians. Our time with Sally was finished, and now was our time to grieve over the loss of the one we both loved so. Later that night, after the funeral home came and took Sally's body away, Bill went out to see one of his friends, and Frank went back to his own house.

This gave us the time we needed to do the last thing we could for Sally. It's an ancient service guardians do for a loved one who has either died in a battle or passed away through illness. The songs we sang that night are sung only at this time. We also sang songs in preparation for whatever was going to befall us next. We had found one of our old songs in Sally's Bible, in the book of Psalms. It was the one we never grew tired of her reading to us, and it was one song which we did teach her.

"Lord, how they have increased who trouble me;
many are they who rise up against me.
Many are they who say of me,
there is no help for him in God.
But You, O Lord, are a shield for me,
my glory and the one who lifts up my head."

You'll have to read it for yourself, but it's one we sang together with Sally, all the time. That night as we sang that song, it had a special meaning for us, because we knew where we were going, just not what was ahead of us, so it was our commitment of ourselves into the hands of the Creator to use us as He saw fit.

* * * * *

This brings us up to our present situation… riding in the back seat of Bill's car. He and Frank talked about us before Bill loaded us into his car. It seemed Frank wanted to keep DJ and let me go with Bill, but, Bill stood his ground on this. "I promised my sister they would stay together until one of them died, and well, it's the least I can do for her now. I'm sorry Frank, but you can't have either of them. They are going with me," Bill told Frank with sympathetic sternness.

Oh, let me tell you, we were both so relieved, because if they had spilt us up, we wouldn't have been able to keep our word to Sally, not only because we're suppose to stay together, but also because no one was going to take DJ away from me. As much as I loved Sally and would have died for her if needed; never would I agree to someone taking DJ away from me. That silly little boy is my whole life.

Chapter Five

At Home With Bill

Bill lived in a big, old house with a large fenced backyard, which is where I figured we would live. You see, Bill really didn't like dogs, and even though he was keeping his promise to Sally by taking us to live with him, I never expected to stay in his house like we did with Sally. The drive back to Bill's house took three hours and he was quiet most of the way. Every now and then he would say something to us, as if by talking to us he was still talking to Sally. We didn't mind that either, because we missed her as much as he did, and it was nice to have someone talking to you even if you couldn't answer them back.

* * * * *

When we arrived at Bill's house, he took us both out of his car. Before he lead us inside, he said, "DJ, you'll have to do your business outside," and then he looked at me and added, "that goes for you too, old girl."

Old girl! who did he think he was calling an old girl anyway, and DJ, why did he look as if he was about to bust out laughing over that. But he knew better. Why, I was only five years old and in very good health.

The house had a big porch and after Bill got everything out of the car, we just sat out there for a while. It was cool and he never really said a word to us about anything. I knew he was missing his sister and thinking about her, just as we were doing. Bill was going to be hard to reach, yet we had made a promise to Sally that we would do everything we could to help Bill find his way back to a life of love.

* * * * *

The first week at Bill's was quite. He took a few more days off from his job and just stayed around the house. When he did start back working, he came home every evening and drank. He liked both beer and mixed drinks. I noticed Bill did a lot of drinking in the evenings, and if he didn't stay home drinking, he would go out with one of his many friends and drink. It was the third day of our second week at Bill's and he had been out drinking most of the night, so the next morning when he got up to hurry off to work, he forgot to feed us… again.

After he left, DJ came over to me and said, "I am not happy here. I don't think Bill likes us very much. I'm so hungry. He never thinks about us, at all. He never feeds us at the same time and I don't like the food he is giving us to eat."

I knew DJ wasn't happy, even before he spoke up, because he was the type of Sheltie which needed a lot of love himself, and he wasn't getting it from Bill. Bill would just walk right by him as he stood there waiting to be noticed. DJ looked at me and asked, "Why on earth, did you promise Sally we would stay with Bill and watch after him? He doesn't want us here and he never talks to us. He never has any dealings with us at all."

I looked at DJ, trying not to be hurt at how soon he had forgotten his own promise to Sally. "We both agreed to do this, so no matter how long it takes or how hard it gets, we're staying," I answered him.

* * * * *

As Bill arrived at work one day, he found the boss wasn't too happy his article wasn't in on time. "I know you have had a lot on you with the death of your sister, but, I have a paper to run and we have deadlines to meet." Bill's boss was a heavy set man named, Joe Rushing, however, sometimes Bill would call him names which we would never repeat. Joe was one of those men who put everything into his job. It was his life. Even his own family took a backseat to his work. That is why he was so short with Bill that particular morning. He couldn't believe anyone could still be upset about the death of a family member. After all, it had been over a week since the funeral. As Joe got closer to Bill he could smell Bill had been drinking again the night before.

Joe admonished, "You're drinking too much, too, and you need to get a handle on it before it takes control of you. I will not stand for you or anyone else coming in here drunk and smelling like a brewery all the time. Stop your drinking or find another job." Joe turned around and walked back into his office and slammed the door shut. There was a silence in the outer office, where everyone was standing. Bill was mad, it was quite evident and he just stood there looking at Joe's office door. Now, Bill was liked by everyone in the office, but even they had seen the change which had taken place in him since his sister's death. Bill just went through the day without really acknowledging he was even in the world. His last family member was gone now and he was all alone. And his parents died when they were young, yet they always had each other. Now, Bill felt he was alone in the world, abandoned by

God and men. Bill now felt like God, along with the rest of the world, was turning His back on him.

Bill did have one true friend there, Tracie Chapman. She was an older woman, who had four grown children and a husband who built houses for a living. They both went to church and they were believers, but Tracie knew Bill was not ready for her to share her faith with him now. She had known he was not ready when they first met. Now, with the death of his sister, Tracie was losing hope that Bill was ever going to be ready. His heart was so hardened.

After Bill went to his desk, Tracie came over to Bill and said, "I don't know why Joe can be so hard nosed. You would think the man didn't even have a heart."

Bill looked up at Tracie, "He doesn't have a heart, all he cares about is this dumb paper, and ever since I walked through those doors, I have worked myself to death trying to make this a better paper than it was. Now, look at the thanks I get for all my hard work."

Tracie leaned over Bill's desk, and said, "Don't take it so hard. Joe is under a lot of pressure here, too, you know. I'm sure when he has had time to think about the things he said, he will come and tell you he is sorry."

"That's the thing I always like about you, Tracie, you never see things as they really are, instead, you see the world through rose colored glasses."

" Well, I will have you to know, Mr. Bill Thomas, I don't wear glasses and if I did they surely would not be rose colored." Tracie turned and walked back to her desk, she was wondering if it was even wise trying to talk with Bill right now anyway?

* * * * *

When Bill arrived home that afternoon, one of his drinking buddies was there waiting for him. It was Mick, who was the kind of guy who could rub you the wrong way really quickly, and he had a habit of doing it to Bill. Mick knew where Bill kept his spare key, so when Bill arrived home Mick and two women were already waiting for him inside the house.

Bill wasn't in a good mood, his head was throbbing, and he felt sick at his stomach. The last thing he wanted to see that afternoon was Mick and those two women. DJ and I didn't care for them either. They were loud and they told Bill to put us outside. Bill tried to get them to leave.

"Mick, I don't feel like drinking tonight. I just want to rest awhile."

"Man, what's gotten into you? Everyone needs to party. Hell man, we have come all the way over here for you to party with us. Don't be such a kill joy, man," Mick jeered.

Bill was starting to feel tense. He hated it when someone tried to push their way off on him, and besides this was his house they had helped themselves into. "Mick, I'm serious. I'm not in the mood to party with anyone tonight," he said.

"Man," said Mick, "you need to loosen up some. And why are you keeping these mangy mutts in your house? I didn't think you liked dogs."

"They are my sister's dogs and I promised her I would take care of them," Bill answered.

"Well, I'm going to do you a favor and throw them outside where they belong." With that Mick reached down to grab me and DJ did something I had never seen him do before. He went after Mick. He tore into him, which startled Mick. He stepped back and kicked DJ, which sent him flying across the room..

Bill came alive with that. He rose up and knocked Mick to the floor. It was as though a raging bull had been unleashed. Bill grabbed Mick off the floor and pushed him toward the door.

"I want you out of my house, NOW and I don't want you or these tramps in my house ever again!" he yelled.

"Yeah, just who are you calling a tramp?" said one of those women. However, as Bill turned toward her, she saw the fire which was burning in his eyes, and decided it was best to leave without trying to start a fight with him. "Come on, Mick, this guy doesn't know how to party anyway. Let's go over to a friend of mine's who will party with us."

With that remark, they walked out the door cursing Bill as they went. I was already over by DJ where he lay on the floor. Bill came over there and put his hand on DJ and told him not to move, "I'm going to call the vet, and we are going to take care of you."

He called the vet, who came right out to check on DJ. Luckily, DJ wasn't hurt, just shaken up a bit.

"Bill, you're sure lucky he didn't receive some broken bones from the blow he received from Mick," the vet told him.

"I know, Doc. What do I need to do?" Bill questioned.

"Well, he seems all right, just keep him quite tonight and lets see how he's doing tomorrow," the doctor instructed.

After the vet left, Bill did something I just couldn't believe; he picked DJ up and held him in his arms. As Bill held DJ, he just broke down and starting crying, "I promised Sally I would look after you and look at what happened here today. I can't believe I let this happen to you, little fellow. I told her I wouldn't be any good at this. I almost got you killed today."

DJ looked up at Bill and just licked his face. Bill broke down again and cried some more, but this time it was as if some dam had broken loose and all the hurt and pain was just pouring out of him. I got up close to him and just put my head on his leg. I knew DJ was going to be all right, and I was starting to have hopes for Bill as well.

* * * * *

The next morning when Bill got up, he called us to go out into the backyard. It was our morning business, as Bill called it. I would have rather he had said nothing about it and just let us out, but he meant well. When we came back in, our food was already in our bowls, the water bowl had fresh water in it too. We both looked at each other and Bill said, as he was getting ready to walk out the door, "Well, don't just stand there, eat your food. I will try to find the kind of food you're used to eating when I get off work today. I'm running late, so let me get going and I will see ya'll this afternoon."

As Bill opened the door, DJ ran up behind him and barked at him. Bill turned and said, "What is it, little man?" As he knelt down to pat DJ on the head, DJ rose up on his hind legs and put his front paws on Bill's leg and licked him one more time before he left for the day. Bill's eyes were tearful as he held DJ close to him. "I will see you this afternoon, little man."

After Bill walked out of the house, DJ came over to me and said, "Now aren't you glad we came here?"

"What? How can you stand there and act that way? Why, I can't believe my ears."

"Oh Maggie, you know I love you. I think we are going to be able to really help Bill."

"Now DJ, its way too early to tell yet, and if I were you, I wouldn't let one day of reversed behavior get my hopes up too high. They just might come crashing down around your head. You must have hit your head last night as well. Who was it just over a week ago, asking if we could run away from here?"

"Maggie, you always remember the little mistakes I make and never remember anything else."

"Oh, now DJ, that's not true and you know it. I remember the first time you

reached over and licked my face."

"Yeah, I see, now you are going to try to sweet talk your way out of this one, aren't you, Maggie?" DJ said.

"DJ, I do hope now we will be able to help Bill. Before, I didn't think we would be successful, but now, I believe we might be able to. Don't you?"

"Yes, I do. But, it might mean telling him everything about us."

Maggie stepped back and said, "We can't, he wouldn't understand. He's not Sally, DJ. He will never accept the truth about us."

"We don't know that yet, Maggie. Besides, the door might not ever open to us, but if it does, we will have to walk through it. We're his guardians now, my love, and Sally was depending on us to help her brother as we helped her," DJ petitioned.

* * * * *

Over the next few weeks, Bill just about stopped his drinking. Oh, he would drink one beer every now and then, but nothing like he had been before. He stopped going out at night and started spending more time at home, just sitting in the back yard with us, or at his desk working on the next day's articles for the paper. You see, one of Bill's many jobs there was to make sure every article was well written, with no mistakes. Bill, having been a professor of literature at a small university, was well qualified to handle the task. However, after Sally's death, he went through a period of time when he wasn't doing his job as he should have, which is why he and Joe got into the altercation that day at the office.

One Monday morning, Bill arrived at work and he realized he was feeling better about life. He could not remember the last time he had felt that way. Right off, everyone seemed to notice Bill's over all attitude was different than it had been. The last few weeks he had not come in one day with the smell of booze on his clothes. Even Joe Rushing noticed the difference in Bill. He asked Tracie, "What's happened to Bill?"

" Joe, all I can tell you is, he has been spending a lot of time with his dead sister's dogs, and for some reason they seem to be having a very positive effect on Bill," Tracie answered.

"Dogs?" said Joe, shaking his head in disbelief, "well, let's see if it lasts. I have never seen anyone who has gone as far down that road as Bill has, ever turn around. Who knows, maybe Bill with prove me wrong, although, I don't believe it."

Tracie looked at Joe and said, "Why can't you believe something good might be happening to someone?"

With a scowling look, Joe nearly took Tracie's head off with his answer,

"Because I'm a newspaper man, and I have been my entire life and I have never seen anything good happen in this rotten world of ours."

Tracie had to hold back the words which wanted to fly out of her mouth. Instead, she quietly replied, "Maybe you have just been looking in the wrong places your whole life." With that, she turned around and headed back to her desk, leaving Joe standing there wondering why she was so upset at what he said. Joe knew Tracie was a Christian, but like most people, he didn't put much stock in that kind of stuff, nor did he understand so many of the things which were happening right under his nose.

* * * * *

It was early in the morning, when Rev. Ron came out of his office, which was located in the back of his church. As he walked into the house and through their living room to pick up the car keys, his wife, Kathy, asked him, "Where are you off to so early?"

"I have to go down to the newspaper office today to see Bill Thomas."

Kathy's mouth flew open, and she just about yelled at Ron, "You are going to do what? Ron have you lost your mind, you know that man hates you and everything you stand for? So please, tell me, what would make you go down there just so he can hurt your feelings again, like he has a thousand times before?"

Ron looked at his wife, still amazed there were times when she still saw things after the flesh. "While I was praying this morning, Kathy; the Lord spoke to my heart and said I was to go down to the paper and see Bill Thomas."

"Ron darling, I know you pray over everything and I do believe you try to listen to God, but this time I think you have missed it for sure. There is no hope for Bill Thomas, he is as mean a man as I have ever seen, and he hates everything that has to do with the church or the Lord," Kathy expounded.

There was sadness in Ron's voice as he spoke to his wife, "Kathy, I have just found out his sister died with cancer, and *I know* the Lord told me to go and let him know he isn't alone, that I understand how he feels."

"No, Ron, I'm begging you not to go. Pray about it some more, and if you still feel this way in a week or two, then go, but don't go right now," Kathy kept on.

"No, this is something I have to do and I have to do it now, today." With that Rev. Ron turned and walked out the door. Kathy went to their bedroom and shut the door so she could pray. She still felt her husband was wrong, but it was her place to stand behind him in prayer and no matter what.

* * * * *

Thus, this was to be Bill's first true test. As he was sitting at his desk working on an article, in walked the Rev. Ron Wilton. Now, ever since Bill had come to the paper, he had nothing to do with Rev. Ron. It was because his wife and daughter had been killed in the car accident. Rev. Ron had nothing to do with the accident, he just represented everything which caused Bill's anger. It might seem strange to some, but when many people fall out with God, they turn against everything that represents Him. Which is why, up until a few weeks ago, Bill hated everything about church and every minister. Tracie tried to head Rev. Ron off so he wouldn't talk with Bill, but he just walked right by her and acted as if she wasn't even there. Jarrod Gilmore, who ran one of the printing presses, was standing by Tracie when Rev. Ron brushed by her. "I believe," he said quietly, "it's time for me to get back downstairs, no use being a witness to a murder. He turned and hurried down the nearest stairs.

Rev. Ron came right up to Bill's desk and held out his hand to him. Bill looked at the man and wondered why on earth he had come in here today. Bill had a befuddled look on his face. He really didn't know what he should feel at this point. Everything had been so wonderful the last few weeks, so how was he going to deal with this preacher?

Then Rev. Ron did what everyone was fearing. He spoke. "I'm very sorry to hear about your sister, Bill. I know how much you must miss her now."

Bill felt the old anger rising up within him and he rose up from his seat and was just about to let the preacher have it, when he stopped cold. He saw that Rev. Ron had tears running down his face. "You see Bill; I lost my brother a few years back to cancer, too, so I know how you must feel. There isn't a day that goes by that I don't miss him."

No one said a word. If was as if the whole world was put on hold. Everyone was watching to see what would happen next. Then, to the surprise of the whole office, Bill came out from behind his desk and threw his arms around the preacher's neck, and they both just stood there and cried. Joe looked at one of the workers and said, "I would have said that hell would freeze over before I ever saw Bill put his arms around the neck of a preacher."

Tracie walked over to Joe, and said, "Well, well, for someone who said people can't change; this ought to make you feel pretty small."

Joe just shook his head saying, "I can't believe it's happening."

* * * * *

When Rev. Ron returned home from the newspaper office, his wife was waiting for him. Before Ron could even get inside the house, Kathy asked, "So, how did it go?" Then she saw his face and could tell he had been crying. "Oh my God, what did he say to you? I told you not to go down there, why didn't you listen to me?"

"Kathy, it's all right. We had a good talk. In fact we are going over to Bill's house tonight for dinner," he informed her.

"We're what?" she asked with shock.

"You heard me. We are going over to Bill's house tonight to eat dinner with him. Kathy, he threw his arms around my neck and we both just cried. I think God touched Bill's heart today, and who knows what God might do next," Rev Ron reported.

Kathy sat down in a chair, and looked up at Ron. She still found herself wondering what he was going to do next. Even after all these years together, she knew deep down that what drew her to Ron when they first met, was that he wasn't afraid to listen to the Lord, nor to act, when he was sure God had spoken to him. She was also thankful Ron didn't allow her to influence him during those times.

That night on the way home, Bill stopped by a restaurant and ordered food for his guests. DJ and Maggie could not believe it when they heard him telling someone on the phone he had guests coming over for dinner and that it was a preacher and his wife. On the way to Bill's, Kathy was asking Ron to tell her everything that happened at the newspaper office, and while Ron was trying to tell her every detail she just kept on saying, "I wouldn't have believed this could ever have happened." At one point Ron just laughed at her, and asked her if he was going to have to change her name to doubting Thomas.

"Well, you have to admit you didn't expect this to happen either, now did you?" she questioned defensively.

"No, I have to admit this has taken me quite by surprise, but it's a nice surprise, don't you think?" his voice was full of joy.

"Yes, it is. But what will we talk about while we are at his house?" she asked, almost to herself.

"We do the same thing we do when we first arrive at a new church situation. We just listen and follow their lead. You see God has prepared us for this day long before we ever arrived here, which speaking of arriving, I think we are here," he stated as he turned into Bill's driveway.

Kathy never would admit to her husband that she was more than a little nervous about their dinner invitation.

* * * * *

When Bill opened the door to let his guests in, he was as nervous as he could be. He thought to himself, "What on earth ever possessed me to ask these people over to my house for dinner?" You could feel the tension in the air, so DJ and Maggie came to the rescue. DJ jumped up in the chair by Kathy, while Maggie went over to Ron for him to pat her on the head.

"I didn't know you had dogs," Ron said.

"Yes, they were my sister's dogs and she asked me to take care of them for her, so I guess you could say I'm now a dog person." The remark made all burst out laughing, Maybe it was just the thought of Bill having dogs, or maybe it was that DJ and Maggie had helped to break the ice on this first meeting, anyway, the air was now clear of any tension, and they could tell Bill was going to enjoy himself.

While Bill and his guests were sitting at the table eating, DJ and Maggie were sitting by, beaming with pride at what their eyes were beholding. Once Kathy looked over at her husband and said, "Ron, look at those dogs, them seem to be hanging on every word we are saying.

Bill laughed and said, "Yes, if they weren't dogs, I would swear they understood everything I said."

Ron laughed along with them, but he had an uneasy feeling that they did understand. Then he laughed at himself for thinking something so strange. "Well, all I can say is they are very beautiful and they do seem to mind you, Bill."

"Yes, they are beautiful, but it was Sally who taught them how to behave as well as they do."

With that DJ, just turned his head and looked over at Maggie, with a look that said, "Is that so?"

Kathy said, "Look at the little one, and see how he just looked at the bigger one." "That's DJ and the bigger one is Maggie, and they love each other, so I guess that's why they give each other those looks at times," Bill explained.

"Bill, are you sure they don't understand?" Kathy asked.

"Oh my goodness, Kathy;" Ron turned "Bill, Kathy reads way too many novels, and while I am a fan of C. S. Lewis, I know animals can't talk." Again, they all broke out laughing. This time DJ and Maggie walked out of the room. As they walked out DJ looked over his shoulder at Kathy and as she was watching them leave the room, he gave her a little wink with his eye. Her mouth fell open, and she started to say something, but Ron stopped her saying "Now don't go and start it up again, dear."

DJ and Maggie went into the spare room of the house where they could talk without anyone hearing them. Maggie said "I can't believe it, DJ. It has happened so soon."

"Maggie, what has happened?" he asked.

"Well, look at Bill. He is talking with a preacher and is even eating at the same table with him and his wife. What did he say her name was?"

"I don't remember, but let's not get too crazy here. For one thing, the preacher's wife is far too observant, and she notices things, Maggie. We need to be very careful around her," DJ replied.

"Oh, so that's why you winked at her as we were leaving the room!" Maggie scolded.

"Ok, I must admit I did let things get away there, but it was funny watching her almost swallow her teeth. But Maggie, we have to remember how we would see Sally began to make changes in her life, and then some guy would come along and away she would go again. Don't forget Bill's enemy isn't going to just let him walk away."

"No, while I have to say, we have seen a lot happen here tonight, I know there can be setbacks. I know the enemy isn't going to just sit this one out and watch Bill turn his life around," DJ said.

"But look at what's happening here, DJ. Can't you see maybe it's time we tell Bill everything about us?" I asked

"No, Maggie, now isn't the time," he answered.

"But why isn't it the time?" she would not give up.

"All I know is, I feel something is coming to try and throw Bill off the path he is on, before he comes to the knowledge of God's love through his Son," DJ justified.

"Oh, don't say that DJ, please don't say that."

"Why not?"

"Because, every time you do, you're always right, and I know the battle has only just begun. It frightens me."

"Yes, but that's why we're here my love, that's why we are here," DJ reminded.

* * * * *

After dinner Ron and Kathy sat around and talked with Bill for about an hour or so before they had to leave. As Ron stood to leave, Bill said, "I am so glad ya'll came and I certainly hope you will come again, soon."

"Well, Bill, you're going to have to come over one night and let Kathy cook a meal for us. I mean, that's the main reason I married her in the first place. I heard she knew how to cook."

Kathy just rolled her eyes at Ron and said, "That's not true and you know it. I learned most of what I know from his mother before she passed away. Now that lady could *really* cook."

Bill stood back watching them tease each other and he smiled, "I can't tell you how much it has meant to me for ya'll to come here tonight. I feel like a great big load has been lifted off me."

Ron walked over to Bill and placed his hand on Bill's shoulder while saying, "Well, let's do it again then."

As Ron and Kathy were driving away, she looked over at her husband, and said, "I have just one question for you, ok?"

"All right, what is it?" he responded without taking his eyes off the road.

"Did you notice anything weird about his dogs?"

"No, why do you ask?"

"Well, for one thing they just sat there for the longest time watching us."

"Kathy, we were eating and they are dogs, now think about it. They were hoping we would drop something on the floor for them."

"No, that's not it either. It was as if they knew everything we were saying, and then as they left the room, the little one winked at me, and don't tell me I didn't see it, because I did. And the biggest one got up and just looked at the smaller one and he followed her out of the room."

"Why is that so weird to you, when all you have to do is to look at me and I will follow you anywhere you want to go,"

"Ron, you're not listening to me. It was like they could understand everything, and I could swear, I heard them whispering in the other room."

Ron just threw back his head and laughed at Kathy, then said, "Oh my goodness." Kathy looked over at Ron who was now laughing uncontrollably, "What does that mean?"

"Oh nothing, other than you were so afraid you let your mind run wild tonight."

Kathy asked, "Afraid of what?"

"Going over to Bill's house. Afraid of what he might do, or how he might act. Kathy, it's all right. God is going to take care of us and Bill."

Kathy looked at Ron with hurt in her eyes, "I'm not afraid of Bill, there are things I am far more afraid of than Bill Thomas."

"Kathy, I told you those days are behind us for good now."

"But every time I see you with those ministers who care only about what position they hold, I see you change Ron, and not for the better.

God has His hand on you; please don't let them push you away from the Lord."

They drove the rest of the way home without speaking. Kathy wondering about Bill's dogs and Ron wondering if he was indeed allowing carnal ministers to pull him away from the place God wanted him to be. Ron knew so many ministers were worried about the size of the church they pastored and they would do just about anything to get ahead, even to the point of lying about other ministers. He prayed as he drove, asking God to give him the wisdom to know how to walk in the world and perform the ministry he was called to do.

Chapter Six

The Enemy at Hand

It was getting close to the Christmas holidays and everyone could tell DJ really liked the holiday season. He was always underfoot, just waiting for some morsel of food to fall to the floor. Sally used to laugh at DJ for following her around the kitchen, always begging her to just let him have a taste of whatever she was cooking. I remember hearing her say more than once, "DJ, you're just thinking with your stomach now, so why don't you go over and lie down." Of course, although I would never follow Sally around the kitchen, I would stay close, watching to see if DJ got her to weaken her resolve about letting us have a taste. And much to his credit, he always did. I always told him with his sweet face, he could get just about anything he wanted from Sally. We both thought the holidays were going to be a time when we would be able to get closer to Bill and hopefully help him move more toward a life of love. He had talked with Rev. Ron on more than one occasion and it seemed as if Bill was really starting to make a change in the way he looked at life in general.

Then it happened. A few days before Christmas, into his office walked a woman named Jane Hendricks. She had blue eyes and dark brown hair. Jane had met Bill through a friend. However, at the time they first met, Bill really hadn't given her much attention; something she had planned on changing. The day she walked into Bill's office, she was wearing a dress which came down to the middle of her calves, but it was a very tight fit. She wanted Bill to see her figure. She had planned this day very carefully, even down to the shoes she was wearing. When Jane walked into the office, every man in the office stopped what he was doing and watched her as she walked so gracefully across the floor. Jane had, more than once, set her eyes on a man and then set out to trap him. The talk is, she had even broken up a few marriages in the past, but all Bill could see was a beautiful woman walking toward his desk. As she came closer to Bill's desk, she held out her hand and said, "Let me introduce myself."

Bill quickly and even nervously said, "There's no need, I remember meeting you some time back."

"Well," said Jane, "I'm surprised you remember meeting me, because you never even spoke to me that night."

"Well, I was sort of... hum... well, I was kind of preoccupied that night."

"Yes, and I can tell it wasn't with me," she replied, pouting her lips.

Bill, looked into her eyes, which was what she was wanted him to do, so she put on her best sad face. "I am truly sorry if I did anything to hurt your feelings that night Jane." Bill was blind to the look in Jane's eyes while he spoke to her; the look certain women have when they know they have a man right where they want him.

"If you take me out to eat tonight, I might find it in my heart to forgive you this once."

Bill almost choked trying to get the words out as fast as he could, "Why yes, sure, anywhere you want to go will be fine with me."

Jane pulled out her card and gave it to Bill. "Call me later and I will tell you where you can pick me up." With that she turned and walked ever so slowly out of the office. Jane was allowing Bill to see her figure as she walked away, so he would be sure to call her back that afternoon.

Tracie walked over to Bill as soon as Jane had walked out of sight, and asked "Bill, do you know anything about her?"

"Well, no, but she seems like a nice lady, and I plan on finding out more about her tonight," he replied.

Tracie had been so happy to see the change which was taking place in Bill. She couldn't put her finger on it, but there was something about this woman which worried her. "You're going to miss the Christmas party for her?"

"I've never have gone to one anyway, Tracie.

" Well, please be careful, there's something about her that just isn't right. Look at the way she dressed to come up here. She dressed so every man would be watching her."

"Oh, Tracie, don't try to mother me now. I'm a big boy, and I have been out with women before."

"Not like this one, Bill, I'm telling you, not like this one."

There was something in the way Tracie said it to Bill that made cold chills run down his spine. Although as soon as he thought about how Jane looked in that dress, he forgot his inner warning and gave in to other feelings which were not the ones the Creator would like for Bill to have toward the woman.

When he came home that evening, he ran in, changed clothes, threw some food in our bowls and was back out the door. DJ looked out the window as Bill drove away. He turned to me and said "Maggie,

I think we had better say more prayers for Bill tonight. I have seen that look before and I am worried about him."

"What do you mean, you have seen that look before?"

"Remember how Sally would look when she would run in and change clothes to go out on a date with a man she had just met?"

"Oh DJ, it's happening isn't it? Bill is under attack from the enemy isn't he?"

"Yes, and I don't know who she is, but she has turned his head terribly. Bill is in danger, Maggie. We must spend more time while he is away at work praying for him."

* * * * *

Bill was unaware of what was going on in his world. He just thought this beautiful woman was after him, and boy did it make him feel special. Little did he know, Jane was under the influence of the evil one and she was acting out of her own lust and greed. She really didn't care for Bill, but the thought of him not noticing her was more than she could endure, so, now he was going to have to pay, and she would take everything he had. No, she was going to have Bill and when she was through with him, she would just cast him aside like all the rest. But not before she had caused him a lot of pain. That was always the fun part for Jane. Knowing she left men in total despondency was what made the thrill of the hunt even more exhilarating. As Bill drove to her house to pick Jane up for their date, he felt a little unsure about himself. He hadn't really been out on a date in years and he wasn't sure just how to act. He really wanted to make a good impression on Jane, but little did he know nothing he did was going to impress her, for she was out on a hunt, and she had heard rumors Bill had a great deal of money hidden away. She was out to get all of it anyway she could get her hands on it.

When Bill knocked on Jane's door he could hear movement, but it seemed he waited a long time before she came to the door. When the door opened, Bill almost lost his breath, for Jane had on a very revealing dress, and her eyes sparkled with pure delight at the look on Bill's face. "Well, I hope you like what you see, it took me hours to fix myself up for you, and I hope you know I wouldn't do this for just anyone," Jane teased him. Bill didn't notice the devilish smile which came across her face. She knew the dress was going to have the affect she wanted; and she lied because she had worn the dress plenty of times before, and always for the same reason. "Let me get my coat, it is supposed to be cold tonight."

"Well, where do you want to go for dinner?" Bill asked.

"I hope you didn't think I got this dressed up to go to some cheap place, no sir, what is the most expensive place in town?"

"Gee, I don't know, are you sure you want to go to one of those places?"

Jane pulled her arm away from Bill's hand and she stepped back to take a good look at him, "I guess by that, you are telling me you are ashamed to be seen with me in public."

"No, not at all, I've just never been to one of those places before."

"Well mister, it's about time you went somewhere with someone everyone will take notice of and envy you." Jane then brushed up against Bill's chest. She knew he would feel her body under her clothes and did not doubt it would send his head spinning. By now Bill's eyes were aflame with passion, Jane reached over and lightly kissed him on the mouth, not lingering, just enough to get her hooks deeper into his heart. "I want to go to the Light Carriage Lounge tonight, my dear."

"Oh, I can't get in there. I'm not a member."

"It's a good thing I am then. I can get you past the front door, but then it's all up to you, Bill. Please don't tell me we aren't going to be able to go there."

"No, no, if that's where you want to go, then I am more than willing to take you there."

Jane took Bill's arm as they walked down the sidewalk. As he held the door for her to get into the car, Jane allowed her coat to fall open and positioned herself so that, as she was sitting down, Bill saw everything he could ever hope to see. His eyes were burning when he shut the door of the car, and she thought to herself this was going to be way too easy.

* * * * *

DJ and Maggie were having one of their worship times when DJ just stopped and laid down with such a heavy sigh. Maggie looked over at him, "What is it DJ, don't you feel all right?'

"I'm fine Maggie, but Bill isn't. Something bad is wrong right now and I feel it so deeply."

Maggie knew DJ had a very sensitive heart and he could feel things most others missed. "What are we going to do, DJ?" Maggie asked with such pain in her eyes.

"Pray harder Maggie, pray harder."

During this time Rev. Ron was walking across the church yard heading home for the evening, when all of a sudden he felt in his spirit that he needed to pray for Bill, and that he needed to do it now! He stopped and turned around and walked back over to the church, unlocked the door to his office, walked in and turned on only one light. He then locked the door again. As Kathy looked out the kitchen window, she watched him turn around to head back to his office, laughing to herself, thinking he had forgotten something again.

When she saw which light he turned on, she knew he went back to pray for someone and he wasn't going to be home at dinner time. A battle was going on for the life of one Bill Thomas, even though he was not aware of it, nevertheless, the war was on. And only faithful servants could see victory in these kinds of battles. Rev. Ron prayed on through the night, unaware he was joining ranks with some special little warriors. For guardians are always watchful in prayer over their charges.

* * * * *

Bill and Jane were enjoying their dinner at the Light Carriage Lounge. Bill had ordered a seafood entree which had a variety of seafood on it. Jane ordered a salad with some other green vegetables. The whole time Jane was eating her food, she was trying to talk Bill into staying at her house that night. When all of the sudden, Bill turned pale and started vomiting violently. It turned out, some of the seafood he had been served was supposed to have been thrown away, instead it got put back into the refrigerator then ended up on Bill's plate. Some folks might say that was just the breaks, but DJ and Maggie knew, when he walked into the house sick as he could be, God had intervened and saved Bill from the enemy's hand that night. As Rev. Ron walked out of his office later that night, he wasn't sure what had taken place, but he felt in his spirit Bill was safe for the moment. Jane sat there after Bill left, thinking to herself, she was having the worst luck with this one man. His money was going to be hers, if it was the last thing she did.

* * * * *

It was a good thing the next day was Saturday, because Bill was way too sick to go to work. Bill thought about calling Jane, but he just never felt like talking with anyone. Plus, there was something in the way she acted when he became so sick at the Light Carriage Lounge which bothered him. It was as if the whole ordeal had embarrassed her even though he was the one throwing up his toenails. Maybe she wasn't all she was making herself up to be, after all. Bill was thinking along these lines when he fell asleep again, only to be awakened by the door bell ringing. Bill got up and stumbled to the door, and there stood Jane, looking as if she were really concerned about him.

"Well, I waited as long as I dared for you to call; then I called the hospital to see if you were there. I guess you're mad at me because you got sick last night," Jane remarked. She was used to twisting things around where one never saw the truth, but only the lie she was painting to be seen. "And Bill, why don't you have your Christmas tree up, tomorrow is Christmas isn't it?"

"Why yes," Bill was shocked, he never for a moment thought Jane would think he was mad at her, and he hadn't put up a tree since his wife and daughter died. Maybe that's why she acted as she did last night.

She reached out and took him by the arm to lead him back into his living room. "Now you just sit right here and I will warm this soup I brought for you." By now, DJ and Maggie were standing in the door watching the whole thing unfold before them. DJ's hair was standing on end. He could feel the presence of evil with the woman, why couldn't Bill? Maggie wasn't sure just what to do, but then she did something which shocked DJ. She walked right up to Jane and looked up at her. "Oh, who are you?" Jane asked.

"Oh, that's Maggie and the other one is DJ. They were my sister's dogs and I promised her I would take care of them."

"Well, how nice, a man who keeps his word, and will even allow dogs in his house." It was her tone which bothered Bill, but he just thought maybe he was reading too much into what she was saying. However, for Maggie, it let her see everything she needed to see to know about what kind of person Jane was. Now all she had to do was figure out why she was after Bill. After the soup was warmed, Jane sat it on the table for Bill and said, "Come and eat before it gets cold." As Bill sat down, she kissed him on the forehead, and said, "Now, if you are feeling better tomorrow, maybe I could fix you something to eat over at my house, not anything heavy, just something light."

"I think I would like that," Bill said.

"Then it's a date," and with that Jane turned to walk out the door; "and the next time we go out, I'm going to let you pick the place. I'm still up-set with the Light Carriage Lounge for giving you that bad seafood."

Bill couldn't see Jane's face, but Maggie was standing where she could, and her face was filled with anger over last night. Maggie shivered as she saw the expression on Jane's face. There was no doubt about it, this woman had to be stopped, and soon. But how? Bill was totally blind to what was happening right under his nose.

* * * * *

Later that night Maggie told DJ about the expression on Jane's face and how she could tell Jane was lying about being upset with the Light Carriage Lounge, "I think she is really upset with Bill and she is out to hurt him for some reason."

"I agree with you, so here is what we are going to do. Every time she is over here, one of us has to stay in the room where she is, so we can watch and listen to everything she is saying and doing. It's up to us to catch her in whatever she is planning. From now on we have to be on our guard when she is over here," DJ planned.

As they worshipped together that night, DJ didn't tell Maggie how he felt such a presence of evil around Jane. There was no use upsetting Maggie any more than she already was. Maggie asked DJ if he thought they would ever have a Christmas tree again. "I hope so, Maggie, maybe next year Bill will see the need to open up his heart for Christmas again."

"Oh DJ, I do love Christmas trees!"

DJ knew how much Maggie loved them. When they lived with Sally, she would lie in the living room for hours watching the lights on the tree. In that respect Maggie was like a small child. She had never lost the wonder of Christmas in her heart.

* * * * *

As Jane drove home that afternoon, she very carefully planned her next move. She had means of finding out about how much money Bill had in the bank, and as soon as she found out, she was going to start going after it, all of it! Afterwards, she would just cast him aside like all the others. Jane remembered the time she felt true love for a man, and how he had cheated on her and treated her as if she didn't matter. Now it was her turn and she was the one who was having fun. She never stopped at just hurting a man, no, she took everything she could get and then some. She was never going to be treated that way again by anyone; she would always do the hurting first.

* * * * *

The following Monday morning when Bill showed up for work, he looked like something the cat dug up. Tracie walked up to Bill's desk with a deep look of concern. "What on earth happened to you this weekend?"

"Bad seafood, I got sick and threw up all over the place. It will be a long time before the Light Carriage Lounge will let me in there."

"You went there? You got sick at the Light Carriage Lounge?"

"Yeah, so let's not talk about it, ok. I'm still not feeling very well. I was sick all weekend and had to cancel out on Jane for dinner at her house on Christmas Day. I don't think it made her too happy, so I sent her some flowers. You think that will help smooth things over?"

Tracie looked at Bill with amazement. How he could not see what that woman was all about. "Bill, let's talk about your newfound friend for a moment." Bill just backed up and gave Tracie one of those looks which told her it was time to back off, "Ok, ok, I won't say anything," and with that she turned and walked back to her desk.

Bill liked Tracie, but he thought she could be pushy at times, and he still wasn't used to letting people in. He still had a wall up, which had kept him distant from people for years. Just about the time he got seated, in walked Rev. Ron. "Now what," Bill thought?

"Hey man, I was just checking on you to see how you were getting along. I know we're not close friends, but this past weekend I had you on my heart and prayed for you."

Bill softened a little and said, "Well, I do appreciate it, Ron. To tell you the truth, I was sick as a dog this past weekend. It was the first date I have been out on in years and I got sick on some seafood and started throwing up right there in the Light Carriage Lounge."

"Wow, now that had to cost you. I mean I couldn't take my wife there. That place is very expensive," Ron exclaimed.

"Yea, that's what they say. I wasn't charged anything and they hurried me out the door before I made any more of their customers sick."

Ron, just laughed, and said, "Man what a first date."

Bill laughed as well and said, "Don't you know it. I doubt that woman will ever go out with me again."

Ron smiled at Bill said, "I bet you she will."

"I hope so Ron, I hope so. You wouldn't mind praying about that for me would you?"

"Bill, you can count on it."

* * * * *

While Bill and Rev. Ron were laughing, Jane was already making her plan about how she was going to find out what was in Bill's bank account. She knew a lady who worked in the bank where Bill kept his account. She had heard rumors about the woman. Jane was certain the woman would not want the rumors to become known. All she had to do was find the right person to check the rumors out to make sure they were true; then she could set her trap. Bill was unaware of the danger he was in. He was so close to finally being free from years of anger and resentment. He didn't know the enemy of his soul was, even now, working at pulling him back into a pit so deep he would never be able to get out. Those who didn't know Jane only saw a beautiful woman, however, those who knew her, saw her as the most evil person one could ever meet.

When Jane walked into Bill's office that afternoon, she was wearing a pantsuit which was very tasteful. This time Jane wanted to give the impression of a woman who knew how to dress for all occasions and one who had refinement. The net was being spread for Bill and he was oblivious to it. "Hi, how are you feeling today? I was so sorry you didn't feel like coming over yesterday. It was because you weren't feeling well wasn't it?" she played her game.

"Oh, yes, you can count on it. I was still too sick or I would have been there." Why did she make him feel so nervous. It seemed every time he got around her, he was stepping on his words and nothing came out correctly.

Jane sat down on Bill's desk and reached out to put her hand on his face ever so lightly, "My poor dear, why don't you come over tonight and let me cook for you." "Jane, I would love to, but I have a ton of work to do. But let's do this, you come over to my house and I will pick something up to eat on the way home. Then after dinner we can sit and talk while I read over some articles."

Jane didn't let her eyes show the disgust she felt on spending an evening that way, but maybe she would find a way to use it to her advantage. "All right, what time do you want me to show up?"

"Let's say around 7:00, if that's ok with you."

"It's just fine with me. I'll go home and throw on something more comfortable and see you later tonight around 7:00 then." With that Jane leaned over and kissed Bill, not a big kiss, light like a butterfly on his lips. It was something Bill would think about all day, and that's just what Jane intended. Deeper and deeper Bill was being blindly drawn into the net she was spreading for him. Luckily there were two little dogs, waiting at home for him, who were not so blind.

* * * * *

Bill was a little late getting home because it took longer than expected to pick up the food. "Ok, now you two are going to have to stay out of the way tonight," he ordered when he came into the house. "I have some company coming over here and I don't want you under foot."

He stopped and thought about what he had said. "Boy, am I losing it or what? These are dogs and yet I am talking to them as if they understood everything I said," he determined. "Anyway, ya'll stay out of the way, ok?" he spoke again.

DJ and Maggie just looked at each other, not giving any clue to the fact they understood. In fact, they understood even better than Bill. As Bill jumped into the shower, DJ and Maggie laid out their plan for the evening.

"If we stay too close, Bill will lock us up in a room, so here is what we're going to have to do. We will take turns staying off to the side, out of the way, but always listening to what Jane is saying. If she goes into a room by herself, one of us has to be there with her. She is up to something, Maggie, and it's our job to find out what it is," DJ stated emphatically.

Right at 7:00, the doorbell rang. As Bill opened the door, Jane reached in and kissed him. It took Bill totally by surprise. Yet it made him feel so good to have this beautiful woman showing him affection.

"Wow, I wasn't expecting this when I came to the door!" smiled Bill.

"I know, I wanted to do something no one else has ever done before." For a brief moment sadness came over Bill. "What's wrong?" Jane asked.

"Well, it has been done before, by my wife when she was alive."

Jane knew how to bounce back, "Well, see, I'm following in the footsteps of a good woman."

With that Bill smiled again, and with a wave of his hand said, "Come on in."

Maggie was behind a chair watching the whole thing. She was shocked at how quickly this woman could bounce back from what seemingly was a terrible mistake. "We surely have our work cut out for us with this one," Maggie thought.

Jane followed behind Bill as he lead the way into the living room, and once again, Maggie saw the look of disgust on Jane's face. It made her wonder just what this woman was after. It was so clear to her Jane didn't care for Bill. Why was she going to all this trouble? She would have to talk it over with DJ later that night.

As they sat down for their meal, Jane just couldn't be complimentary enough about the food. "Oh, I just stopped by O'Bryans and picked up something. It's nothing really," Bill said.

"No it isn't," thought Jane, but to see her face, one would have thought she was enjoying herself. "Bill, you went to way to much trouble just for me. I would have been happy with just a peanut butter sandwich." With that, Maggie got up. Even though DJ looked at her as if to say what on earth or you doing; she just walked out of the room. She wanted to walk in there and ask Bill just how blind he really was. Anyone with only half sense could see this woman would never be happy eating a peanut butter sandwich. Jane looked at Maggie as she walked away and said, "What's up with that one?"

"Oh, that's Maggie. I think she just gets tired of lying in the same place, so sometimes she gets up and moves."

"Oh, good answer," DJ thought, "Maggie is going to have to be a bit more careful around this woman. They had a job to do and now was not the time for Maggie to let feelings be visible."

Jane moved closer by Bill and said, "You know, I have my night bag out in the car. I could spend the night if you wanted me to."

The very thought of Jane spending the night made Bill's head spin, but then, he thought about his wife and daughter, and about Sally. He knew it wasn't something any of them would want him to do. Bill reached out and took Jane's hand, "Let's take a rain check on that right now, if it's ok with you."

Jane had a look of total shock on her face, then one of anger, "You mean you are going to turn me down?"

"Oh, please don't take it like that… it's just that… well… I don't know if I'm ready right now," Bill stumbled.

Jane knew how to make her point, and she also knew how to set the stage for another day, "Well, I don't know *when* I have been so offended." She jumped up and ran out to her car. Of course, Bill was right behind her.

DJ looked over at Maggie and said, "Well, I don't care how she leaves, just as long as she goes."

Maggie walked over to DJ and giggled, "You're such a silly boy. Oops, someone is coming back in!" They both quickly lay down and looked toward the door.

Bill walked in alone, with such a sad look on his face. "I think I might have blown it with Jane tonight. She said she didn't know if she ever wanted to see me again. I tried to make her understand, but I didn't seem to get through to her," he mumbled as if seeking comfort from his own words. He walked into his room and looked down at the picture of his wife and daughter. Why did life have to be so difficult? Why did he have to lose the ones he loved?

Jane was laughing as she drove home. Oh, this is going to be much easier than I had hoped it would be. And just think, I'm not going to have to sleep with this jerk, just take him for all he's worth. Her laugh would have sent a cold chill down anyone's spine. It was a laugh filled with evil, and one devoid of any love or compassion. Bill had taken another step deeper into the net, and still, he wasn't aware of the danger.

* * * * *

The next morning Rev. Ron was walking through the kitchen when the phone rang. He stopped to answer it and by the tone in his voice, Kathy could tell he wished she weren't in the room right now. "Oh yes, that's fine. I'll be over for coffee to discuss the bishop's up-coming work day. Ok, I'll see you in just a little while." As Ron hung up the phone, he could see the look on Kathy's face.

"How could you? You promised me we would never have to go through this again, and now I hear you planning a meeting with people who would just as soon cut your throat as look at you," Kathy exclaimed.

"Kathy, you have to understand. If I don't stay in the loop some, I will never get a better church."

"Ron, do you remember the person you became? How you lied and for years and treated people who were your friends as if they were dirt under your feet? And if you want to tell me getting back in that group is going to help us down the road, then maybe you need to remember the road we were on. It was heading toward a divorce court and our marriage was just about over." By now, Kathy was crying too hard to even speak, she just held up her hand and walked out of the kitchen.

Ron stood there, not knowing what to think any more. He had been told if he didn't get back into the loop, he would be passed over for the better churches, but then he did remember the effect it had on his life. He never pondered the past and you could forget praying about it. His life was one big mess, however, he believed since he knew what the dangers were, he could prevent it from happening again. Like most people, Rev. Ron believed he could walk right next to that fine line without crossing over, and like most people, he was dead wrong. He had given most of his life to the Lutheran church, and had always served where they sent him. But this time, he wanted to make sure when they moved him; he was going to be closer to the top. The one lesson Ron needed to learn was being on top of things in the religious world did not necessarily mean you were on top of things in the kingdom of God. He turned and walked out the door while Kathy was in the back bedroom crying.

She listened as he drove away and she prayed, "Oh God, please don't let this happen again. I don't know if I can go through it again. Please open Ron's eyes to see all that matters is his faithfulness to You, not what some group of spiritually dead preachers think." With that Kathy started crying again, "Oh God, please send us someone who will pray for us and who will truly care about what is going on in our lives."

DJ and Maggie watched Bill as he drove away, heading to work. Maggie said, "Well, at least last night ended ok. Maybe we have seen the last of Jane."

"No Maggie, we haven't seen the last of her. But there is something else bothering me right now."

"What is it DJ, do you feel all right?"

"Yes, I feel fine, but this is something deep inside of me."

"Something else about Bill?"

"No. But I do think we should add Rev. Ron to our prayer time too. Something's going on in his life right now, and I just feel the need to lift him up in prayer."

"DJ, that's silly, he is a minister, and you know how he and his wife got along. Why would he need prayer, or what could possibly be wrong with him?"

"I don't know, but the same enemy who is after Bill, is after Rev. Ron as well; as he is all of God's people, Maggie."

"DJ, Bill's car is out of sight, so lets get started."

With that, they joined together in prayer and singing of the old songs guardians have been singing for centuries. Maggie started singing, "Blessed is he who walks not in the counsel of the ungodly,"

Then DJ added, "Nor stands in the path of sinners." It was going to be a long time of prayer and worship that day. In the end they would have comfort in knowing they did all they could do for their charge.

* * * * *

It wasn't until Wednesday that Jane made her next move. She called Bill at work and asked him if he still wanted to see her, or was he just playing games with her. "Oh no," Bill said, "I would never play games with you--- you know I want to see you, but I'm just not ready to go that far in a relationship now. It was so painful when I lost my wife and daughter, and I guess there is something in me that's still holding back. Maybe… I don't know… I just don't feel comfortable sleeping with anyone right now. I hope you understand."

"Yes, I think I do, and I don't want you to think I go around asking every man I meet to hop into bed with me, because I don't." This was one of the biggest lies Jane had ever told, in fact she knew how to use her body to get just what she wanted from just about any man. Bill was the first who had ever turned her down which made her wonder at times if this was going to be more difficult than she had hoped. Bottom line was, she was after whatever money he had and she was going to get her hands on it one way or another. "I tell you what Bill, why don't we meet somewhere, let's say Friday night for dinner, and we can take this thing a little bit slower this time, that way no one will feel rushed, ok?"

"Yeah, that sounds like a good idea, Jane. I knew you would understand. I'll call you later on and we can decide where to go and eat."

"Bill, you pick the place and I will meet you there at 7:00. Just call me to let me know where, or better yet here's my e-mail address." Jane had such a sinister smile on her face as they hung up the phone. Maybe it was going to be easy after all. Bill was just about falling all over himself trying to make things right with her, and with his e-mail address, maybe she could get into more of his life.

Bill was just about on cloud nine when they were through talking. "She isn't what I had feared, and she is going to give me a second chance," he thought. Things couldn't be going better.

* * * * *

As Bill sat at his desk working, he kept trying to think of ways to impress Jane. Then it hit him, he remembered Sally telling him how much she loved taking DJ and Maggie to the nursing home. They were both certified and the elderly loved them. He picked up the phone and made a few calls and the next thing he knew, he had them lined up for that Thursday afternoon at 4:00.

When Bill got home, he was still so excited over his idea he just couldn't help sharing it with DJ and Maggie. After all, what could it hurt, they didn't understand what he was saying. Bill was getting a drink of water and talking as fast as he could about how much fun it was going to be for them. DJ and Maggie were already looking forward to going when he let the cat out of the bag. "Maybe it will even impress Jane, and who knows where that might lead us. I know ya'll can't understand, but this is really going to help a lot with her."

When he turned around, Bill noticed DJ was holding his head down. He didn't appear excited any more. "Was it the tone of my voice?" Bill wondered. "It's ok little fellow, we're going to have a great time." Maggie walked over to DJ and just put her face next to his, she made noises which Bill thought were just some kind of grumbling noise, however, it was the ancient language know only to guardians.

"It will be alright DJ. Maybe the Creator has something in mind for Bill at the nursing home." DJ just rubbed his face next to Maggie's, their love went deeper than Bill could understand right then. They were hopeful one day he would begin to understand the true meaning of love again.

Chapter Seven

A New Friend

The next day, Bill left work early and hurried home to pick up DJ and Maggie. "We're heading to the nursing home I told ya'll about, so please do everything right for me." Bill paused a moment, "I'm talking to these dogs like they're human or something. I used to think my sister was crazy for talking to them like she did and now here I am doing the same thing."

The name of the nursing home was Peaceful Shore. Once a week they had 'A Day at the Beach' theme where all the workers dressed up as if they were going to the beach. Those living there loved it. During the holidays the staff would have hot chocolate and set up back drops as if the residents were on the beach sitting by an open fire. Bill was quite impressed when he walked in and saw how much time had been extended to the care of the elderly, but he was even more impressed with Paula Welch. Ms. Paula Welch was the administrator of the nursing home and since she wasn't married, she put all of her time and energy into her work. Bill first saw her as he walked around the corner of the entry hall. Paula was about 5 feet 9 inches tall. She was slim, with long jet black hair. Her green eyes could be spotted from a block away, and when she smiled, it made Bill's whole world stop in place for a moment. At least that's what happened when he came around the corner and saw her for the first time. Paula looked up and smiled, and Bill just stood there, as if he didn't know where he was or why he was even there.

"Well, I see you brought your dogs with you today, now who are they?" she welcomed him.

Before Bill could say a word, Paula was down on one knee patting DJ and Maggie on the head, which of course gave DJ an open door to lick her right on the face. Paula laughed at him, and just held DJ close to her. "Hey now, I don't kiss on first date." DJ's tail was just a wagging as Paula held him. Maggie got up close to her, so Paula could put her arm around her as well. "My goodness, aren't you two the friendliest dogs I have ever seen?"

Bill just stood there, not knowing how to introduce himself. Finally he said, "My name is Bill Thomas, I belong to these two."

Paula looked at him and laughed, "Well, Bill Thomas, who belongs to these two, I'm happy to meet you."

As she stood, Bill took her hand and helped her up. Something happened when they touched. It's a magical moment when two heart's come into contact, yet neither of the two really knows what has happened…and that's what happened to Bill and Paula.

Paula blushed for a second, then she turned and started walking down the hall. "If you would, follow me to the room at the end of the hall. You will find a large number of people waiting to see you." Paula stood aside as Bill walked into the room. Their eyes met, and DJ was wondering to himself, if maybe Maggie was right, coming here was all for the purpose of getting Bill here to meet Paula.

The room was full of elderly people. When they saw DJ and Maggie they all clapped their hands with joy. Bill let DJ and Maggie off of their leashes. DJ went to one side of the room while Maggie went to the other. Paula stood there shocked by their behavior. "Did you train them to do that?" she asked Bill.

"No, I don't know where they learned it. They belonged to my sister before she died, and I promised her I would take care of them for her. I think Sally used to take them once a month to a nursing home in her home town. In fact, I remember Sally telling me how she was invited to a seminar once and she carried DJ and Maggie along. It was about how animals could help the elderly."

"Oh my God, I was there. Now I know where I saw these wonderful little dolls, and I met your sister, Sally, too. She was such a wonderful person." At that moment DJ turned around and ran up to Paula. He just stood there waiting for her to look down. When she did he just barked once, "He knows me. I mean he remembers me. Do you see how he is acting toward me? I believe he knows me." Maggie walked up about then and licked Paula on the hand. Paula bent over to pat her, but Maggie turned and ran back to an elderly man, who was calling her by name. "Bill, they know me, they remember me after all this time." Without thinking Paula reached out and took Bill's arm in hers and just stood there. Everyone in the room watched them standing there. Paula was usually real reserved and strictly professional in her actions toward men. She had been hurt a few times in the past, and had made herself a promise she wasn't ever going to let it happen again. Yet, here they stood together, talking as if they had known each other for years, not even aware of the fact most of the people in the room were talking about them.

Bill was only supposed to stay there an hour, but he ended up staying two instead. Paula led him around to the rooms of some of the residents who couldn't get out of their beds, and they both watched with amazement at how the elderly people responded to DJ and Maggie. As they walked back down the hall, Paula said, "Bill, it was wonderful of you to bring these precious little fellows. I hope you will bring them back really soon." "Oh yes," he thought he might have answered her a little too quickly, but he couldn't help himself. As he looked into her green eyes, he had a new feeling, but he wasn't sure just what it was. It felt like something he had felt long ago, but he couldn't remember exactly what it had been.

Paula went back down to one knee to hug DJ and Maggie goodbye, which gave DJ another chance to lick her on the face. Maggie just stood there and wagged her tail, "Oh Maggie, I'm not going to forget about you either," Paula hugged Maggie also.

Bill was really confused when he left the nursing home. Here was this beautiful woman, whom he liked a lot, and then there was Jane who made him feel alive, but not in a good way. There was something in the way he felt about Jane which made him feel uneasy, but she knew how to come on so strong and forceful. It was something he had never experienced before. Which one was he going to choose? What made him think he had a choice to make right now? If Paula would go out with him, why not see both of them to see which one he liked best. Bill was playing a deadly game, and one he had never played before. He didn't know just how much pain this little game of his could bring to him and Paula. He didn't see that by even thinking those thoughts, he was setting things in motion to kill what could be the best thing which had come along in his life since his wife had died.

That night as Paula laid in her bed, she opened a small box and took out a letter which was written to her a few years back. Sally was thanking her for all her help with DJ and Maggie the day of the seminar. As she closed the letter, Sally had written, *I do wish you could meet my brother Bill, he is such a nice guy, and he is so lonely.* Paula thought about Bill as she fell asleep. She marveled at the way DJ had acted toward her. What was it about those two dogs? What was it she had forgotten about them? There was something, but she just couldn't remember it now.

* * * * *

The next morning Rev. Ron was walking through the kitchen, heading to one of his meetings which his wife was so against. Kathy knew better than to say anything now. She knew her husband, and when he got like this, there was nothing she could say to him. His mind was made up. He was going to do what he thought was best for them. However, it all truthfulness, Kathy sat there praying, asking God to open her husband's eyes. Ron drove down to the coffee shop where the meetings always took place.

As he walked into the room, he heard some of the ministers talking about some of the other Lutheran pastors who worked in their area. "Yes, I know him, he is one of those who believes he is so spiritual. He is always studying and praying. Well, look at the church he is pastoring and the one I serve, and tell me who has the better situation." It was Pastor Steve Godwin. He was the Area Rep. and the one who could make your life miserable if you didn't play ball the way he said you should. Ron walked up to the table and asked if he was late for the meeting. "No Ron, of course not, we're just talking about how some of these spiritual guys make us sick, that's all. Why, I remember when I went to seminary, I thought the Bible was true and a book you should believe. Boy am I thankful they set me straight on some things." Ron, sat there not knowing what to say, primarily because he still believed the Bible was the Word of God from beginning to end. It was times like these, when he wondered if he was doing the right thing. Then Steve would reach over and hit him on the arm and say something like, "I don't care if you believe that way yourself, but don't go around trying to tell me that I should."

Ron knew this wasn't correct behavior, but these connections could help his ministry. He didn't know why Kathy couldn't understand it.

"Ron," Steve spoke.

"Yes Steve,"

"Are you dreaming over there boy?"

"No, I was just thinking about what I had to do today, that's all," Ron answered. "Well boy, if you join up with us, all you will have to dream about is moving up to the top. Bigger churches, larger pay checks, and the bishop will take notice of you, of that you can be sure."

As Ron finished his first cup of coffee, he sat there and listened to the other minister's talk about how they wished they could get rid of some of the ministers in the area. "But wouldn't that be wrong?" he asked at one of the openings in the conversation. "Look here Ron, you're new to this game, so let me help you understand it better. There are certain ministers whom we feel they have no place in the ministry."

"Yes, but I know one of the guys you are talking about and he told me how he knew God had called him to preach the gospel," Ron explained.

"Well, let him go somewhere else," Steve yelled across the table. For just a moment, Steve's face looked as if it was filled with hatred toward Ron's friend. "Ron, you're going to have to decide whose side your own in this, either our side or theirs. There can be no middle ground here. We intend to see this thing through and get rid of as many of those Bible carrying guys as we can. This is, after all, the twenty-first century and we all know better than to put our faith in an old worn out book."

Back at Ron's home, Kathy was in the bedroom on her knees, praying for her husband. She knew it was all she could do now for him, but she had the strangest feeling she wasn't alone in her praying, that there were others praying along side her. As she finished her time in prayer, she walked to the kitchen to start lunch. However, the feeling that she was not alone wouldn't leave her. Kathy stood looking out the window, still praying and still thinking about the strange feeling she had felt all day. "Oh Lord, I know you are always with me and I do feel your presence here, but there is something else as well, something I can't put my finger on right now. However, thank you for whomever, you have praying with me for Ron."

As Kathy turned to cut the fire down on her peas, DJ and Maggie were walking out of the room where they prayed.

"DJ,"

"Yes love,"

Maggie always liked it when DJ called her that. "Didn't you feel the Creator's presence strong with us today?"

"Yes, I did; and remember we have to keep praying for Rev. Ron also. Something is going on in his life right now and he is in danger of falling into a pit from which he might never be able to climb out."

Maggie walked close to DJ and just pushed him a little with her body, "Always my dear, we are in this thing together. We're guardians and nothing will keep us from our charge."

* * * * *

On Friday morning, Bill's phone rang at his office. "Hello, Bill Thomas speaking."

"Well, I guess I'm not very important to you, since you've forgotten to call and tell me where to meet you tonight. Are you trying to send me a message or something?" was Jane's greeting.

"No, Jane that's not it at all. I have been buried under this work load and to tell you the truth, I forgot about our date."

"You did what?" Jane's voice was filled with anger. How could he forget about a date with her? Why, there were a lot of men who would be thrilled to hear her voice on the other end of the phone. How could he say he had forgotten all about their date? "So, I guess we're not going out tonight then?"

"Oh Jane, please don't be mad at me, I'll call right now and see if we can get reservations. I'll call you right back."

"No, just e-mail the information to me, Bill. But if I don't receive an e-mail from you this afternoon, then I will be going out with someone else." At first Jane's statement made Bill mad. Then fear set in. What if he lost her and why did he think anything would ever come of this Paula girl? 'A bird in the hand is better than two in the bush,' he had always heard. So as soon as he got off the phone from making the reservations, he e-mailed Jane the information. Now all he had to do was get his work done so he could leave on time.

* * * * *

It was around 7:00 p.m. when Bill arrived at the restaurant. It was a small, quaint restaurant called Mom & Pop's Place. They served really good food. As Jane walked in the door a few minutes later, Bill walked up to her and said, "I hope you like this place, it was our favorite place, my wife and daughter's, that is."

Jane bit her bottom lip, she was just about to blow him out for asking her to step foot in such a place. "Oh, I think it's the cutest place, and it's so sweet you would invite me to your family's favorite restaurant." Bill never caught on to the fakeness in Jane's voice. Maybe it was the way she was dressed, very revealing as usual, or it could have been just the plain fact that Bill was allowing himself to be blinded by her. The food there was just good ole home cooking, and while Jane picked at her food, she was planning her next move.

"You haven't eaten your food, Jane" Don't you like it?" Bill inquired nervously.

"Bill, the food is fine. I guess I am still upset about you forgetting our date tonight. I mean, how would you feel if I had forgotten about coming to meet you and had gone out of town. Then, when you e-mailed me, I wouldn't have been there to receive it? But, as it was, I sat there all day just waiting for your e-mail," she put on her pout face.

Bill felt really bad now and Jane liked watching him squirm. "I am so sorry Jane, can you ever forgive me for acting like such a fool?"

"I might this once, if you promise to help me with something?" she played.

"Name it and if I can do it, I'm your man."

"Well, I know you know a lot about banking and all of that, and I need a good bank, so I was wondering if maybe you could tell me which bank you preferred."

"Is that all? Sure, that's no trouble at all. I bank with the First Home Trust Bank." "Do you really? I have often wondered if they were any good. I mean you can get into real trouble if someone messes with your account now days."

"Oh, don't worry about that. They have one of the best security systems in town." "You know what, Bill dear?"

"No, what Jane?"

"I think I know a girl who works there and you're right, they do have one of the best security systems in town." As Jane put her drink to her mouth, she once again thought of the rumors about the girl at the bank, knowing if the rumors were true, the girl would do just about anything to keep them quite. Jane laughed out loud.

"What's so funny Jane?" Bill asked.

"Oh nothing, I was just thinking how nice it was going to be, you know our banking together."

* * * * *

It was late when Bill arrived home, but DJ and Maggie were thankful he came home alone. There was a message on his phone. It was from Paula, just thanking him for bringing DJ and Maggie to the nursing home and asking if he could bring them again next week. Bill played the message twice, then a third time. He was hoping to hear something in the message which would tell him what to do in his situation, but nothing was there. How could he be so confused? Why was he letting himself be drawn to Paula? He had only decided to do this to impress Jane. Bill didn't know Jane's true character. If she had known he was visiting the nursing home with his dogs, she would put a stop to it at once.

Bill didn't get up early that Saturday morning, it was the first time in a long time he had slept in. But when he did get up, DJ and Maggie were waiting for him to open the door and let them out into the backyard. Bill took his coffee and sat outside while they walked around the yard, as he always said, 'doing their business.'

DJ was at the back of the yard when Maggie came up to him. "DJ," she said in a very low voice.

"What is it, and keep your voice down."

"I was going to ask you if you thought Bill looked worried about something."

"Yes, Maggie, he is worrying about why his dogs are at the back of his yard talking to each other. That's what's worrying him."

"I have my back turned toward him so he can't see me talking with you,"

"It doesn't matter Maggie. We can't even let him think about our talking. It's not time and it might never be, so get back over there and act normal," DJ stated curtly. As Maggie walked away, she said under her breath, "Act normal? I always act normal. Who does he think he is anyway?"

* * * * *

The phone began ringing. Bill went inside to answer it. DJ went to the back door to see if he could tell who it was. "Oh yes, I think I could do that. Yes it is my day off, but I will give an hour of my time to help the elderly." Maggie had reached DJ, and by the look on his face, she could tell it was good news. As Bill opened the door for the dogs to go back inside, he told them, "Well, I hope you two are up to putting on your best behavior today, because we are going back to the nursing home. That was Paula and she asked if I could bring ya'll out there today. So let's get ready."

While Bill loaded DJ and Maggie into his car that Saturday morning, Rev. Ron sat in his office with his head in his hands. "Oh, God, please help me. I think I might have gotten myself into a fix with the wrong people. These men may be ministers in name, but by their actions, there is no outside evidence they know you at all. They are the most self-seeking men I have ever met, and now I have gone and gotten right in the middle of them. I don't know how to undo what I have done, please help me, O Lord."

At the same moment, Jane was lying in her bed waiting for the phone to ring. As soon as it rang, she picked it up, "What took you so long? You know I don't like to be kept waiting. Yes, I know it could cost the woman her job, why on earth would I care about a thing like that? Now, tell me what you found out and don't make me mad again. You would hate for me to tell your wife about the young lady I saw you with a month ago." Jane knew how to get what she wanted and she didn't mind stepping on someone to get it. She knew this man was going to do whatever she asked; because she knew something he didn't want his wife to find out. As Jane listened to the information she was almost beside herself with excitement. "This is going to be too easy," she said out loud. Maggie shivered as they drove over to the nursing home. DJ looked over at her. Maggie knew by his look, he had felt it too. It was like a darkness had passed over them. They both knew after Bill went to bed that night, they were going to be up late praying and worshipping. There was much to pray about these days, and they still had Rev. Ron on their list, as well.

* * * * *

When they arrived at the nursing home, Bill took DJ and Maggie out of his car. Paula came out and asked him if he needed any help with them. "Oh, no, they pretty much know what to do. In fact, I'm more or less just their driver."

Paula laughed at Bill. She thought to herself, that to have the reputation of being hard and cold, he surely did seem to be friendly. Of course DJ and Maggie were taking everything in, but they still knew they were there for a reason, so as soon as Paula opened the door they started walking down the hall toward the large room. "How do they do that?" she asked Bill, "it's as if they know why their here and where they are suppose to be."

"All I can say is that since they came to live with me, I have learned never to underestimate them. They are very remarkable dogs, although, there are times I feel they are much more than that." Bill laughed at himself, and said, "My sister would say she had finally won me over."

"What do you mean, 'won you over'?

"Well, I didn't really want to take them when she first asked me, but I promised her and now I'm glad I did. I don't know how to explain it, but they have made a change in my life. For the first time, I'm beginning to believe in love again," Bill stopped and then he turned a little red in the face. He couldn't believe he had just told this woman something so intimate. It wasn't like him at all to share his innermost feelings, or at least not the current 'Bill.'

Once again Paula took Bill by the arm and they walked down the hall following DJ and Maggie. She remarked, "If my boss saw us following these two dogs, he would ask me who was leading whom."

Bill didn't answer her, but he thought to himself, "If anyone could lead, they surely could." The day was a wonderful day for Bill. DJ and Maggie were hits once more. Everyone asked Bill if he could bring them back again to visit. As Bill drove home he was quiet. He was thinking about Paula and how she made him feel. She made him feel good about himself. It pleased him a woman like her could show some interest in him.

DJ just sat there wishing he could ask Bill what he was thinking, but he knew now was not the time. They would have to do the best they could to show Bill all the love they could. Look how far Bill had already come in this trek of his. No, he and Maggie would have to work harder to show Bill more love. That would have to be the way they would help him see the difference between Paula and Jane.

Paula had not moved from her office window where she had stood to watch Bill drive away. She wasn't sure how long she had stood there, but this was the first time she could remember taking so much time to think about a man. Yet, try as hard as she could, she just couldn't remember what it was about those two dogs she was supposed to know. She could almost remember, but it was as if it was just out of reach deep in her mind.

* * * * *

When they arrived home, Bill fed DJ and Maggie their food. They just looked quizzically at him as if to ask, "Didn't you feed us this morning?"

Bill laughed at himself again. "My goodness, I think I know what you two are thinking and yes I did feed you this morning, but ya'll did such a good job today, I thought you deserved something….more food, or maybe a treat. I don't know, I just wanted to show you two how much you mean to me, that's all."

As DJ walked over to his bowl he looked at Maggie. Bill didn't see it, but if he had been looking, he would have seen them wink at each other. Bill sat down and was reading the paper when the phone rang. "Hello," he said. Then DJ could tell it wasn't the call they had hoped Bill would receive. "Jane, why yes I have thought of you today. What was I doing? Well, you might think this is neat. I have been at the nursing home today with DJ and Maggie. They are so wonderful with those elderly folks and everyone loves them."

Jane felt sick. What kind of fool was this man anyway, and how could she be seen out with him? But she would do just about anything to get her hands on Bill's money. "Bill, you must be tired, so let me come over there and take you out for a good meal. My treat. Now don't say no, because I won't offer this very many times"

"Ok, I'll be ready when you get here." Maggie stood there wanting to get in Bill's way as he went to his bedroom, and ask him why he couldn't see the evil in that woman. When Jane arrived, she came to the door and rang the doorbell. Bill hurried to get the door and when he opened the it, there stood Jane, like a picture of beauty, only this picture was so deadly. At first, Bill didn't say a word. Then he said, "Wow, you look great!"

Jane had hope for something better than 'wow,' but it would do. It was the look in Bill's eyes that was what she was after. She could tell over the phone something was wrong and that she needed to get back close to Bill, if she had any hope of carrying out her plans. After dinner Jane walked Bill back up to his door, "Bill may I ask you something?"

"Yes, Jane you may ask me anything."

"Well, is there someone else? I mean you sounded so far away when I talked with you earlier, and I became afraid I was losing you, so, I hurried over here. I guess that makes me sound pretty stilly doesn't it?"

Bill was more confused then ever, but before he could say anything, Jane reached out and pulled him close to her and kissed him. It was a long, hard kiss. Jane was hoping she was sending Bill a message, not the real one but the one she was trying to blind his eyes with. After she kissed Bill, Jane turned and walked away as fast as she could. If there was one thing she knew, it was how to act.

Bill ran after her and when he caught up with her he took her by the arm and pulled her close. This time, Bill was the one sending a message with his kiss. Jane was laughing inside. She had played her cards just right that night and it looked as if it was going to pay off.

Jane pulled away from Bill, "I need to go, I feel so vulnerable right now and I hate feeling that way."

Bill held on to Jane, which if he had noticed she wasn't pulling away that hard. "No you can't leave like this."

"You mean, you want me to stay with you tonight, Bill?" Jane kissed him again before he could answer her. "Oh, I want to stay here with you tonight, Bill. Please say that you want me to," she pleaded huskily.

Bill looked at Jane and for a moment he came so close to asking her to stay, but then he remembered Sally. Her last words to him were, "Bill, I will always love you, no matter what you do." He looked away from Jane, which made her blood boil.

Jane jerked away from Bill's hold and asked him, "Who is she?"

"What? I don't understand you ,Jane."

"Yes you do. Tell me who she is."

"There isn't anyone, I promised my sister I would take care of DJ and Maggie and I know she wouldn't want me to sleep with you either. I mean, oh, can't you see what I'm trying to say?"

"Sure, you're not interested in me. How about that. Thanks for the nice meal, but boy, glad to see you leave. Your sister is dead Bill and those dogs in there could care less what you do, their only dogs!" Jane turned again and ran toward her car. She listened to see if Bill was coming after her, and sure enough, he was.

Bill caught up with Jane just about the time she reached out for the car door. "Jane stay with me tonight, please, I'm asking you to stay with me."

The smile on her face would have made every devil in hell rejoice, but Jane was a master at playing men, and she knew what it was going to take to get this one. Jane turned around and looked at Bill, she had tears running down her face, "No Bill, if I stayed with you now, it would make me cheap. You had your chance. I'll have to think about our relationship, I'm not sure I'm going to call you again, ever." She pushed him back and jumped into her car, Jane speed away leaving Bill standing there on the sidewalk. As soon as she was out of sight of Bill, she broke out into an evil laugh. "He was begging me to spend the night with him, how rich. I'll have his money before he even knows what is happening to him."

* * * * *

While Bill's world was being turned upside down by Jane, Paula was sitting in her chair by the window. "I wonder if I should call Bill," she thought. "I have never asked him if he has a girlfriend, so I might be stepping into something I don't want to be involved with. But on the other hand, he has always seemed so friendly when he brings DJ and Maggie to the nursing home. I just wish I could remember what it was about them. There is something, but I can't remember." With that, Paula picked up her phone and then she put the receiver back down. "No, my mother said a lady should always wait for the man to call. If Bill is interested in me then he will have to call me first."

DJ and Maggie were looking out the window the whole time Jane was putting on her act. "DJ can't he see what she is up to? If she thinks she is sleeping here, well, she had better think twice."

"Maggie, my sweet love, you know we can't say anything, besides staying the night isn't what she wants."

"Then what does she want DJ? I mean she is doing everything she can to get Bill to beg her to stay."

"He's already done that, girl, and I don't know what she wants. From now on, we are going to have to keep a closer eye on her when she is over here. I hope Bill does what he was talking about earlier and goes to church in the morning. Maybe he will go to Rev. Ron's church, DJ. They seem to hit it off. Maybe he will talk with him."

"That might help, it sure couldn't hurt anything."

* * * * *

It was sunrise when DJ asked to go outside, he just kept whining until he woke Bill up. "Ok DJ, I'm up, let's go outside. Maggie, get up. You might as well go too since we're all up now." He opened the backdoor and DJ and Maggie went outside.

Maggie walked to the back of the yard and waited for DJ to come back where she was. "Please tell me why you woke everyone up so early? You know I hate to get up early, and I was sleeping good, DJ. So, why on earth did you do this, couldn't you have waited a little while longer?"

"Oh, I didn't need to go out Maggie."

"You what?"

"Keep your voice down girl."

"If you didn't need to go outside, then why on earth did you wake us up?"

"So if Bill got up, maybe he would go to church this morning. I just couldn't get it off my mind. So I thought, if he was up, maybe he would get ready and go to Rev. Ron's church."

"Well, couldn't you have waited an hour or so longer? I mean the sun isn't up yet."

"I'm sorry my love, I just thought if he was up long enough, he would think about going to church. I promise when he leaves, you can go back to sleep and I will not make a sound."

"When he leaves? Boy, as soon as we get back in that house, I'm carrying myself back to bed."

"When Bill opened the door to let DJ and Maggie back in the house, he had made coffee and had already drunk two cups. "You two know what? I'm going to get ready and go to church this morning. I surely hope the roof doesn't fall in on me. It's been so long since I've been to church." Bill looked down at the floor. "I haven't been since that dark day when I lost my wife and daughter. We used to go all the time, but I stopped going and left the university and moved here to work at the paper." Bill's eyes were starting to water when he said, "Well," taking a deep breath, "I need to go and get ready."

DJ looked over at Maggie, who stuck her tongue out at him and walked off toward the bedroom. DJ loved Maggie and he knew she was only playing with him. In all truthfulness, they were both very excited about Bill going to church. Maybe this was going to be the breakthrough they had been praying for.

* * * * *

As the sun was coming up, Ron was still sitting in his office, thinking about the phone call he received last night which had kept him from falling asleep. It was from one of the ministers whom Steve had said they wanted to get out of the association. His name was Tom Dixon. He and Ron had attended the same seminary. It was a very conservative one, not like the one Steve Godwin and some of his friends had attended. They went to the one which would help them along in their bid for larger churches and climbing higher up the ladder in their chosen field. It was there they had lost what little bit of faith they had in their hearts. Now, all they had was their own ambition and they were out to get ahead, even if it meant getting rid of people like Tom Dixon.

Tom had called Ron to tell him about the charges which were being brought against him. In Tom younger days, before he became a Christian, he had a drinking problem, however, when he came to Christ, he put all that behind him. Now, here he was being charged based only on what Steve and some of his friends were saying. They were saying Tom had been seen at a bar drinking a lot. Tom knew they couldn't make the charges stick, but just the fact he was being charged was going to hurt him later on. It would close some churches to him, because the higher ups would look only at his file and never ask him if the charges were true or not. Tom was so upset when he talked with Ron.

It made Ron sick. He could have warned Tom, but instead he did nothing, and now he sat in his office realizing he was as much to blame as anyone. How was he going to preach this morning? How did men like Steve preach, or make an attempt at preaching? He knew somehow, he was going to have to do something, but he just didn't know what to do right now.

As Ron stood behind the pulpit that Sunday morning, he looked out and saw Bill. How was he going to lead someone like Bill back to the cross when he was selling out, and for what, higher pay, and bigger churches? Where did the words of Christ fit into all this mess he found himself in? Maybe it was because Ron had already made his mind up to set things right, maybe it was because God knew Bill needed to hear the word of God that morning. Whatever the reason, when Ron read his text that morning he felt God's Spirit there with him. "Turn with me to Acts, chapter nine. Read with me the first nine verses."

After the service Bill walked up to Ron standing at the back door greeting folks as they left, "Hi, Ron,"

"Hello Bill, glad you could make it this morning. Would it be possible for me to take a moment of your time today? I'll tell you what, why don't you come over and eat dinner with us? I think we owe you a meal anyway."

"Oh, no ya'll don't owe me a meal. I was glad to have you and Kathy over, in fact, I need to have ya'll back over again soon."

Ron looked at Bill with amazement. Here was a man who, just a year ago, wouldn't even speak one kind word to him and now he was asking to have him and his wife back over for dinner."

"Bill, lunch is on us, and I won't take no for an answer. Kathy," Ron, called out to her as she was walking by. "Bill is coming home for lunch today, tell him it's all right."

Kathy looked at Bill and smiled, "Bill Thomas, you are welcome at our house any time. You come on with Ron when he is through here. I'll go on and start setting the table." As Kathy walked out of the church, she still couldn't believe what had happened in the life of Bill. "Maybe God, you are going to use Bill to help Ron keep his feet on the right path," she mentally communicated with her Creator.

* * * * *

Paula was driving home from church. She couldn't help thinking about the pastor's sermon on following Christ with our whole heart. She also couldn't help thinking about Bill and what he was doing this Sunday morning. "Maybe I should call him and see if he could bring the babies out to the nursing home this week." She thought of DJ and Maggie, as sweet little babies. Again she was mentally reminded there was something about them she was supposed to know. She tried so hard to remember, but it seemed the harder she tried the more it was impossible to do so. Yet, there was something about Bill which kept drawing her thoughts to him. Paula found herself spending more time thinking about Bill Thomas than she would like to admit.

Out on the back deck of her house, Jane sat with a glass of wine reading the paper. She was planning her next move in her quest for Bill's money. While she felt she was making headway with him, there seemed to be something which was always in the way of her getting him to just fall head over heels for her. It had never been this difficult in the past to get into a man's life. She didn't understand why it was so with this man. It didn't matter though, because once she had set her sights on something, she wasn't going to detour from her prize. She had never given up before and she wasn't about to start now. If Bill had all that money, just sitting there, in the bank well, if he didn't know how to enjoy the better things of life, then she was going to. Jane laughed as she thought how foolish he would feel when it dawned on him later how she took him for everything he was worth. To hear the wickedness in her laugh and to see someone who had given themselves over to evil so completely, made the angels shudder. Truly Jane would do just about anything to reach her goal, which was to come out ahead in this life with more than anyone else.

* * * * *

DJ and Maggie were still sitting in their room worshipping. They knew Bill was planning on talking with Rev. Ron, so most likely he wasn't going to be home until late afternoon. Maggie was singing one of their old songs. It was one her mother had taught her. DJ just sat there and listened to her while she sang. Maggie stopped singing and looked at DJ, "Is everything all right, why aren't you joining in with the song?"

"Maggie, my love, there are times I could just sit and listen to you sing for hours. It's the sweetness that comes across in your voice, but even more the expressions on your face."

"What do you mean DJ?"

"Well, it's as if your whole face just lights up, from the inside. "You're so beautiful when you sing Maggie, please continue, I promise I'll join in this time."

Together they started singing and the room was filled with the presence of the Creator, who loves to inhabit the praises of his creation. Bill had already put their food out, but they always waited until after their time of worship before they ate. Later, when they were eating, Maggie asked DJ if he thought everything was going to be all right with Rev. Ron.

"We're doing all we can, Maggie. We're praying for him, and I know the Creator has many more praying for him as well."

As they laid down for their afternoon nap, DJ told Maggie one of their stories, about guardians who lived long ago. They learned their many lessons by the method of telling and retelling old stories about guardians who had lived in centuries past.

* * * * *

After lunch, Bill and Ron walked back over to Ron's office. "Now, what seems to be troubling you Bill?"

"I never said anything was troubling me, Ron." While Ron stood there holding the door open to his office, Bill asked, "Is it that noticeable?

My goodness, I must have it written all over my face. Ron, I feel like a fool, I mean, I don't know what I am doing."

"Well, at least your half way home, most people have a hard time admitting when they are wrong or that they don't have a clue what's going on around them. Why don't you tell me and let's see if I can help you make any sense of it all."

"I don't know where to start, but it started about the time Jane came walking into my office. You don't know her do you?"

"No, I can't say that I do, but you can tell me about her if you want to."

"Well, she makes me feel alive, she is so exciting, and she would have already been in my bed if I had gone for the idea."

"What made you say no, Bill?"

"I guess even though I was mad at God and everything about church, there was still something in me that remembered the good times I had with my wife when we would go on mission trips."

"Now wait a minute, Bill, you used to go on mission trips, and work on churches and things like that?"

"Yeah. I know it sounds so farfetched from whom I am today. That's how far I have gone from whom I once was, Ron. I let bitterness eat me alive, even to the point that I hurt my sister many times with my words, and Sally didn't do anything to deserve it, Ron."

"You know the old saying, Bill, 'we always hurt the ones we love the most,' even when we don't want to or mean to. So go on, tell me more about this lady friend of yours."

"Jane is well bred and she does have an air about her sometimes, but I think she really does care for me. Then there's Paula."

"What, you mean you're going to sit here and tell me you have two women on the string?"

"I don't know if I would call it having them on the string, neither of them knows about the other one. At first there was just Jane. Then I got this bright idea about how I was going to impress her by taking DJ and Maggie to a nursing home to visit with the shut-ins. Well, that's when I met Paula. She is one of the nicest women I have ever met. When I am around her it's.... I don't know.... There's something about her that makes me remember the way things used to be in my life. Do you understand Ron? I mean am I making any sense to you?"

* * * * *

As Bill was driving home, he didn't feel any better about his situation. It seemed to him Ron was preoccupied with something and he couldn't seem to keep his mind on what they were talking about. I wonder what has him so bugged out. I mean, he has everything any man could want. He has a beautiful wife, a great job, and more friends than any man I know. So what's eating him?

Ron stayed in his office after Bill left. He needed time alone before the service that night. He knew he wasn't any help to Bill. He felt so guilty about his friend, Tom. He could have helped him, but now he didn't know what to do. Even if he came forward, Steve and the others would deny any dealings with what was happening to Tom, which would make Ron look like the guilty party. He looked out the window, then looked upward in the sky toward heaven. "God, please help me to get my life back. Why did I ever go down this road? I couldn't see at the time how it would lead me so far from you."

Kathy knew something was troubling her husband and she figured it had something to do with the phone call he received the night before. But she knew this wasn't the time to ask questions. Ron was in a war of his own making, and all she could do at this point was to pray for her husband.

* * * * *

DJ and Maggie were waiting for Bill when he arrived home. DJ sensed Bill was getting close to home when he was about ten minutes away. DJ would always pick at Maggie and tell her males had a stronger gift in that area. Maggie just raised her head up into the air and walked away, and as she did she said, "You tell yourself whatever you need to, DJ, to get through the day, but we both know it isn't true."

If Bill could see the way they picked with each other, he would understand why Sally loved them so. It was through their picking and playing games on each other, that she began to see the possibility of finding love. For Sally, breaking up with Frank had been so difficult. It was out of her love for Frank that she did it. Then it was out of love for both Sally and Frank which led Maggie to use her gift to call him and bring them back together before Sally died. Bill would understand so much more if only he knew, but the time wasn't right, and it might never be.

As soon as Bill walked in the door, DJ was there to greet him with a healthy sounding bark. "Well, hello to you too, little man. I know I've been gone a lot longer than I had planned on today, so let me tell you what; I'll let ya'll out and then lets see what we can snack on later."

DJ and Maggie always loved to watch TV with Bill. Sometimes he would watch shows about history, which DJ loved. Or, if he was planning on remodeling a room, he might watch a show which showed how to do the work yourself. Maggie loved watching those type of shows. It was one of Sally's favorite kind of shows. Maggie still loved watching, because it made her feel close to Sally. Tonight though, they were watching a show about the life of C. S. Lewis. Bill talked endlessly about this person. It seemed he knew so much about him, and all the books he wrote. Bill looked at DJ once while he was explaining on and on about C. S. Lewis. "I wrote a paper on him in college. I had to do a lot of research on his life and works and I got to where I liked his writings, so I used to read them a lot. As a matter of fact, there are a lot of his books on the bottom shelf of the bookcase in my office. I never mentioned it the night Ron and Kathy were over here. I guess I wasn't ready to open up to them, then."

DJ sat listening to Bill thinking about what they were going to do tomorrow. It was getting close to ten when the phone rang.

"I wonder who that could be at this hour?" Bill asked. "Hello." For a moment there wasn't any sound, then Bill heard her voice.

* * * * *

Ron was sitting up looking out the window in the living room when his wife Kathy came into the room. "Are you coming on to bed Ron, it's getting late?"

"I'll be on in a little bit. I just need some time to think."

"I'll be glad to listen to anything you have to say dear, all you have to do is talk to me. I feel like you have shut me out the last few weeks. I know we have had some cross words, but Ron, I still love you and I don't want to go on like this."

"It's not you Kathy, and this had nothing to do with our having some harsh words. By the way, I am sorry for the things I said to you, and for the way I treated you," Ron replied in a soft, mournful tone.

Kathy walked over to her husband. She could sense he was hurting, but didn't know why or the cause. "Can't I do something to help you dear? I'll do anything you want me to, you know that." As she reached over to kiss Ron on the forehead, he looked up at her and kissed her very softly. The look in his eyes troubled her. She could see the pain. She didn't know what else to do but to go on to bed and pray while he sat up looking out the window.

Ron had preached on the power of guilt before, but it had always been one of those sermons he preached from notes about what others had said about it. Now, he knew its power and how it could take peace of mind and heart away. What he feared most was becoming what he saw in men like Steve, who had so hardened their hearts to the extent guilt no longer had any effect on them. Their conscience was seared. They felt nothing anymore.

* * * * *

While Bill was driving to work on Monday morning, he thought about the phone call he had received. It left him more confused than ever and he still didn't know what to do. If only he could talk with someone who could understand what he was going through. If only he knew someone who would listen to him. Bill had forgotten the days in his past when he faced days just like this one. Those were the days before the accident, when he would walk and pray for hours, and he always found the answers. Since then, the darkness he had been living under had robbed him of those memories. Now, he was stumbling over something he should have known from the very beginning. If he had not been in such darkness, he would have known what type of person Jane was from the very beginning. As it was, he wasn't sure about anything at this point. All he knew was, he was taking DJ and Maggie to the nursing home that afternoon, and Paula said last night she was looking forward to seeing him as well.

When Bill arrived at the office, Tracie Chapman was waiting for him. "I hope you're in a good mood today?" she said.

"Why?" Bill asked,

"Because Joe's on the warpath. It seems someone forgot to turn in their work on time, so we had to run an old add to fill up space on page nine of the paper."

"Who forgot Tracie?" Oh, no! It just hit Bill like a flash of lighting. "I forgot to turn mine in, their right here in my briefcase."

About that time, Joe came out of his office. Just one look and Bill could tell he was mad enough to kick something or someone. "I hope you know how much trouble you caused me today, Bill. I thought you always put the job first and you would work on into the night to have your work ready. Isn't that what you told me when I hired you a few years back? That I would never be sorry for giving you a chance?" Joe just stood there waiting for Bill to come up with some kind of excuse he could tear into.

However, all Bill did was to hand him the work and say, "Joe, I am so sorry, I forgot and there isn't any reason good enough for what I did. I promise you, I will not let it happen again."

Joe stood there, not really knowing what to do, he wanted to chew somebody out, but Bill wasn't acting the way he had thought he was going to act. When Bill got back over to his desk, Tracie came over there and said, "I'm so glad you didn't try to blow up on him, Bill. He would have fired you for sure."

"I was in the wrong, Tracie. It was my fault and I should have done my job better. Joe didn't deserve this from me and he's right, I did promise him he wouldn't be sorry he gave me a job. Now look what I've gone and done. I'm sure at this moment, he is sorry he did."

"Bill, you have picked this paper up from the dirt. People in this town only bought the paper to count how many mistakes there were in each article. Joe knows that, he might be a good office manager, but he's a far cry from a literary professor."

"Well neither am I Tracie,"

"Now Bill, I know where you came from, even though you have tried to keep it hidden."

Bill thought as Tracie walked back to her desk, how he did miss those days. Something deep inside of him missed the days when he taught at the university. He didn't understand what was going on in his life right now, he was seemingly at a loss for understanding of just what was happening to him. It was as if he didn't even know who he was anymore. The world he had created for himself was no longer satisfying to him. He didn't know where to go from here.

Jarrod Gilmore came up to Bill later that day, "Hi Bill."

"Hi yourself, Jarrod. What can I do for you today?"

"Nothing, but I might do something for you."

"Really and what might that be?"

"Well, a woman gave me a note to give to you. But I almost forgot, so I ran right up here as soon as I remembered," Jarrod handed the note to Bill and waited to see if it was as important as the woman had implied.

The color left Bill's face for a moment, then he just blew, "Whew-w-w- What next? I just wish someone would tell me what to do next," he thought.

* * * * *

Bill thought he had his day all planned out, but now from this note, he wasn't sure what was going to happen before the day was over. He had already made a commitment to the nursing home to take DJ and Maggie for one of their visits, so Jane would have to wait. He e-mailed her to let her know he would be an hour late meeting her. Something inside him told him she wasn't going to like it very much.

DJ and Maggie sat in the backseat of the car listening to Bill as he talked to himself. DJ felt really sorry for Bill and wished there was something he could do to help him, but right now all he and Maggie could do was to show Bill all the love and understanding they could, without giving away their secret.

Paula was waiting outside when they drove up. Bill took a deep breath when he saw her. Was it something she had done to herself or was he seeing her in a different light. Whatever it was, Paula was one of the most beautiful women he had ever seen. Why hadn't he noticed it before now? Paula reached out and opened the door to help get DJ and Maggie out of the backseat. DJ jumped up and licked Paula on the face as she was bending over.

Bill laughed and said, "His breathe can take some getting used to. I have tried everything, but nothing helps.

Paula laughed also, "Well, I guess I should get use to it then. Anyway, Sally told me the first time he licked me, she had tried everything and she hadn't found anything to help his bad breath. But, with someone as sweet as DJ, you can overlook it."

Bill took Maggie's leash, then stopped and looked at Paula. "What's the matter Bill? You look as if something is troubling you," she asked.

"No, nothing's troubling me. I'm just wondering why I hadn't noticed before how beautiful you are."

Paula stopped and looked at Bill for a long moment, then smiled, "Thank you for the compliment, Bill. Even if it isn't true, a girl still likes to hear it." Paula turned and walked as fast as she could without looking as if she was running away. Paula had hoped to get Bill to notice her, but she never thought he would say something like that to her.

The elderly were waiting for the loving couple, so when DJ and Maggie walked in they just clapped their hands. DJ knew when it was time to put on a show, and he went right into his act. He went around to everyone with Maggie following right behind him. "Bill look at them," Paula requested.

"What is it Paula?" he asked.

"Well the last time you brought them, they went around the room with DJ on one side and Maggie going around the other. Why are they following each other this time?"

"I wouldn't know. Maybe they were trained to do it that way." Each time Bill got near Paula, he could smell her perfume. Something about it made him remember, even more, the days when his wife dressed up for one of their Friday night dates. Bill felt sadness, yet at the same time, he was drawn to this woman.

Then there was Jane, what was he going to do? When he was with Paula, he knew he would be happy with her. Every time he got around Jane, he became confused. He wasn't sure what he wanted anymore. There was something about Jane which made him nervous when he was around her, yet excited at the same time.

The time he spent with Paula at the nursing home went far too fast. As Bill was loading DJ and Maggie up in the car, Paula came out to say goodbye, "Bill, I know this isn't lady like and I don't do this, believe me, but would you like to go somewhere and get something to eat?" she asked him.

DJ thought to himself, "Good, this will be an end to that Jane woman once and far all."

Bill stopped and looked up at Paula, "I would love to, but, no..."

"Bill, don't finish it, nothing good as ever come out of a statement starting with but."

"I already had a meeting scheduled or I would Paula, I promise. Would you let me make it up to you?" Bill asked.

"Well, since I sprung it on you without warning, yes. I understand, in your business you have to meet with people about the paper."

"Thank you for understanding, Paula. "I'll call you tomorrow when I'm at the office. That way, I can look to make sure nothing will stop us from going out, I promise." As they drove away, DJ had a sinking feeling tomorrow wasn't going to turn out the way Bill wanted. He didn't understand why Bill didn't just drop Jane like a bad habit. As Bill drove away from the house, Maggie asked DJ if they were ever going to be rid of Jane.

"I hope so Maggie I sure hope so. I just hope Paula doesn't find out he stood her up to go out with Jane."

"What do you think she would do, DJ?"

"Well let's just say, I doubt we would be going back to the nursing home anytime soon."

"Oh no, DJ, those poor people love us and we do so much for them. Surely Paula and Bill wouldn't let something stop us from ministering to those dear folks."

"Maggie, you know how funny people can act when they are hurt. If Paula finds out, she is going to be hurt.

* * * * *

Bill met Jane at the Light Carriage Lounge, where they had their first date, which ended with Bill leaving there throwing-up his toenails. Jane was sitting at the table waiting for Bill, "Well, I hope you aren't going to tell me you are going to have to leave early or something like that. I'm beginning to think you don't like me."

Bill looked at Jane.. She was wearing a black dress which fit tightly to her body, in fact, everyone could see every curve of her body. Jane had worn this dress many times when she thought things weren't going well with a man she was trying to gain control over, and it always got her what she wanted. Tonight though she had planned a little insurance, Jane had found out about Paula and she wasn't going to let this miserable little do-gooder stand in her way. Jane knew someone who owed her a big favor, so she had them bring one of Paula's friends to the Light Carriage Lounge. Of course, they were sitting right across the room from Jane and Bill. Paula's friend's name was Lisa Ellis. She had known Paula since they were children and they talked about everything.

They had even talked about the way she was feeling about Bill. When Jane saw that Lisa was watching them, she reached over and kissed Bill. It was a long kiss, one that stirred a fire in Bill and confused him even more than before. When Jane stopped kissing Bill, she started to pull back and sit back in her seat, but Bill pulled her back to him and kissed her again. Lisa sat there hurting for Paula. She wanted to walk over and give Bill a piece of her mind, but instead she planned to call Paula just as soon as she got home. Jane could tell by the look in her eyes she had accomplished what she had hoped, and now that the do-gooder would be out of the way, she was going to step things up a bit.

* * * * *

Paula hung the phone up and just started crying out of control. Why was this happening? Why did Bill act as if he liked her, only to go out with this particular woman, whom everyone knew was nothing but trouble? Was he one of those guys who liked to have a good girl for the public to see, while he had a buddy to sleep with on the side? Well, if that was what he was looking for, he could just take that tramp and leave her alone. Paula cried most of the night. She had promised herself she was never going to allow herself to be hurt like that again. Then Bill walked into her life and she thought he was different. Sally even said he was. Boy was she wrong!

The next morning Bill arrived at work a few minutes early. He saw Paula sitting at his desk waiting for him. "Hello, I'm glad to see you! I'm sorry about last night."

That's when she did it. Paula hit Bill as hard as she could right across the face. She hit him so hard it hurt her hand, but it didn't matter. Bill looked at her wild eyed, not knowing what to say.

Paula said, "How dare you say you're sorry about last night. How dare you play with my feelings as if it was all a game for you. I know you were out with that tramp, and you were making out with her right there in the Light Carriage Lounge, in front of everyone there. And you are going to tell me you're sorry about last night? I don't ever want to see you again. I don't want to ever hear your name again as long as I live. Damn you Bill Thomas, I hate you for the way you thought you were going to use me." Paula turned and ran out before Bill could even think what to do.

He was shocked. How did she know, and what was he going to do now? Bill sat down at his desk and just looked out the window.

Tracie started over to his desk, but when she saw the way he looked at her, she knew this was not the time to try and comfort him. She didn't understand Bill either. This was so unlike him. Bill was the one guy one would always think of as a one woman guy. What has happened to him? What had changed him so? Then she thought of Jane and all the pieces were starting to fall into place.

Jane knew when she saw Paula running out of Bill's office building, it was over. She drove off laughing. I knew she would go to him and make a spectacle of herself, do-gooder, they're all alike. Jane called her friend on the phone. I need the information on the person at the bank and I need it today. I'm going to get this guy's money and then I'm going to throw him back to that little goody two shoes. She can have what's left.

* * * * *

DJ and Maggie knew something was wrong when Bill got home. The first thing he did was to open a beer he had brought home with him. He set there and started drinking and he didn't move all night, in fact he fell asleep in the chair. After he fell asleep in the chair DJ and Maggie went into the other room to talk. "What happened today DJ? Why is Bill so upset? He isn't saying a word, just drinking. Remember what

Sally told us about how he behaved when he lost his wife and daughter. She said he just sat in a chair and drank for days.

"It's his only way to deal with what has happened in his life. I bet you, it has to do with Paula. She must have found out about his date with Jane. Let's keep our ears open, and we will be able to pick up on what happened today. But, for now I'm going back in there to sit by him tonight."

"Why DJ? He isn't going to wake up."

"No, maybe not, but he is still our charge and he is my friend as well, Maggie."

"I'll come too then. We're in this thing together, and maybe we will be able to help Bill work this out. Maggie followed DJ back into the room where Bill was sleeping. Together they sat there, all night, taking turns watching over him. Bill was unaware of the true friends he had in those little creatures, but maybe one day he would know.

* * * * *

The next morning when Bill woke up, DJ was sitting right there beside him. As soon as Bill moved, DJ looked up at him. There was such sadness in DJ's eyes, it hit Bill really hard. "I see you've been here all night. I did it again, didn't I? I messed things up with Paula. She hates me, that's for sure now. I couldn't blame her. Why did I go out with Jane in the first place, and to sit there and make out with her like a lovesick teenager. What was I thinking?"

Maggie was taking it all in. She was thinking about a way she could help Bill, but it wasn't the right time yet. First they had to catch a rat.

Bill called in sick, which he really was, he sat there all day, not knowing what to do. When he did get up enough nerve to try to call Paula, her assistant said she was unavailable. In fact, she told him he had lots of nerve even trying to call Paula. Then, she hung the phone up on him. The sun was going down when his phone did ring. Bill grabbed the phone, "Hello."

"I knew you were glad to hear my voice, but never in my wildest dreams did I expect to hear you so excited." Jane was doing all she could not to laugh. She knew exactly what he was doing and whom he thought was calling him. "How about if I come over and pick you up and go out for something to eat?"

"Not tonight, Jane. I must have gotten a bug at work yesterday. I came home last night and when I woke up this morning, I was sick."

"My darling," what can I do for you? Tell you what, I will bring you some chicken soup over. That will make you feel better."

"You don't really have to Jane."

"But darling, after that wonderful night we spent together, how could I do anything else. Now I'm not going to take no for an answer, I'll see you in just a little while," she insisted.

Bill didn't know what to do. Maybe he should just stay with Jane. It looked as if he had messed things up real good with Paula. A bird in the hand, he had always heard, but this relationship with Jane just didn't feel right. What else was he going to do? Bill got up and took a shower before Jane got there.

When the doorbell rang, DJ and Maggie didn't run to the door, nor did they bark. They slowly walked toward the door and stood where they could watch everything Jane did and listen to every word she said. They had to find out what she was up to and do it as soon as they could, for Bill sakes as well as their own. Jane didn't stay long, she acted as if she didn't want to catch whatever he had come down with. "Then why did she kiss him before she left?" DJ asked later, as he and Maggie were reviewing the situation. "Why did she wait until it was late in the evening, and did she know Bill was home all day?"

Bill had gone back to bed. He wasn't feeling well, but it was more from the night of drinking than anything else. "Maggie, I think we are going to have to use your gift tonight, my dear."

"What do you mean DJ? What are you talking about," Maggie tried to understand.

"You, love, are going to make another phone call."

Maggie wasn't too happy when DJ told her his plan, not that she didn't think it was a good plan. However, she didn't want to copy Jane's voice. Realizing it had to be done, they went upstairs. Maggie reached for the phone with her mouth and took it off the receiver. Together they dialed the number of the newspaper office. Jarrod was working late and he answered the phone. Maggie asked him if Bill was still working late.

He asked, "Who is this?" Then he said, "I remember you, you called early today. Look lady, I told you then Bill called in sick, he's at home." Jarrod hung the phone up and so did the dogs.

"DJ, did you hear?"

"Yes, I heard. She knew he wasn't at work all day, so why all the make believe? What is she up to and why? Maggie, don't you think it strange that one of Paula's friends just happened to be at the restaurant the other night?"

"You know, now that I think about it; it does sound strange to me. Maybe there is a rat in the wood pile, DJ. We are going to have to keep our ears open, and our eyes too. This woman is evil, but she is well versed at what she does, and if we're not careful, she will pull whatever she is planning off, before we know it."

"That's not going to happen, DJ. She's up against two guardians, and we're not going to let her hurt Bill. We will find a way to fix things with him and Paula."

"I hope so, Maggie, I hope so."

Chapter Eight

The Battle Lines Were Drawn

Rev. Ron was sitting in his office. He still didn't know how he was going to make things right with his friend, or if he could even stop what Steve had started. However, something deep inside of him was troubled, and he knew he had to do something. When it all came down to it, money wasn't worth it. Money wasn't worth the price of a friend, nor was it worth the price of his own soul. Ron felt he had failed Bill. He came to him for help and because he had been so heavyhearted, he wasn't able to minister to Bill. Ron's own heart was breaking over the situation he had allowed himself to get into. Ron's phone rang in his office, "Hello," he answered, wondering who could be calling him at such a late hour.

"I know you've heard the good news by now."

"What good news is that, Steve?"

"Why, your old friend Tom Dixon, of course. It's sad to hear that his drinking problem is getting the best of him again," Steve replied gleefully.

"Steve, I know Tom and he has promised me he hasn't had anything to drink in years, and I believe him."

"Well, that really doesn't matter does it? It's on his file now, and that's all we wanted. When he comes up for a move now, they will always send him to some small, out of the way church . You see Ron, you have to get rid of anyone who might take a church you want, that's how the game is played. You have to network you know. You have to have the right connections, if you're going to get ahead in this game," Steve went on.

"Why was it called a game, what ever happen to the ministry?" Ron sat there with a sick feeling coming over him. He now saw just how far he had been pulled into this trap. He was the one who told about Tom's being set free from drinking when he came to Christ. He meant it as a witness to Christ's delivering power in one of their conversation over coffee. Little did he know they were going to use it against Tom. A lie meant nothing to men who were out to 'get ahead' anyway they could. Ron fell on his face and prayed. He spent the whole night in prayer. He begged God to help him find a way to make things right, to do the right thing, no matter the cost.

* * * * *

Friday morning Bill walked into the office. He was early and he still did not want anyone asking him about Paula and what happened the day she came into his office. He had never been so sick over anything in his life, and every time Jane called him, he always had a reason for not going out with her. Maybe if he went by the nursing home he could talk to Paula and tell her he had acted like a fool and he knew it.

However, when Bill arrived at the nursing home, he got there just in time to see Paula getting into a car with another man. "Well, I must not have meant that much to her if she's out on a date so soon," he mused. Bill got back into his car and drove away from the nursing home. He was mad and hurt, but madder at himself than he would like to admit or was going to admit at the time. He reached for his cell phone, "Hello Jane, do you still want to get together tonight? I think I'm feeling a little better if you're up to it," he reacted to his confused emotions.

Jane was smiling when she put the receiver down. "He's mine, now I can start bringing my plans together," she thought slyly.

They went back to the Light Carriage Lounge for dinner and Jane took Bill by the hand and asked him if he wanted to dance. "I haven't danced in years," he hesitated.

"Well then, it's about time you start back, don't you think?"

"Yes, I do think it's about time I start living again. I've been shut away far too long. Yes, it's time for me to have some fun," he stated somewhat rebelliously.

They had danced for over an hour when, at last Jane said, "I'm about given out. Boy, when you start something back up, you really know how to do it right."

"I'm sorry. I didn't mean to wear you out."

"Oh no, I'm not worn out. How would you like to go back to my place for a nightcap---just one little drink?"

"Ok, but just a small one. I'm not drinking these days. That's one thing I don't ever plan on taking back up."

"I understand and I would never ask you to do anything you didn't feel comfortable with."

When they got back to Jane's house, she turned the lights down low and turned the music on. They sat down together and Bill took a drink from his glass. He felt nervous about being there, but then he thought about Paula getting into that man's car. Why shouldn't he be here? He was a grown man. It was his business what he did and not anyone else's.

"What are you thinking about Bill? You're not talking much tonight," Jane asked sweetly.

"Oh, nothing, I was just listening to the music. It does make you feel so clam doesn't it?"

"It makes me feel alive," and with that, Jane leaned over and kissed Bill. She pulled away and took his drink away from him and kissed him again, this time it was a really long kiss.

When Bill woke up the next morning, he felt so guilty. There was Jane sleeping right next to him. How did he let this happen, and more importantly, what was he going to do about it? He was dressed and trying to leave without waking Jane. "Hey, where are you going and why are you leaving so early?" she roused.

"I have to get back home to take DJ and Maggie outside. They will think I have forgotten all about them."

"Bill, their only dogs. I doubt if they care or even know you weren't there last night."

"You don't know these two. They not only care, but they know. Jane, they're different from any dogs I have ever been around."

Jane jumped out of bed and ran over to Bill to give him a good-bye kiss. She knew Bill was having feelings of remorse, and she knew just how to put those fires out. She held on to Bill as she kissed him as if he was the most important thing in the world to her. For a moment, Bill almost stayed when she asked him to, but DJ and Maggie would be hungry and they needed to go outside.

Bill didn't listen to any music nor did he listen to the news, he just drove in silence, his heart was waging a war within him. He had never felt so low, and he still didn't know why he had stayed. He liked Jane, but he knew this was wrong. Why didn't he stick to his beliefs? Why did he give in to her? He finally had to admit it to himself, it was all about lust. The way Jane was dressed. The way she had rubbed up against him while they were dancing. He just gave in to lust, and he hoped she didn't blame him for staying overnight. Perhaps she only asking because she thought she had to for him to continue being interested in her. My goodness, what would he do if he blew this thing with Jane like he had with Paula?

When Bill walked into the house, DJ and Maggie both ran up to him. They were barking, but deep down inside they were glad to see Bill home safe and sound. He opened the back door to let them out. Maggie ran out first and then DJ started out, but, he stopped in the doorway and looked back at Bill, "What is it little man?" Bill reached down to pat him.

DJ, turned quickly and walked away toward the yard. DJ was hurt. He knew where Bill had been. He knew the enemy had won a victory last night. Bill wasn't aware of it, but DJ and Maggie could see it. A darkness had come over Bill's face, not necessarily something just anyone would notice, but they did, and it cut both of them to the heart.

Bill got his coffee and sat out on the back deck. It was cold, but not enough to keep Bill off the deck. DJ and Maggie both stayed away from him while they were outside. They had talked a little before Bill came outside, but they still hadn't worked out a plan yet. Bill just sat there alone, his heart was waging its own little war, and he still didn't know how he was going to tell Jane they couldn't sleep together anymore. He just knew she would take it as rejection.

* * * * *

Paula was at her cousin's house. Bill didn't know the man who picked her up was her first cousin, and they had been best friends since their childhood. Paula loved his wife and their two children. When she woke up the morning after her arrival, she thought it had been a mistake to come there, because the children were going to be a reminder to her that she was probably never going to have any of her own. She didn't understand how Bill could have been so nice when he was around her and lead her to believe he was really interested in her. Well, it was better she found out before it went too far and she really fell in love with him. The sad thing was, even though Paula had lied to herself about being in love with Bill, she was already in love with him and the more she tried to turn her feelings off, the more she was going to hurt over Bill.

* * * * *

Tracie talked with her husband that Saturday morning as they were eating their eggs. "Earl, I don't understand what has gotten into Bill Thomas lately."

"What do you mean? I thought he was always kind of 'out there' from what you've told me in the past."

"Well he was, but then he changed and you could see perhaps what the real Bill was like. Then the other day, a really nice looking woman came up to the office to see him."

"Now Tracie, you can't blame the man for seeing a nice looking woman."

"No, that's not it. Let me finish, will you, before you butt into what I'm saying. This lady rared back and slapped him so hard it about took his head off. I have never seen anyone as surprised as Bill was."

"What did he do? I mean, what did he say to her to make her do that?"

"Nothing, she didn't give him anytime to say anything, she just blew him out real good and left."

"Wow, maybe I need to come to work with you. I never get to see anything that exciting at my office."

"Earl, I'm being serious here. I think Bill was really hurt over what Paula did, even though I couldn't blame her."

"Why is that?"

"Oh, let me tell you the good stuff now. It seems Bill was leading Paula on, or maybe he was just dating two women at the same time, trying to decide which one he liked the best. That *never* works, especially when one of the women finds out about the other one. You remember that little red head you were trying to date when we first started dating don't you?"

"Tracie, that was a long time ago. When are you ever going to forget it?"

"Oh, I have. I just have fun reminding you sometimes."

"Who was the other woman Bill was seeing?"

"Oh yeah. I almost forgot, it's Jane Hendricks. She's a looker too, but there is something about her that makes mc nervous when she is around."

Earl looked pale and sat there for a long time saying nothing. "Earl, do you know her? What's the matter with you?" He looked up from his cup of coffee, tears were running down his face. Tracie drew a deep breath, afraid of what was he about to tell her.

"Earl, what is it?"

* * * * *

Saturday morning found Ron in his office working on his sermon for the following morning. He had stayed away from the coffee drinking club all week. He felt it would make him too sick to even be around those guys. How could they just sit there and plan to ruin someone's life and not see how wrong they were? Truly they had to believe something, or had they arrived at the place where they no longer believed anything in the Bible. Did they see themselves as the only rule of conduct and morality? Ron knew what he had to do, but first he had to talk with Kathy. She had been right all along. He had made a bad decision and now he was going to have to 'eat crow.' He just hoped he wouldn't lose a friend in Tom.

When Ron walked in the back door he mentioned the cold morning they were having. Kathy sat there drinking her coffee. She didn't speak as she would have done before the last few weeks. Ron had been keeping his distance from her. Kathy hated what they were going through and had been praying it would end soon. She saw no way she could help change it. Ron stood there and looked at her. How was he going to admit to her he had been a fool all the time? How was he going to tell her he had missed the mark?"

"I need to talk with you if you have the time."

Fear filled Kathy. She wasn't sure what he was going to say next, since they had some harsh words lately. She was afraid Ron might be pulling away from her even more. Her voice was trembling as she said, "What is it Ron?"

"Kathy, I have been a fool. I have done something, or rather I was used by those men and now a good friend has been hurt. I should have listened to you. If I had, none of this would have happened."

Kathy jumped up and threw her arms around Ron's neck, she burst into tears, "Oh God, and I was so afraid you weren't going to want me anymore. I'm so sorry for the things I said to you, please forgive me."

"No, it's I who should be asking you to forgive me. I should have listened to you. Instead, now I have caused a good friend to suffer and I'm not sure what I can do to undo what I have done."

Kathy held Ron close, "Together, we'll face it. Together, Ron, and no matter what happens, we're never going to let anything come between us again."

They just stood there and held each other for the longest time. Slowly Ron told Kathy how something he had said had been used against Tom. Ron broke down crying while he was telling her, "I feel so ashamed of myself. Tom is my friend, and I would never do anything to hurt him."

Kathy put her arms around Ron and held him close to her, "You're a good man, and I know you will come up with the right thing to do. The first thing I think we need to do is have Tom and his wife over for a meal. Only then can we come up with the right plan."

* * * * *

Earl took a deep breath. He didn't know how he as going to tell Tracie about Jane. He knew it would upset her so. "Darling, you remember my old partner Shawn Whitehead don't you?"

"Of course, how could I forget him? He's the one who killed himself over some woman who broke up his marriage and stole most of his money. That's when you took the business over. I remember how hard you had to work to turn things around. But why are you bringing Shawn up now?" Earl just gave Tracie a strange look as he took a sip of his coffee. Tracie dropped her cup to the floor as it hit her. "Oh my God! The woman was Jane Hendricks, wasn't she?"

"Yes she was, and now it seems she has her eyes set on your friend, Bill."

"I've got to warn him about her. He has to know."

"Tracie, you can't say a word to him, that woman would take us to court. She would swear it was all a pact of lies, and the only one who could prove her wrong is dead."

Tracie put her head in her hands and started crying, "Then Bill might end up like Shawn and there is nothing we can do to stop it, is there?"

"No, at this point there isn't a thing we can do. If ever a man needed an angel in his corner, Bill surely does."

They sat there the rest of the morning drinking their coffee, trying to think of someway they could help Bill out of the mess he had ended up in, but there isn't much one can do to help someone who hasn't a clue he is in need of help. Finally, Earl took Tracie's hands and together they put Bill into the hands of God, knowing only there, would he find the help he needed.

* * * * *

Paula's trip back home was overshadowed by the cold day with over cast skies, and by the time she arrived home, it was late Saturday afternoon. She was tired and wondered why she even went to visit her cousins. All it did, was make her even more depressed about the whole situation with Bill. The more she thought about the way she acted at his office, the more she regretted her actions. What Bill did was wrong, but that gave her no reason to burst into his office and slap him as hard as she could. It was so out of character for her. Maybe she cared more for Bill than she would like to admit, even to herself. Paula took a card and wrote a short note on it. In it, she told Bill how sorry she was for the way things turned out between them. She apologized for hitting him and yelling at him. *Please*, she wrote, *If you can find it in your heart, please forgive me for the way I acted that day. I know there will never be anything between us, and now I guess there never was. I let my own imagination run away with me and thought there was something there, when it is quite clear now there wasn't.* It was a very hard thing to do, but she signed the card and put it into the mail. "Why did she let herself fall for this guy, and how did it happen?" she asked herself. "How could she ever ask him to bring DJ and Maggie back to the nursing home? She just couldn't face him again, not after what had happened." Paula started crying again, "Why did I let myself fall in love with Bill? Why go through this again," she thought to herself. "Is love really worth all this? Is there really a thing called love?"

* * * * *

Bill's phone rang and as he reached over to pick it up, he knew inside who it was. "Hello."

"What happened to you? I haven't heard from you all day. Don't tell me you hated being with me *that* bad."

"Jane it isn't that... it's just,... well... I'm not comfortable just hopping in and out of bed with women."

"Who have you been in bed with besides me?"

"No one, but I shouldn't have been in bed with you either."

"Oh, I see. You had your fun, so now you are going to just cast me aside, and be off to the next one. Is that how it is, Bill?"

"No, it's not that way at all. However, if we are going to keep seeing each other, we have to reach an agreement that we are going to stay out of bed. Jane, I like you a lot, but I don't believe people should sleep with just anyone."

"Well, I didn't think I was just anyone, Bill."

"You're not. Now don't go and try to make this harder than it already is. All I am saying is that... well... lets take things slower, ok?"

"Ok Bill, I can live with that. But don't let me catch you in bed with someone else."

"You won't, Jane, I promise. How about if we meet tomorrow for lunch, say around 1:00 in the afternoon." When Bill got off the phone with Jane, something was wrong; he was no longer excited to be around her. He had seen a side of her which he had not known was there. Even in times like these, men can lie to themselves, which is what Bill did that day.

"She was upset," he thought, "she thought I was just out to get her in my bed. Maybe, now, she will know I am not that way. Maybe now, we can have a good relationship where there is no pressure being put on anyone to do something they are not comfortable with."

Jane was at home sitting in her favorite chair. She was laughing out loud to herself, "I know what I'll do, I'll play the 'you were using me' bit a little more until he is so guilty, he will open the door wide open for me to go through his house without him thinking anything about it. I'll have his records, his money, and then I will kick him back to that little Miss Priss." One thing Jane never had any trouble with, was her conscience. No one knew just how far she would go to get what she wanted, but when it came down to it, Jane would go to any length to reach her goal.

* * * * *

Joe Rushing sat in his office late that Saturday evening. He was known to work late sometimes, but it wasn't something he often did . He had a lot on his mind that Saturday night. The paper was doing really well, and he wouldn't admit it to anyone, but it started to turn around when Bill came to work for the paper. Why, Bill could take a story and dress it up so everybody was talking about it for days. Yeah, he was surely glad to have Bill working for him. He just couldn't figure out what had been going on in Bill's life since his sister died. He had seen people do some pretty strange things over the years, but by taking those two dogs of his sister's he had stopped drinking, and was even starting to show up to work on time. Then, what happen the other day with that woman named Paula? Yeah, he was just sitting trying to figure out what was going on in the life of Bill.

* * * * *

DJ and Maggie went into the other room after Bill went to bed. Luckily, he was not in the mood to stay up late and watch TV. "We have to keep our voices down Maggie, so we won't wake Bill up," DJ cautioned.

"I know DJ, but answer me, do you think Bill is going to get up and go to church in the morning?"

"Nope, I surely don't my dear."

"Why not? He went last Sunday morning."

"I know, but he hadn't slept with that evil woman either, and you know how humans are. When they feel bad about something they've done, church is the last place they want to be. Most likely we will sit outside in the morning while he drinks his coffee and then come in and watch TV all afternoon."

"You mean you and Bill will sleep, while the TV is on, don't you?"

"Maggie it's time we started our worship."

"Hum… couldn't answer that could you little boy?"

"Yes, I could, old girl, but I choose rather to get to the task at hand."

"Who are you calling old anyway?"

"Who are you calling little boy? Ok, let's get to our business," and with that, DJ started to sing in a very low voice so he would not to be heard. He sang an ancient old hymn, long forgotten by men, even though it was in God's book, but still sung by the guardians.

"He sent His word and healed them, and delivered them from their destructions. Oh, that men would give thanks to the Lord for His goodness, and for His wonderful works to the children of men!"

Maggie joined in and together their voices made such a sweet sound. Bill didn't know why he had been sleeping better lately, but it was due to the presence of the Creator who filled his house while DJ and Maggie worshipped.

* * * * *

On Monday morning while Bill was driving to work, he thought about the sermon Rev. Ron had preached the day before. He had to admit, it did seem as though Ron was in a better frame of mind this time. Maybe, whatever had been troubling him was over and now he could keep his mind on his work. Bill laughed to himself, "Maybe I could go and talk with him and he would remember I came by this time." Bill also thought about his dinner date with Jane yesterday. She seemed to be surprised by the fact he had been to church that morning. She came to the restaurant dressed very conservatively. Jane wasn't wearing a lot of make-up and it looked as if she hadn't slept much in the last few days. "What's the matter, are you alright?" Bill asked her.

"Oh yeah, I just made a complete fool out of myself by going to bed with you and now, I suppose you're going to tell me, it was fun while it lasted but now the fun is over, so, see you later." Jane knew Bill was feeling guilty over their having slept together and she was a master when it came to playing this game. She knew how to use his own guilt against him and make him think it was all his fault.

Bill sat there with his head down while she talked. Jane had gotten so good at her debauchery, she could even cry on demand. When Bill looked up at her, tears were running down her face. What makeup she had on, was running.

"Bill, the only reason I went to bed with you in the first place, was because I was afraid of losing you. I know how men are. They aren't going to go out with a woman without going to bed with her. I have lost more than a few men because I refused to go to bed with them, only to watch them go out with someone else who would. That's why I put so much pressure on you to go to bed with me in the first place. I liked you and I was afraid of losing you to someone else."

Bill thought if there was a rock somewhere, he could just about walk under it right now, he felt so low. Jane was also a master at reading the face of the man she was trying to fool, and she could tell Bill had taken her hook, line and all. Bill thought about their conversion and if only he had taken the time to think back, he would have realized he had tried to keep sex from happening, while Jane was the one being so forceful. But no, he just felt so badly he had hurt this beautiful woman with his overactive sex drive. It seemed like every time the truth tried to surface in his mind, Jane's voice would drown it out. Yes, DJ was right about her, she was evil, just about as evil as they came.

* * * * *

Tom Dixon opened the letter he had received from Ron. He didn't know why Ron was writing to him. By now, he had heard Ron was the one who had spread the lies about him. (You see, if you're going to smear someone's good name, you first have to lay the blame on someone other than yourself, in order to keep from being drawn into any conflict which might arise over it.) Steve had taken something Ron had said, twisted it until it wasn't even close to being the truth and then, he went around telling everyone Ron had told him all about Tom's trouble. The only sad thing was, Tom did not know who was really behind it all, so it was understandable how he would get most upset when he received Ron's letter. "How could he have the nerve to write me and say we need to get together to talk? I thought we were friends. We went to seminary together and even preached revivals for each other. I should have known when I heard he was hanging around that group he had changed. Networking is what they call it these days. Well, I know what it really is."

Beverly, Tom's wife, walked into his office as he was walking back and forth, talking to himself. "My goodness, what has you so upset this morning?"

Tom handed her the letter to read. He just stood there and waited to see how it would affect her. Beverly looked up after reading it with a clam look on her face, "Tom, I think we should go and meet with them."

"How in the name of all that is holy, can you expect me to go and sit down with that Judas?"

"Because, I want to find out if he really is a Judas, or if someone else has done this to you and is laying blame on Ron."

Tom, thought about it for a moment. It did sound like something Steve would do and had done to others in the past. "Ok, we'll go. You call and make the arrangements with Kathy Wilton, and we'll find out who's the Judas in this whole messy affair."

* * * * *

Steve Godwin had called some more of his friends, and they were planning to meet together later the next week. He thought about inviting Ron, but he knew Ron was having second thoughts about everything, and once he found out how they had used him…well, it's best to keep him at arms length now. That way, he wouldn't know anything he could use against them. Steve was going to get to the top and he didn't care who he had to step on to get there, or how it affected their lives. The 'ends justify the means,' did it not, or at least that was what one of his seminary professors told him. Steve had long ago stopped believing anything that was written in the Bible. After all, he was taught it was only a book written by men, who had limited knowledge and understanding about the world *we* are living in, so in fact, it was an out of date book. He would read a scripture every Sunday morning for his text, then he would tell stories about his hunting trips or what he did back in his school days. Steve, like most in our world today, gave very little lip service to the Bible, and he never preached it. "Marshall, this is Steve Godwin, we need to get together and talk over a few details. Yes, I think we need to keep a close eye on Ron as well. So, let's say I will see you around 1:00 then."

* * * * *

Paula arrived at work that Monday morning wishing she had thought more about sending that card to Bill. It sounded like the right thing to do, but what if he called her and blows her off. After all, she was the one who walked into his office and hit him right across the face. She sat at her desk, with the door to her office closed. She didn't remember anything the preacher had said the morning before. Her mind was so troubled over all of this. "Why couldn't she just let go and walk away? Why was she so drawn to Bill anyway?" her mind kept churning. Over the next hour Paula got very little work done. Employees kept walking in with information or wanting her to do something for them. Normally, it would have been just another Monday, but today it had an extra weight added to it. The phone rang and as Paula reached over to pick it up she thought, "Who could this be? I'm so tired of everyone pulling at me today. "Hello," aggravation could be heard in her voice as she answered.

"I hope I'm not troubling you, Paula."

"No, Bill, not at all, in fact I'm glad you've called."

* * * * *

Tracie had watched Bill as he arrived at work. She had seen the card on his desk waiting for him. Everything inside of her wanted to pull him aside and tell him everything she knew about Jane, but Earl was right. All it would do was to land them in a lawsuit and most likely push Bill more into her arms. Earl told Tracie how Jane had operated when she was going after his old partner. Every time Shawn's wife found out something about Jane which should have opened his eyes, Jane was there with such a convincing lie. Poor Shawn was so confused that by the time it all came out in the open, Jane had taken him for most of his money. Shawn's wife had endured enough and left him for good. He was only going to get to see his kids once a month. Then, when he confronted Jane with what he was going through because of her, she laughed in his face and told him to go back to his wife if she would have him, because she was through with him. Jane told Shawn to tell his wife she was sending him back to her with a lot more experience, which should make her happy.

Tracie had gotten so upset she had to go to the ladies room. She just stood there and cried, "Oh God! Please don't let this happen to Bill. You have answered so many of my prayers for him lately, don't let the devil win this fight."

* * * * *

"I've received your note today and I wanted to call you to try and explain it all to you as best as I think I understand it, Paula. I wasn't trying to lead you on, nor was I trying to use you. I'm not sure what happened, but I was seeing this lady before we met, and I, well, I guess I was afraid of making a commitment. It was still too painful. I didn't realize how much pain I was still carrying over the loss of my wife and daughter. I think that is why I could never break it off with either of you. It was like, as long as there were two of you, then, I didn't have to make any commitment to anyone. That way there was no chance of being hurt again. I'm so sorry I was so selfish, because I never once thought about how I could hurt you."

"Well, At least you weren't trying to just lead me on Bill, and for that I am thankful."

"You are too wonderful a woman, Paula, and I am so sorry I hurt you the way I did."

They talked for almost an hour. Finally, Bill had to get off the phone and get some work done, and Paula needed to go out onto the floor to see that everything was going well. Before they got off the phone, Paula did do one thing she was led to do, even though she was unaware of it. "Bill, please bring DJ and Maggie back again. The elderly here love them and I can't tell you how many times they have asked me when their next visit was going to be."

"How about this Wednesday afternoon, if nothing happens here at the paper, and if it does, I'll call and we can set another time?"

"That's great. Thank you for calling me Bill, I feel much better now." After they hung up the phone, it hit Bill that Paula had said, "I feel much better now." What was she talking about? Why did she feel better after they talked? There were times Bill was sure he would never figure women out.

* * * * *

At their meeting, Steve and Marshall both ordered a beer. They didn't see anything wrong with it, and they didn't think it was anybody's business either. They had started drinking long ago as well as doing other things which no minister should do, or Christian either for that matter. That's why they always went to an old lounge out in the country, far enough out where no one would spot them.

"Now tell me what you think about Ron, has he gone soft on us?" Steve asked.

"Yeah, but I told you in the beginning he might do that. All that matters is that he can't trace anything back to us," replied Marshall. "Well, we were there the day he told about how Tom was freed from his drinking problem."

"I know, but so were about fifteen other guys so no one can trace it back to us," Steve replied.

"You mean, *you*, don't you Steve? I never said anything to anyone about Tom. You didn't give me any time."

"Well, you seemed to be taking your sweet time about spreading the lie to the right people."

"Steve, you know I don't believe like Tom and Ron, but there are times when I wonder if what we are doing is right."

"Now don't you go and get a conscience on me. It certainly hasn't hurt your feelings that you are the pastor of a large church. And we both know there were others who could have gone there, but we pushed them out of the way. So don't forget the part you've played in all of this, my friend. If I go down so do you."

"Steve, I didn't say I wasn't going through with it, and you're right, I am the pastor of a larger church than I might have been. So, how do we neutralize Ron if we need to?"

* * * * *

When Ron walked in the backdoor, Kathy met him, "We are going to have dinner with Tom and Beverly Thursday night. We are going to meet at the Ole Farm Steak House, around 6:30."

"Beverly called, not Tom?"

"Yes, why do you ask?"

"Tom is upset, or he would have called. I don't blame him. I would be upset, too. I just hope I will be able to undo what has happened to him."

"Well, Beverly told me Tom was asking for a move this time and they told him he was going to have to stay there until some things could be straightened out. Tom is very upset over it. They are going to send him to a psychologist for an evaluation. Beverly said it would follow Tom the rest of his career, so he is depressed over it all."

"It will follow him, but maybe there is someway I can set things straight. I would love to see Steve take the fall for all his lies."

"Ron, let God keep the record and set things right. You help your friend."

* * * * *

"Long after Bill got home, there was a knock at his door. DJ and Maggie both ran to see who it was, and they were not happy to see Jane at the door. "Bill, if I didn't know better, I would swear your dogs don't like me," was her first remark when Bill opened the door.

"Jane, they just don't know you. Give them some time to get use to you, and before you know it, DJ will be following you around the house everywhere you go." When Bill said that, it hit DJ and Maggie at the same time, they had been going about this all wrong. They needed to get as close to Jane as possible. Only then, would they be able to find out what she was up to. DJ waited for about an hour, then jumped up and sat down right by Jane.

"Bill, this dog is on the couch beside me."

"Good, he is finally warming up to you. See, I told you once he did, he would stay right by your side."

Jane thought to herself, "Boy isn't this my lucky day. I have to put up with his flea hounds now, as well." She sat on the couch while Bill finished fixing their meal. She thought about the phone call she had received earlier in the day. It was from the man she had some gossip about. He had the name of the woman at Bill's bank and even the information Jane needed about her. It seems, when she was younger, she lived a loose life style and she had to give up a child. She did what she felt was best for the baby, but now she was starting all over. She had been to college and was married. However, her husband didn't know about her past. She had lied to him about so many things and now she would do just about anything to keep her past hidden. Which was what Jane was counting on. This was going to take a little time. She had to get all the information together before she went to see Louise Hayes.

* * * * *

Louise was in her late twenties, she was about five feet ten inches tall, with light brown hair and hazel eyes. Louise grew up in a broken home and had to learn early in life to take care of herself. She also learned early in life, men would lie to you just to use you. It was from her lifestyle then that her son was born. As much as she loved him, she knew she wasn't fit to be his mother. So when he was born, she signed papers and gave him to a good family, one that could give him everything he would ever need. It was from the pain of that moment Louise made the decision to change the way she had been living. She wasn't going to let men use her anymore, so she went to college and that is where she met her husband. He came from a good family, one which would never have agreed to his marrying her. So she hid her past and all the pain and shame which went with it. Louise thought she would never have to face her past again. She was happy now, with her new life and her daughter. She and her husband were even talking about having another child in a year or so. The future couldn't have looked any brighter. Now she had a new position in the bank, making more money than she had ever hoped. Louise truly believed her past was buried so deeply no one could ever dig it up. The only trouble with Louise's reasoning was that she was lying to her husband. She should have trusted him when they first met and been open with him. Sherman Hayes was a good man, but he did not like anyone lying to him. He fell in love with Louise, and he wouldn't have cared about her past.

* * * * *

Tuesday night Jane was back on the phone with her contact at the bank, "Why don't you have the information I want? What do you mean it's not in her file? So, the little tramp lied about her past did she? Said she came from another town? Oh no, I doubt you could find your own car if it was right in front of you." Then she thought, "I know someone who is very good at digging up a person's past. In fact, he loves his work. He had made a large sum of money before by going to families selling them the information he found, to keep it from falling into the wrong hands, as he put it."

When he heard Jane's voice on the other end of the receiver he said, "So tell me, who are we going after this time?"

Jane told him everything he needed to know to do his search on Louise Hayes. The only thing he hated was the fact she didn't come from a family with money. This one job could make him rich. He knew just how to hold information over a family's head so they would give him any price. Since there was no outside money to be made, he told Jane it was going to cost her more this time.

"How much more are you talking about?"

"I won't know until I have the information!"

"You have never done this to me before, so why are you doing now?" she complained.

He had Jane right were he wanted her. She had slipped up. She had let him know how very important this was to her and that she couldn't let just anyone do this job. "Take the deal, or find someone else."

By now Jane realized she had messed up, she had given out far too much information and she had let the importance of the job become known to the one person she could not afford to. But it was too late now. This time she would just have to deal with it, but he would pay for making her pay a higher price this time. Jane also had a file, and in it she had every bit of information she could get on how he had been blackmailing families. Yes, he would hate for that to fall into the wrong hands. She would wait until the job was done, and then sell him her file for the information. That way it wasn't going to cost her one red cent.

* * * * *

Bill arrived home Wednesday afternoon but he hadn't said anything to either DJ or Maggie about going back to the nursing home, primarily because he didn't know how much they understood. He knew they were different and that they seemingly knew more then he realized at the time, but let's face it, they were his dogs. Would they really understand it if he just said it to them? As he was getting out of his car he laughed out loud, "My goodness, here I am wondering how much my dogs will understand. Boy, I know what Sally would say right now. 'See, I've won you over'." He was still laughing as he walked into the house. DJ and Maggie were just standing there looking at him, wondering what was making him act so strange. Well, here it goes then, "Guess where we're going today?"

They both just stood there with no expressions on their faces. "Ok, I can see the excitement building in you, so let me get right to the point. We're going back to the nursing home today!"

With that, Maggie and DJ looked at each other and Maggie barked and started spinning around with pure joy, while DJ barked and ran around Maggie. They were like two kids who were excited about getting to go to the park on a Sunday afternoon.

Bill stood there speechless. "They understood, I mean, they really understood." He got down on one knee and Maggie came right over to him, and then DJ ran over and started licking him on the face. "All right, now let's get ready to go, and children, please help me look good today. I don't want Paula to stay mad at me forever."

DJ stepped back and gave Bill a strange look as if to say, "You can count on us, we'll do everything possible to help you out there."

When they drove up in the driveway at the nursing home, Bill felt a little nervous about seeing Paula again. He knew he had hurt her and he didn't want to reopen any wounds in her heart. He surely hadn't meant to cause them. He was still not sure how it all happened or why. He still felt something special each time he thought about her or heard her voice. He was getting DJ and Maggie out of the car when he heard a friendly voice behind him.

"Hello is there anything I can do to help?"

Bill turned around to see one of Paula's staff members. He was a tall fellow and had a big smile across his face. "So, this is DJ and Maggie. I've heard so much about you two." DJ wagged his tail and Maggie stood back a little, "I'm sorry, I must have made them nervous or something."

"No, not at all," Bill said, "I think they were expecting Paula to greet them."

"Maybe later, but right now Paula had one of her bosses show up, so she is tied up and asked me to show ya'll to the room. Everyone is waiting. Why, you would think we had someone famous coming to visit these folks. Once they heard DJ and Maggie were coming today, everyone started making plans to be free for the afternoon so they could see them. I was kind of glad Paula was tied up so I could watch, I mean, I want to see what it is they do that makes everyone love them so much."

"Well, DJ and Maggie, let's show him shall we?" Bill opened the door and in they walked side by side right down the hall to the large room. As soon as they entered the room, everyone cheered and with that DJ barked and Maggie spun around. Then they both started going around the room, DJ took one side while Maggie went up the other side of the room. They stopped and loved each one of the elderly, causing some of them to shed a few tears.

"We have missed ya'll so much, one lady reached down and kissed Maggie on top of her head. I love you little girl." Maggie stood there and wagged her tail at the lady, then she did something that was totally out of character for her, she reached out and licked the lady on her hand. "Oh, look everyone. Maggie is kissing my hand and she never does that to anyone."

An old fellow said to someone sitting by him, "Now, we'll have to listen to her go on and on about that the rest of her life." They both laughed and Bill was standing over against the wall laughing also. He wasn't sure who it helped the most, the elderly people living there or himself. There was something about watching those two strange little dogs loving these people that made him feel better about himself. Yes, he was glad he was able to patch things up with Paula if for no other reason than to bring DJ and Maggie back here for these good folks. He didn't hear Paula walk up behind him, but he could smell her perfume.

"Paula, thank you for asking us back. I think DJ and Maggie missed it more than I did." How did he know she was behind him, she had walked up as quietly as she could, and what did he mean they missed it more then he did? Bill turned around, there were tears in his eyes, "It makes me feel more alive to stand here and watch these dogs help all these people here feel better about themselves than anything I could ever hope to do. And all I have to do is drive them over here and sit back and watch. They show more love than any two people I know. If only people could learn how to love like that, without walls being built up to keep people out because of past hurts." Bill stopped, he realized he was saying far more then he intended and he was letting his wall down as he was speaking. He slowly turned back around to watch DJ and Maggie, only to see them standing across the room watching him and Paula.

"I swear, sometimes I feel like they know way more than they are letting on." Paula walked out to the car with Bill and the dogs. DJ was keeping his eye on them to see if they were going to make up. "Bill, thank you for bringing DJ and Maggie back out here, the elderly do love to see them."

"Thank you for asking us to come back. I have missed it and I know DJ and Maggie have. Why, when I told them we were coming back out here today, you should have seen the way they acted. Maggie spun around and DJ just went to barking for pure joy."

"Now, how do you know he was barking for pure joy?"

"Because, the expression on his little face was one of such delight, Paula. They love to come out here and meet the people here, and they missed seeing you also, and so did I."

Paula's emotions were like a raging sea right then, she wanted so to just grab Bill and kiss him, but at the some time she wanted to run away from him. Never in all her life, had she felt this way about a man. She held out her hand to Bill, trying to be very professional, "Then please, bring them again next week on Wednesday if you can."

"I'll be glad too, thank you for asking us. Did ya'll hear that? We are coming back next week."

DJ walked up to Paula. As he did, she bent down on one knee to pat him on the head, but DJ just pushed by her hand and reached up and licked her on the face. Paula reached out and held him close to her. "Oh, I have missed you too, little fellow."

Maggie walked over as if to say, "What about me?"

"And I have missed you too, girl. Let's face it; us women have to stick together." As Bill drove away, he couldn't help wondering if Paula felt the way he did when they were together. It made him feel warm inside, and at peace with himself. There was just something about being around her that he missed when he was away from her.

* * * * *

Thursday morning after Bill had left for work, DJ and Maggie went into his office to find the book they had been reading. Ever since Bill had mention he had quite a few of C. S. Lewis books, DJ had been after Maggie to see if they could reach them. Luckily, they were right where Bill had said, on the bottom shelf, so it would be easy for them to find one they wanted to read first. DJ, of course, wanted Maggie to read the *Chronicles of Narnia*. With Maggie's gift for doing voices, she could make every character come alive. DJ would lie on the floor just listening to her as she read the story. Something in the *Chronicles of Narnia* fed his soul and DJ loved a good story as much as anyone. He remembered how Sally would read to them and try to make different voices as she read. "Maggie, why didn't you tell Sally you could do voices? That way she would have let you be the reader?" he asked.

"Of course she would, but then you wouldn't have the memory of her reading to us would you?"

"No, you're right and I do miss her so, my dear. You are wise beyond your years."

"If you keep using that term, years, like that, you might wonder if you're going to see another year!"

DJ laughed at Maggie. They did have so much fun picking at each other, and it was times such as these that he wondered himself what life would be like without Maggie? How could he handle the task before them without the one he had grown to depend on so? They were more then just a pair, they were a whole, two halves that make a whole, yes, that is what they were. But for now, he would put that thought out of his mind. "Go on my dear, read some more of the story."

Maggie cleared her voice and started off again. My, how she seemed to capture the personality of each character. No wonder DJ loved hearing her read. Maggie loved to read to him, as well. Yes, they were two halves which made a whole.

* * * * *

Kathy and Ron showed up to the Ole Farm Steak House early. Not only did they want to get a table away from everyone else, but they also thought it would be better if they were there waiting for Tom and Beverly. Six thirty came and Tom wasn't there.

"This is so unlike Tom, he is never late," Ron said.

"Let's wait a little while longer before we order, I'm sure their coming. Beverly was the one who called me, remember?" Kathy responded.

"I know, but let's face it, Tom is hurt and mad, and I wouldn't blame him if he never spoke to me again."

About that time Tom and Beverly walked in. Ron waved at them, but one could see from the expression on Tom's face he wasn't happy with Ron. As they walked up to the table, Ron stood up and went to Tom. Before Tom could say anything, Ron burst out crying. "Tom, I didn't know what they were up to, I swear that to you. What I said was all good, I promise. All I did was tell how God had set you free from drinking years ago, and I made it plain that it was years ago."

Tom stood there as if he had been hit with a block of cement. "Well, just tell me why you had to say anything about me around that pack of wolves anyway?"

"They were talking about miracles and how some of them didn't believe in miracles. I called myself standing up for the truth. I had no idea they were just out fishing to try and get something on someone they could twist around."

Tom backed away from the table. "Beverly, I think we should go now. I'm not sure this was a good idea. It might be another setup."

"Tom we have been friends for a long time. You know I would never do anything to hurt you, and I am willing to do whatever it takes to make things right, even if it hurts my ministry. I'm serious about it, Tom. That's why I wrote to you asking if we could meet. I'll go to the bishop with you and clear your name, I promise, just tell me when you want to go."

"I have to be in the bishop's office in the morning."

"I'm going with you then and Tom, no matter what happens, before we leave his office your name is going to be cleared."

The rest of the evening Ron confessed how he allowed ambition to cloud his thinking and pull him away from the things which were most important. "I forgot that I was first called to be a follower of Christ and then a pastor and minister. Tom, can you ever forgive me and trust me again?"

"Ron, if you will go with me tomorrow, that will be proof enough for me that you were being used by some very unscrupulous men, who should never be allowed in a pulpit."

"Tom, I can't prove Steve had anything to do with it though. He has covered his tracks pretty good."

"That doesn't matter, Ron. All that matters is that my name is cleared and that I know I haven't lost a friend."

"I promise you, Tom, I'll always be your friend."

The next day Ron walked into the bishop's office with Tom.

* * * * *

The bishop's name was F. L. Langley, and he was the most conservative bishop the denomination had. Bishop Langley was an older man and was known to be a very open and fair minded individual. As Tom and Ron walked into his office, Bishop Langley stood up to greet them, but said, "Ron, you aren't suppose to be here."

"Well bishop, if you will give me just one minute of your time, I think I can clear this whole mess up before it gets anymore out of hand."

"Then by all means, sit down, both of you and let's hear what's on your mind." An hour later, the bishop leaned back in his chair and said nothing. Then he sat up and said "Tom, I can see that a very grave injustice has been done to you, and it was designed to hurt your ministry. I hate to admit it but there are some men who are in need of Christ, and it's sad that they stand in the pulpit every Sunday. Tom, you're going to get the move which was withheld from you this time. Now, it's not going to be the church you wanted, but I think you will like the move anyway. Let's see, you're at a small church with about 75 members and the one I am going to send you to has around 190 members, with twice the pay. I hope that will make up to you any hurt we may have caused you."

"Ron, what you did took a lot of guts. Most men would have thought more about their own career than that of a friend's. I know you didn't ask for a move, but I was thinking about it anyway. So now, I feel like it would be the best thing for you."

"Bishop please, I didn't come here asking for a move, only to clear my friend's name. Besides, I don't feel like I should leave this town yet."

"Oh, you're not leaving, you know about the church across town don't you?"

"Why yes, it's the one Steve is going to, isn't it?"

"He thinks he is, but nothing is written in stone, you know. Although I can't prove it, I think we both know who started this vicious lie, and I don't think he is the man for that church. Go home, both of you and start packing for your move. Tom, you'll only be about forty minutes from Ron, I hope ya'll stay in touch with each other."

"Bishop, I don't think you have anything to worry about there."

"Ron, stay away from that group. I was about to call you in to have one of my fatherly talks. Believe me, you don't want *that* to happen."

Ron and Tom both were laughing along with the bishop. "Maybe it wouldn't have been such a bad idea, Bishop."

With that, they walked out of the bishop's office… two men whose friendship had gone through fire and had come out stronger than before. Tom looked at Ron, "Well, what do you think Steve is going to have to say when he finds out?"

"I'm not sure, but I'll bet you won't be able to find his words in the Bible. Let's go and pick up our wives and go out to dinner, shall we?"

"That is one great idea, Tom."

Friendship is like a strong cord, it's not easily broken and both of these men knew, now more than ever, the value of friendship.

* * * * *

Steve was in his office when the phone rang. He was down-loading his sermon for the week. He thought, "This makes things so much easier. I don't even have to read that old book any more." He reached over when he saw it was the bishop's office calling. "Now, he was going to get the good news about his new appointment. "Hello Bishop, good day to you sir."

"Why, thank you, Steve, and a good day to you as well. I am calling about your new appointment."

"Yes sir, and let me say I am going to do the very best job for you sir."

"Why, that's fine, Steve, although, I think that promise should be made to the Lord instead of me."

"Oh yes, I mean that too, Bishop. I was just wanting you to know I will always do my very best."

"I'm glad to hear that, Steve, because you're not moving this time."

"What?" he just about yelled it out.

"Steve," the bishop said, "You're not yelling at me, are you?"

"No sir, but what about the church across town, I mean I really wanted that church."

"I know you did son, and believe me, the man who is going there is the right man for the job. And I know you will do a good job where you are. Besides Steve, that church didn't really want you to come there. It seems they have heard some things about you that have them worried. If you feel you need to talk with me more about it, then I will be glad to make some time next week so you can come in."

"Oh no sir, that won't be necessary. I'm happy to stay here for another year if I need to."

"That's good Steve, but if you need to talk, just drop by any time."

When Steve hung up the phone, he was so mad, he couldn't see straight. Who? How did he lose that church? Who cared about what a few old members said anyway? All he wanted was to get higher up the ladder and that church would have been just the ticket. Steve picked up his phone again, "Marshall, this is Steve. I need you to do something for me."

"Sure, what is it?"

"I'm not being moved. That old fool of a bishop gave my church to someone else and I need to find out who it is."

"Steve, you might want to back off this one. If the bishop did that, then it means there is something going on here we are not aware of and it could bite both of us. Tell you what I'll do, I will talk with a friend of mine and not ask any questions. If he knows anything he will tell me. The guy can't keep his mouth shut."

"Well, as soon as you find out, let me know, ok?"

"Yes, sure thing, I'll call you as soon as I find out something." Marshall put his receiver down and looked out his window. He was wondering how Steve was going to take the information that Ron was going to the church he had worked so hard to get. Marshall's friend had already called him to let him know the bishop was going to be looking into who started the vicious lie against Tom. Marshall's friend had told him the bishop had a good idea it came from Steve, so to stay clear of him for a while. Or you could find yourself going down with him."

Well, Marshall thought, "We were going to get rid of all the ministers we didn't like and it looks like they are the ones who are being moved up the ladder while we are staying in the same churches. I think I will drop Steve a note to let him know, but also tell him right now, it's not safe to be seen in his company. That ought to set him off for about a month. Plus, if the bishop takes the Area Rep. job away from him, then he will be just one of the many, not on top as he thought. Isn't it funny that the ones who believe the Bible are the ones who are being blessed, and those of us who are suppose to know better are still in the same churches and might even lose them? Maybe I need to start reading the Bible again, take a more serious look at it, because I think some of my teachers must have lied to me, because it sure is working for those who believe it. What translation will I start with? I guess it doesn't matter,

I'll start with the old King James and then work my way through some of the newer ones."

Marshall pulled out some paper to write a short note to Steve. A friendship which was built upon deceit and ambition had ended; it was never built upon good soil, for love is the only soil in which lifelong friendships can grow. Marshall stood looking out his window. Would he have the guts to walk into the bishop's office and lay his career on the line for a friend, or did he even have anyone he counted as a friend he would be willing to do that for? He reached over and picked up a book he had long neglected. Lets see, I think I will start with the book of Matthew.

Chapter Nine

Memories of the Past

It seemed as if the weeks just flew by, before Bill even knew what had happened. It was already the first of March, and just like every year, he received the same invitation in the mail. It was from the community he had lived in for all those years while he was teaching at the University. Every year about spring break, the town had one large spring yard sale. Every vender in the town and the surrounding area would come and have booths where they would sell whatever they made or sold in their stores. Bill had never returned for one of these spring yard sales, primarily because it would have caused him too many painful memories. He read the invitation and started to throw it into the trash, but then he thought about something, maybe he should go, maybe he would ask someone to go with him.

As Jane picked up her phone, she could hear the excitement in his voice. "I have some place I would like to take you, and we can get separate rooms so there won't be any trouble there," Bill said.

Already she hated the idea, but she was waiting for a phone call which should be coming any day now, and then she would be able to move forward with her plans. "Well, that's wonderful dear. You mean you want us to go back to the small town where you used to teach and go walking around a large flea market?"

"Yeah, it will be wonderful and you can meet all the people I know there, plus they will get to meet you as well."

The last thing Jane wanted to do was to go up to some small town in North Georgia and meet a bunch of small town hicks. "Bill, I hate to have to tell you this, but I was planning on going out of town to spend time with a very dear friend of mine. She just lost her husband and I felt she needed someone close by her right now. But if you feel like you just have to have me with you, then I'll call her and tell her I have other plans."

"Oh no, I wouldn't want you to do anything like that, Jane. If your friend needs you, then you should go. I remember what it's like to lose someone, and yes, you're right, you need to be with your friend."

"Oh Bill, you are so understanding. What did I ever do to deserve you?" Jane was smiling as she was speaking to Bill. If only he knew the whole story.

* * * * *

Bill woke up the next day. It was a beautiful Wednesday morning. It was cool outside, but not too cold, and the weatherman was promising it was going to get as high as the middle fifties. "Let's see," he said, "oh yes, this afternoon we make our trip back to the nursing home." The day was filled with business as usual. Bill worked hard all day trying to get everything done so he could make it to the nursing home on time. When he ran into the house, he yelled, "DJ and Maggie hurry up and let's go."

They came running to the door as if they had been waiting for him all day. Bill laughed, "What have you two been up to all day?"

They just looked at him as if to say, "What us? Why nothing."

"Yeah, just what I thought, ya'll never tell." He didn't see the look Maggie gave DJ. If only he knew how much they had to tell.

As they pulled into the driveway of the nursing home, Paula was standing outside waiting on them. "Oh, I was afraid you weren't going to make it this week, either."

"I'm so sorry about last week, Joe called a meeting and I couldn't get out of it to save my life."

"Bill, that's ok. I know you have a job, but it is nice when you can bring DJ and Maggie. As you know, the elderly here love to see them whenever they can come." Paula opened the door and said, "You two know the way." And down the hall they went as if they knew this was their job for the day, to minister to these people. "You know Bill, I still can't get over how they act as if they understand so much more then they are really letting on."

"I feel the same way. Why, there are times I find myself talking to them as if I expect them to understand every word I say."

"I know. I feel the same way when I'm around them. It's kind of weird in a way." DJ and Maggie were just about to walk into the hall where the people were waiting for them, when DJ just turned around and looked at Bill and Paula. "See," Paula pointed at DJ, "there he goes, as if he knows what we're saying about them."

Bill laughed, "If only Sally could hear us now. She would say we had been won over."

"You miss her don't you, Bill?"

"Yeah, more than I ever thought possible. I have missed her a lot more lately. She was the one person I could always go to and talk with. And Sally would never tell you what you wanted to hear, no sir, she would shoot straight with you. I wish I had her right now to talk with."

"Bill, you know we're friends, you can talk with me, I mean if you want to, that is."

"No Paula, there are some thing's a guy needs to workout on his own. I'm half way thinking about going back to a town where I use to live for a visit. I taught there for years, before I came here to work for the paper. Well, they have this large flea market there every year and they have been writing to me asking me to come back and visit the town, but I haven't gone back there." Bill grew quite for a moment, "Well, let's just say in a long time."

Paula knew why Bill had stayed away. Sally had talked with her the day they met and told her about her brother and how he had lost his wife and daughter in an automobile accident. "Why don't you go? It sounds like it would be so much fun."

"I don't know if I could go back there alone. I'm just being a coward I guess."

"Why don't you take a friend?"

"I asked, but they had other plans."

Paula said, "I use to love to go to flea markets. Why, when I went to college, I even worked in one for a friend of my mom. I ran it for two whole weeks, and I met people from all over the country. I still get postcards from some of them. Oh, I have to say, it was one of the best times in my life. Bill you should go, it would do you good."

Bill looked at this woman, who lit up like a Christmas tree as she was talking about her college days. Why was it, every time he was around her, he found more things about her that he liked. And she made him feel so comfortable in her presence? Nothing like Jane. Why was he still holding on to Jane? It seemed every time he was around Paula, he was asking himself that question.

"Paula, I have an idea."

"What? You act as if you just had a brainstorm."

"I did. Why don't you go with me?"

Paula stepped backward away from Bill, "I… well… I'm not sure that's a good idea. I mean, what about your girlfriend? I wouldn't want to cause you any trouble with her, Bill. So, I don't think so." Paula turned and walked away as fast as she could, her heart was racing, her mind was all fuzzy, "I need to get away from him right now," was all she could think. Paula walked into her office and shut the door. She sat down at her desk and felt like crying, but before she could, there was a knock on her door.

"Paula, its Bill, please let me in. I really need to talk with you."

She opened the door, only because she didn't want every employee hearing him talk to her through the door. Bill walked in and sat down in a chair across from her desk. "Paula, I wasn't trying to hurt you. I can see now that it was the wrong thing for me to ask you to go, not after I hurt you the way that I did. I just wanted to tell you again how sorry I am for the way I hurt you, Paula. I never meant to hurt you. I hope one day you will be able to believe me."

Paula was crying now, not out loud, but there were tears running down her face. Bill's eyes were teary as well. He got up to walk out, when Paula asked him, "What do I wear?"

"What? I don't understand?"

"Bill, I need to know what the weather is going to be like there, so I can know what to wear."

* * * * *

Jane was sitting on a boat with her friend, Lisa Ainsworth. Lisa's husband, number five, had just died. He was very rich, which meant now Lisa was even richer than before. She was five feet two inches tall, with brown eyes and wavy blond hair, which came down past her shoulders. "Tell me Lisa, how many does this one make?" Jane started laughing before she could even finish the sentence.

"Number five, if I remember correctly. But then again, who's counting, just as long as they leave me their money, that is."

Jane and Lisa had been friends since their college days, where both of them realized they had more in common with each other than with any other girls on campus. It was while they were sitting up late one night, that they hatched their plans on how they would use men to get what they wanted. They both had been hurt at one time or another by some guy, so now it was up to them to get even. Lisa looked over at Jane, "Now tell me about this new fish you have on the line."

"Oh, he is… well… maybe I shouldn't tell you anything, you might set your eyes on him yourself."

"How old did you say he was?"

"He is in his late forties."

"No, too young for me. I would have to put up with him for too many years, and you know how I hate to do that."

They both laughed, as Jane took a sip of her drink, "Well, he was a university professor, that is until his wife and daughter were killed in car accident. He left everything and moved to South Carolina to the little town of Green Haven, which is where I first met him at a dinner party. He showed no interest in me whatsoever, which meant, I had to go after him. At first, I was just going to date him, then drop him. Then, I heard about his money, and well my plans changed, as you can imagine. Anyway, he wanted me to go with him back to North Georgia to the town of Whitworth. That is where the university is. I told him you had just lost your husband and you were all alone down here by yourself just grieving your heart out."

About that time, a young man walked by, who spoke to Lisa. "Oh yes, I am," she said as she was getting up to follow him below deck. Jane and Lisa were both laughing as she walked away. Jane was more determined than ever to get the information and finish this thing with Bill. Another young man walked by and took Jane by the hand, as he looked into her eyes, he asked her if she was going to stay by herself all day. With that, she grabbed him and kissed him. "Oh no," she said, "I plan to get to know you better by morning."

* * * * *

The following Friday afternoon, Bill picked up Paula at her house. After they loaded her luggage into the car, they began their journey to Whitworth. "I didn't know you were going to take DJ and Maggie along with you, as well."

"I hope you don't mind. I thought they could use the break from the house and besides, they didn't want to stay with the vet. I have a small cabin rented for us." Paula looked at Bill with a strange look on her face. "Oh no, you will have your own cabin right across from mine.. No Paula, we're not going to share cabins, but if DJ asks you, tell him he can't spend the night with you either."

Paula laughed at Bill, knowing if it were anyone but him, she would be expecting him to do something underhanded. Maybe this would be a good time to really get to know him better. "How long will it take us to drive to Whitworth, Georgia?"

"I guess about a couple of hours, but I'm not in a hurry, so it might take an hour or so more. I love this drive in the mountains, and this time of year is beautiful. Everything is starting to warm up for spring, life is about to burst forth from every tree and plant. God's creation is waking up." Bill was quite from a minute, "Well, that is what my wife used to say."

"Bill, would you tell me about her… your wife, I mean? She sounds like such a wonderful person and I would like to hear more about her."

For the first time in years, Bill opened up and let someone in. He shared his heart with Paula that day as they drove through the mountains. By the time they arrived at Whitworth, Paula felt as if she understood Bill better. She knew why he had such a hard time when his wife and daughter died. They were a close family and it hit him harder than anything else could have, which is why it took several years, plus two special little friends, before he could begin to move on in his life.

* * * * *

When they arrived at Whitworth, Paula immediately fell in love with the town. It was a small town nestled right in the mountains of North Georgia, with a population of around twenty-seven thousand, and when the students were at the school, the town had a population of around thirty thousand. Whitworth was one of those towns where you just felt at home the moment you arrived. The people at the Hotel knew your name by the second day you were there, and the guy who ran the coffee shop, dried his own coffee beans. Paula looked out the window of the car as they drove through the town, "Bill look at this place. Why, it is beautiful! No wonder you loved living here as much as you did."

Bill looked over at Paula and saw the wonder in her eyes. It made him think about the first time he brought his wife to this place. As they pulled into Whitworth Mountains Resort, Bill pointed out the two cabins he had rented for them. "See, our cabins are up on the hill, like I said, across from each other. I think they will give us a great view of the town."

John Reinhart and his wife, Janet , were on the lookout for Bill. As soon as he drove into the parking lot, they came out the door to greet him. "Dr. Thomas, it seems as though it has been ages since we last saw you." John hugged Bill around the neck while Janet gave Paula a great big hug as well.

"Bill, you didn't tell us she was as pretty as this. Had we known, we would have really put on the dog for you folks," Janet teased.

Bill turned a little red in the face. He was afraid his feelings for Paula might be showing, even though he tried to deny he was falling for her. However, there was still that strange hold Jane had over Bill. Even he didn't understand why.

"Now Janet, don't go and embarrass the boy, he hasn't been back here in years and there you go before he is even unpacked, sticking your nose where it doesn't belong. Dr. Thomas you know…"

Bill held up his hand, "John everything is all right. Paula is a good friend, and we're here for a few days of fun, that's all."

Paula thought to herself, "Is Bill embarrassed? Did his face turn red? I wonder what it means?"

Janet said to Paula, "I'll help you unpack, and John can help Dr. Thomas."

John walked by and took hold of Janet's arm, "No mama, we're going to get the other cabins ready for our other guest, these kids are on their own."

As they walked away, Paula looked over at Bill. "It looks like you still have a lot of friends here."

"Yeah, I guess I do at that, but then that's the way this town has always been. They will open the door of their heart to you and invite you to come on in. I can truly say, I have never found any place like it anywhere else."

* * * * *

Saturday morning Bill knocked on Paula's cabin door to see if she was awake yet. "Come on in, its open."

Bill opened the door just a little and asked, "Are you ready to go into town?"

Paula came bouncing around the door of the bedroom, "Ok, lets walk into town."

"I didn't say we were going to walk, rather, I thought it would be a nice day for a drive."

"Oh Bill," Paula took him by the arm, "today is just the kind of day you want to walk into town."

"And why is that?" Bill asked, looking at Paula with a smile.

Paula's eyes sparkled as she led Bill down the steps. "This way, you can tell me about everything in town, and we can meet more of your old friends."

Bill knew it was no use to try and talk her out of it. He had seen that look before, and he never won those battles then, so he knew he wasn't going to win them now. "Ok, where do you want to start?"

"Well, how about walking somewhere to get something to eat?"

"That's a great idea, and I know just the place. But, it's going to take us about ten minutes to walk to it, maybe more. We could be there quicker by car."

"No sir, we'll walk."

So, off they started toward the Heartland Grill, where Fay and May were the owners. The Heartland Grill had been in Fay and May's family for years, but they were the only ones left, now. The two sisters had never married. They took care of their parents and ran the family restaurant when their parents were no longer able to. As Paula and Bill walked into the restaurant, Bill heard a familiar voice calling out, "May, I hope you have pancakes this morning, because Dr. Thomas has just walked in."

May and Fay both ran out and hugged Bill around the neck. They were crying and telling him how glad they were to see him again. No one even noticed Paula standing there. Finally Bill pulled away and said, "This is my friend, Paula. And, Paula, these two ladies are about the best cooks in the whole state, plus, they make the best tea cakes anywhere on this earth."

Fay took Paula's hands and just stepped back, "Why May, just look at those eyes, and her hair is so black, it looks like night. I can see why the Doc. fell for you, Honey."

"Oh no," Paula said, "we're just friends. I rode up here with Bill so he wouldn't have to ride by himself. He has a girlfriend."

May looked at Paula; "Well, if you asked me, he picked the wrong one."

Paula asked, "Why do you say that May?"

"Because you're the one who is up here with him, not her."

As they sat down, Bill said, "I'm so sorry about those two. I forgot how they could carry on about things. If you want to go somewhere else to eat, we can."

"No, I like them Bill. Their honest and they will tell you what they think, not what they think you want to hear. They remind me of my grandmother, and she was such a character."

* * * * *

Just about the time their food was brought to them, Dr. Harry Pittman walked in. "Bill, I thought I would find you here this morning, and this must be the charming young woman I have heard so much about."

Paula looked at Dr. Pittman and said, "Excuse me, but I just arrived here yesterday, how could you have heard about me?"

"My dear, this is Whitworth, and it's not the largest town in the mountains, so when anyone arrives here, its news. Especially someone as pretty as yourself, and with our own Bill. Why, I should hope I would hear ya'll had arrived."

Paula liked Dr. Pittman. He was an older fellow, and very likeable. He stood about six feet tall with gray hair. His presence made one aware this man didn't take a whole lot of nonsense from anyone. Paula asked Dr. Pittman, "How long have you been the president of North Whitworth University?"

Before Dr. Pittman could answer, Bill piped in, "About the time Noah got off the ark." They all broke out laughing, then, the three of them sat there talking for over two hours. Fay and May looked out from the back once and asked each other if it was a reminder of the past.

May said, "Remember how Bill and his wife, Rachel, use to sit and talk with Dr. Pittman every Saturday just like this?"

Fay said, "Mark my words, those two are meant for each other."

* * * * *

DJ and Maggie were sitting on the screen porch of their cabin. With no one around, they were able to talk freely. "Maggie, don't you like the view of the mountains? We can see most of the town from here."

"Yes, but Bill said he was going to take us walking at some point. I hope he doesn't forget us and we just have to sit on this porch all the time."

"Oh Maggie, he won't. Paula won't let him forget us."

"That's why I said I hope he doesn't forget us, love."

They both laughed and sat there taking in the sights. They even had their time of worship sitting on the porch. "I think it makes you feel the Creator's presence even more when you're close to nature like this."

"Wouldn't it be good if we moved back here with Bill? Don't you agree, DJ?"

DJ was looking off in the distance. Maggie knew there were times he felt things which would happen in the future, but he didn't always feel free to share them with her. At least not until he knew it was the right time.

* * * * *

Ron sat by his wife on the porch late that Saturday evening. They had been making plans all day about their up coming move. Kathy looked over at her husband as he sat there just looking out at the stars in the sky. She was so glad to have him back. Ron turned and looked at her as if he knew what she was thinking.

"I promise you, I'll never get mixed up with that group again," he said.

She moved over closer to him, "I'm not worried about that. I heard how the bishop was about to call you into his office for one of his talks." They both burst out laughing.

"Honey, do you think you'll like this move?"

"As long as it's with you, I know I'll like it. How are the people here taking the news?"

"Well, some are upset, and others said they knew it was about time we were moved to a larger church. So, I guess it depends on who you're talking to. The new church is a little bit bigger, but it is a strong church, and one that wants to hear the Bible preached every Sunday. That's the reason I could never figure why Steve thought he would do well there."

"Oh please, let's not bring his name up. I have heard his name all I ever want to, believe you me."

"Whatever happens to him, well, he brought it on himself."

Ron got a far away look in his eyes. "What is it Ron?" Kathy asked.

"I feel sorry for him dear. He is so mixed up and he doesn't even know it. He thinks the Bible is make-believe. He doesn't know Christ. He is just in the ministry for the money he thinks he can make."

Kathy thought about what Ron said. She knew he would pray a lot for Steve, but he had better stay away from him. "Ron, he will hurt you if he is given the chance, you know that don't you?"

"Yes, but I can still pray for his soul, in hope that one day he might turn to the Lord. They say Marshall has made a complete turn around in his life. I hear his church attendance is up and they say, he has been preaching from the Bible…no notes, just what he has been studying during the week."

Kathy looked at Ron, "Well, maybe there is hope for Steve after all."

* * * * *

Marshall Wiggins stood in his office with his Bible in hand. He had spent the whole day reading over the gospel of John. He looked out the window at the stars, "O Lord, help me to proclaim your word tomorrow. Help me to hear what you are saying to us through the gospel of John." Every time Marshall started to read the Bible now, he always started with a prayer. "Lord open my eyes to see what you want to show me, and let my heart hear what you are trying to say to us through your Word."

He couldn't remember when the Bible had such meaning to him, but now, every time he picked it up; it was like a living book in his hands. Gone were the days of getting his sermons off the internet, or from some journal. Now, his sermons came from one of the texts he had been studying during the week.

He looked once more at the note from one of his members. *Bro. Marshall, we just want to tell you how much your preaching lately has meant to us. We feel like God has answered our prayers. We ask you to please keep it up; our church has been needing this for so long.*

"Amen," he said as he put the note back on his desk. "God, help me never to forget what you have done in my life through all of this." Once again he turned to John chapter nine; the story of the blind man who was healed. "I was that blind man Lord, and you have healed my eyes to see how far I was from you."

* * * * *

Bill walked Paula back to her cabin. "Well, I hope you're not too tired from all our sightseeing today?"

"I'm tired, but I don't remember when I have enjoyed myself more. Thank you for asking me to tag long."

"Look, you have been a big hit here. Why, I think everyone here loves you already."

Paula was thinking as Bill was speaking to her about asking him if he really thought Jane was the right one for him, but then he said, "And I believe they will like Jane once they meet her too. Maybe I can get her up here before the end of the year."

Paula felt a sharp pain shoot through her as Bill said it. She was finally realizing she was falling in love with Bill, but she had never been one of those women who tried to break someone up.

Bill tapped her on the arm, "Paula, are you all right? I asked you what you wanted to do tomorrow and you acted as if you didn't hear me."

"I'm sorry, Bill." She didn't know what to say, then it hit her. "I was just wondering if you caught it, that Dr. Pittman wants you to come back and teach here."

"Yeah, I got the message loud and clear."

"Well, are you? I mean, are you thinking about coming back here to teach?"

"I miss this place so much, and I would be lying to you if I said I didn't, but I'm not sure if I'm ready." What Bill didn't want to say was, he was afraid Jane would leave him if he said anything about coming back here. Maybe after they were together, she would see how important it was to him to go back.

As Paula walked into her cabin, she felt so frustrated. Why couldn't he see what that woman was? How long was it going to take for Bill to wake up? She got down beside her bed to pray, "Lord, help me to understand what you are doing in my life. I mean, Bill doesn't want me; he is all about that other woman, so why do I keep feeling this way about him? Please, remove these feelings if he isn't going to leave her on his own. I'm not going to do anything to change his mind about her. If that happens it will have to be Your doing, not mine."

Bill sat on his bed with DJ and Maggie looking at him. "I wish there was someone I could talk to, who would understand. No, I wish I understood how I felt. When I'm with Paula, I feel so comfortable and easy inside. But, when I'm with Jane, she makes me feel so alive. There is something about her that is very intoxicating, and I'm not sure if that is a good thing or not. I just know how it makes me feel when I am around her. But is she the right one for me, or is the right one across the yard in the other cabin?"

DJ wanted so much to tell him Paula was the right one for him and even a blind man could see it, so, why didn't he?.

* * * * *

Sunday morning came and DJ and Maggie were both sitting out on the porch with Bill while he was drinking coffee. He heard Paula stirring around over in her cabin, so he called out to her, "Hey, I have coffee if you want some."

Paula poked her head out the door, "Just give me a minute, I'll be right there." Before she pulled her head back in the door, she said, "Good morning, DJ and Maggie." DJ sat up and waged his tail. Maggie was still waiting for Bill to feed them. As Paula walked across the yard, she asked, "Bill what time does church start here in the mountains?"

"About the same time it does anywhere else, why do you ask?"

"Today is Sunday isn't it?"

"Yes, it is, but I didn't think you would want to attend church on your time off from work."

"Bill, I attend church no matter where I am. It's a part of my life. It's a part of who I am."

Bill could remember hearing something like that years ago from his wife. There was just so much that made him feel comfortable with Paula. After church, as they walked back to the cabin, Bill asked Paula if she had something against his car. "No, why do you ask?"

"Well, it's just that ever since we have arrived here, you have wanted to walk everywhere we go."

"I'm sorry, I didn't think about you not wanting to do that. I just want to see everything about this town, Bill. This is like a wonderland to me."

Bill looked at her and again, he felt so confused, "How about our taking DJ and Maggie on a tour of the town today? I promised them a walk, and they will get their feelings hurt if I forget to keep my promise to them."

For a fleeting moment, Paula was reminded there was something about those two she was supposed to know and it's right on the end on her brain, but she just never seemed to be able to recall it. "Bill, I know this sounds funny, but there is something about them I am supposed to know, but I can't remember it. It happened when I met Sally that time."

"What happened, I mean, what do you think happened?"

"Now see, that's why I have never said anything to you before now. I can't remember, but there is something about those two."

"Oh, I know that. They are special, and I wouldn't take a million dollars for them."

Paula didn't say anything more. She wanted to remember, but she couldn't. It was like a fog over her mind. However, the more she was around them, she was sure it would clear one day and then she would be able to remember just what it was about them.

As they walked down the road, DJ and Maggie walked side by side. Paula said to Bill, "Look, they act like an old married couple."

DJ just looked back at Paula, and then he looked at Bill.

"What's the matter with him?" Paula asked Bill.

By now Bill was laughing, "Well, have you noticed we're walking side by side too, so I guess DJ was trying to point that out to you."

Paula stopped and burst out laughing with Bill, "Oh my God, these dogs are too smart for me."

* * * * *

The week Bill and Paula spent in the mountains was wonderful. As they drove home, both of them were quite, not saying much to each other. Bill didn't know how he was going to tell Jane about taking Paula with him to the mountains, but then he didn't know if he wanted to tell her.

Paula felt like she knew Bill felt something for her, but then there was that other woman. It was clear to everyone in Whitworth she really did care for Bill, so why couldn't he see it?

Bill wasn't sure if he truly felt something for Jane, or if it was guilt over their having slept together. He wasn't aware of the evil one's working in his own emotions and guilt. DJ and Maggie had been praying very hard for Bill and his emotions. They were very worried over his situation. They knew all too well, how people can let their emotions lead them down the wrong path. Bill was confusing his own guilt with what he thought he felt, when in all honesty, it was only lust which kept him tied to Jane. He was heading home to try and find out if he truly did feel anything for Jane or if it was Paula he really cared for.

Chapter Ten

Strategies Renewed

By the time Jane arrived home the next Saturday, she was ready to finish this thing with Bill. She had tasted what it was to have her fun while she was on Lisa's boat and she wanted to have some time to kick her heels up and party. The last eight years she had gone after one man after another, and she had enough money to live 'high on the hog,' as her poor old daddy used to say. Jane rarely ever thought about her daddy. She was ashamed of the way they lived. He was poor and worked so hard, he had died early in life. The thing she had really lost sight of, was his love for her. The few times Jane did allow herself to think about her father, she was very fast to push it from her mind. Mainly, because she knew he would be ashamed of the way she had turned out.

She was so angry when she arrived home because she had allowed her thoughts to wander over to her father, and by the time she had pushed them out of her mind, she had already began to feel shame for the life she had lived. Jane dialed the number and listened as the phone rang. She heard a familiar voice on the other end, "Well, I hope for your sake, you have the information I wanted weeks ago."

"Keep your shirt on, Jane. I have what you want and believe me, that woman will do whatever it is you want to keep this from leaking out."

"When can I pick it up?"

"I can meet you in about an hour at the park. You just park in the same spot and I'll walk by and drop it into your window and you can mail me my money."

"It had better be worth what you're asking."

"Oh believe me it is, and more."

Jane took a sip of her coffee, it wouldn't be long before she could start the wheels rolling, and then she would have all of Bill's money, and that Louise Hayes was going to take the fall for it all. This was going to be too easy and more fun than she had hoped. And who knows, she might just get ole Bill back into her bed before she kicked him out. That way, he would be killed by his own guilt, and maybe even do himself in.

While Jane waited at the park, she kept her window rolled down just enough for an envelope to be dropped in. She heard a noise, then, a tall man wearing a dark overcoat walked by and dropped a large envelope into her window. Jane started her car and drove home as fast as she dared. She was fighting within herself, wanting to open the envelope as she drove home, but reason told her she needed to wait until she was home. That way, she could sit down with her coffee and look over the information slowly and carefully. Then and only then could she plan her next move, because it would have to be done in such a way no one could trace anything back to her.

It was then, Jane came up with her brainstorm. She would call from Bill's house. Yes, that would be great. If anyone ever traced the number, it would be coming from Bill's own house. As Jane pulled into her driveway, she was laughing out loud. Little did she realize she was in a war, and Bill had two very faithful guardians watching out for him. Jane's brainstorm was, in fact the results of their faithful praying, for now things were about to turn in their favor. The wicked one had used Jane for years and she had gotten away with a lot of evil, but her time was just about up.

* * * * *

Bill dropped Paula off at her house. "I had a great time, Bill."

"I did too, Paula." Bill felt as if he had been kicked in the head. Why didn't he just go ahead and break it off with Jane? Surely this was the one he was supposed to be with. When Bill walked into his house, Jane was sitting inside waiting on him. "How did you get in my house?"

"Oh, I found the spare key you have hidden outside. So, I let myself in. I didn't think you would mind. Jane then jumped up and took Bill in her arms and kissed him. It was a long kiss. Jane wanted to turn Bill's head with this kiss, so she kept holding on to him. By the time the kiss ended, Bill had forgotten all about dropping her. His head was spinning out of control. She made him feel so alive. It was a passion he had never known before, but what he didn't know was it wasn't real passion. It was just a mirage, an illusion to keep him from asking himself the questions he really already knew the answers to, but did just not want to hear. Such is the condition of the human heart; it will lie to itself, if only to keep its illusion.

Bill stepped back, "Wow, now that's worth coming home to. I mean, what a kiss!" Jane stepped up beside him and kissed him again, this time even longer and with more passion, but Bill didn't know all the while she was planning how she was going to use his phone. "Please let me stay for a little while tonight. I know you're tired, but I have missed you so."

"Ok, do you want something to eat? I could run down to a little place I know."

Jane put her finger over his mouth. "All I want is right here," she pushed Bill back onto the couch. His head was spinning while she kissed him. How could he stop this from going any farther, and did he even want to? Jane was a mastermind when it came to playing with men's emotion, and she knew how to get a man so confused he would think it was all his idea.

Maggie asked DJ in a low voice, "What are we going to do, you see what she is trying to do don't you?"

"Maggie I'm not blind. I just don't know what we can do at this point."

"Well, I'm not going to just sit by and watch this wicked woman worm her way into this house." And with that Maggie ran in there and started barking as if the house was on fire.

"Maggie shut up, we're home."

It was no use, she wasn't going to stop. Jane sat up and yelled at Maggie, "If you don't shut up, I'll throw you outside!"

Bill, felt a little angry at Jane's reaction toward Maggie. "She just needs to go outside and she is doing the right thing by asking." Bill felt the same anger he had felt when his friend had kicked DJ. Jane could see in Bill's eyes she had overstepped herself. "Jane I'm tired and maybe it would be better if we just met for dinner tomorrow."

"Bill, I'm sorry I yelled at your dog. It's just that I have missed you so much and I wanted to show you how much. I'm sorry."

Bill reached out and kissed Jane with a very gentle kiss, "It's all right, but I am tired and I think we had better stop before things get out of hand."

As Jane walked out to her car, she cursed those two dogs, "I ought to have them shot for what they did tonight."

Bill let DJ and Maggie outside to do their business. He thought again about how confusing things were in his life right now.

Outside, Maggie said to DJ, "See, we can do something if we will just try."

"I know love, I just couldn't think of anything to do at the moment. Thank God for your quick thinking. It saved Bill, that's for sure."

With that, Maggie reached over and licked DJ on the side of the face. "What's that for Maggie?"

"Just because I love you and you make me feel special, that's all."

DJ got closer to Maggie and said in a low voice, "My dear, when the Creator made you, he broke the mold. There will never be another one like you."

Bill walked out onto the back porch, "Hey, are you two ready to come inside?"

DJ and Maggie walked into the house to find Bill had them a special treat. He knelt down and patted them both on the head, "Ya'll kept me from making a big mistake tonight, and I just want to thank you for it. I don't know why, but for some reason, I think you knew what you were doing, Maggie." Bill hugged them both then turned out the lights. After he had fallen asleep, DJ and Maggie went into another room where they could spend their time in worship.

* * * * *

Paula unpacked her clothes and thought about Bill. I wonder if he is going to be home tomorrow, or should I even call him? He might call his girlfriend and eat dinner with her. Oh why am I even doing this to myself? Maybe I should just walk away from Bill and learn my lesson.

You can't change a man's mind when he has his head turned by some tramp.

She went to bed but she couldn't go off to sleep. Instead, she thought about their trip to the mountains and how much fun she had. It was the kind of relationship she had been looking for, only he had a girlfriend. Paula shut her eyes once again trying to go to sleep. Finally, she got up to make some tea. As she sat in a chair looking out of her window, she prayed asking God to show her what to do, if there was anything she could do, or if things were not going to change, would He please change the way she felt about Bill. Then she thought about how much she already loved DJ and Maggie, and there it was again, what was it that she couldn't remember? It was something she saw or overheard, but what was it?

Sleep did not come until early Sunday morning, nevertheless, she got up and went to church. Maybe there would be something in the sermon which would throw some light on her situation. Paula went home feeling about the same way she was when she arrived at church… confused about everything, and not sure about anything. How in the world did she ever allow herself to get into such a mess?

Bill got up and went to Bro. Ron's church. It was there he found out Ron was moving across town to a larger church. After the service, Bill walked up to Ron, "Hey, Ron, I'm glad to hear about your new move. That's great, or at least I hope you think it's great."

"Yes, it is going to be a good move, Bill," Ron reached out and took Bill by the arm and led him away from all the people standing around.

"Did I do something wrong Ron?"

"No Bill, it's just some of the people are having a hard time with our being moved and well, to put it lightly, it's probably better if you don't talk about it in the church right now."

"Right, I understand."

Ron looked at Bill and he could still remember how Bill use to talk so ugly to him, but here they were now friends. Truly God's grace had been good to Ron and his wife.

"Bill," Kathy said as she walked by, "why don't you come over and eat lunch with us and Ron can tell you how God saved his skin and gave him a bigger church to boot."

Bill looked at Ron with a big question mark on his face, Ron just said "Well, you might as well know too, so come on over and lets talk."

Bill said, "For some reason, I know I don't want to miss out on this."

Kathy laughed as they were walking across the church yard.

"What's so funny dear?" Ron asked.

"We are!"

"How's that?' Bill piped in, "does that mean me too? I mean, have I done something I didn't know about?"

"No, ya'll two silly gooses, we're what's funny."

Bill looked at Kathy; "I don't understand what you are talking about, Kathy." "Well think about it Bill, a year ago would you have been coming over to our house to eat lunch?"

Bill laughed when it hit him, "You know, you're right. We are funny, but it the best kind of funny, don't you think?"

Kathy put her arm through Ron's arm, "Yes I do, Bill, yes I do."

While Kathy put the final touches on lunch, Bill sat listening to Ron tell him how he almost messed up not only his friend's life but his own as well. "Man, it took some guts to go and face the bishop. Was he mad at you?"

"No, Bill, the bishop is a fine man and a wonderful Christian. In fact, he has been a big help to me through all of this."

Bill sat there thinking how he would like to have someone he could go to and open up to, but he didn't feel like now was the right time to talk with Ron about Jane and Paula. After all, he wasn't sure which way he might go himself. There was no use in bringing someone else into the picture at this time. By the time Bill left Ron's house, he felt like he knew Ron better, and he liked him even more now than he previously had. Maybe he would call Paula when he got home. About that time, his phone rang. "Hello," Bill answered. He could hear Jane crying on the other end. Then, it hit him he had forgotten all about meeting her for lunch. "Oh Jane, I am so sorry, I forgot about our plans for lunch. Please forgive me."

"So, is that's how it's going to be now? You have had your fun. You know what I'm about, so you will just throw me aside and forget about me. I have been crying all afternoon. I promised myself I wasn't going to call you, but I had to know why you were being so mean to me, when I have done nothing to you but show you love." One thing about Jane, she knew how to act, and she could cry on a dime if the need demanded it.

Bill felt sick about this, he wouldn't do anything to hurt her or anyone, "Jane, please, let me make it up to you. Meet me for dinner tonight. I'm on my way home and after I change clothes, we can meet for coffee then go out and get something to eat."

Jane was still crying, her voice was breaking up she was still crying so hard. "You mean that Bill, you aren't lying to me are you?"

"No Jane, I promise, I'll come by and pick you up just as soon as I change clothes, I promise."

After they hung up, Jane wiped her eyes, and started to laugh, "Girl, you still got it. They don't come any more foolish than a man who has a crying woman on his hands. It was only five minutes after Bill walked out of his house his phone rang. This time it was Paula. She left a message, but all she said was that she had a great time and thanked him again for allowing her to go along. It wasn't what she wanted to say, but you couldn't open up your heart to someone's voice mail. No, she would wait for the right time. Paula sat there with her Bible in hands. "God, please show me when it is the right time to talk with Bill and prepare his heart to hear me when that time comes."

* * * * *

While Jane waited for Bill to arrive at her house, she looked over the information she had on Louise Hayes. I'll call her tomorrow, and we will get this ball rolling. Maybe in a month or more, I will be able to turn ole Bill lose and let him go back to Miss Priss. Maybe she will take him back. Then she smiled, thinking, "Maybe I will work it out so she won't even speak to him again, ever." Jane laughed. She was so proud of herself. She had thought of everything, or so she thought. But that's when we can make the biggest mistakes, because we always leave out the One who controls the universe. Jane had long forgotten about God, and she never gave him one thought, but God has a way of changing that, and He knows how to get our attention.

When she heard Bill in the driveway, Jane put the papers away. No need to chance him seeing them now, was it? Jane was dressed to kill. She was wearing as little as you could get by with and still go out in public. Bill was taken aback when he saw the dress she was wearing. "I hope you like it. I know it shows more of me than you want to see now," leaving that statement open as if to imply now that he had slept with her, he didn't want her anymore.

Bill felt so guilty; he wasn't trying to say that at all. He knew she was going to feel that way if she ever found out about Paula going with him to the mountains. So, right then and there, he decided not to tell her, and he wasn't going to call Paula later like he had planned.

He couldn't let Jane think he was just trying to take advantage of her. Maybe things would be better after a little more time. After all, wasn't he drawn to Jane first? Even though it was wrong, he had been in her bed. So, they did have a connection. It is always strange how people will lie to themselves, even when deep down inside they know what's right, but sin can so blind the eyes that a person will think he is acting honorably, when in all truthfulness, he is just following after sin.

Bill was still caught in the web of sin, and every time he saw Jane dressed the way she usually dressed, he would forget about following his heart, and lust would take over. Bill's honorable act was nothing more than his head being turned by Jane's provocative attire. It was going to take a lot more to wake him up from the sleep he was in. Sin can put a soul into a sound sleep, even to the place where the heart no longer hears the Word of God calling them to return back home.

* * * * *

Tracie and her husband Earl had stayed home from church that Sunday night. Earl went down to the store to pick up a pizza. When he arrived back home Tracie was all excited. "Earl, guess what I just found out? A girl from work called me and guess who Bill took to the mountains with him?"

"I have no idea, dear. Who did Bill take to the mountains with him?"

"He took Paula, so maybe that means Jane is out. Thank God it's over between them."

"I wouldn't be so fast to thank God just yet, Tracie."

"What do you mean? What do you know about this?"

"I just passed him on the road, and he was with Jane, not Paula. Sorry, but it looks like Jane has her hooks in deeper than you thought."

"Why doesn't that woman just go somewhere and fall off the planet? Why is she out to hurt Bill anyway?"

"I don't have the answers to those questions, but remember we are praying and I believe God cares more about Bill than either one of us does. Besides, you're the one who told me about the change which has taken place in his life."

"Well, a lot of good that's going to do with Miss Tramp of the Year hot on his trail."

"Don't forget what the preacher said this morning, Tracie. Things always look darker before daylight."

"Well then Earl, it's midnight for Bill, ok. I mean, this woman causes men to kill themselves after she is through with them."

Earl could tell Tracie was upset. He walked over to her and she fell into his arms crying, "I feel so helpless, Earl. Bill's my friend and I can't do anything to help him."

"Your praying for him, Tracie, and that's more than ten thousands words, believe me."

"But it didn't help Shawn," Earl looked down at the floor, there were tears falling from his face now. "What is it Earl?"

"Tracie, I was so upset with Shawn for having an affair with that woman I never once prayed for him. I have felt so guilty all these years. What if I had prayed for Shawn, he might still be alive. I let my pride get in the way, and I didn't stand by him in prayer when he needed me the most."

By now Earl was crying uncontrollably. Tracie held him as close to her as she could. "Don't blame yourself honey, I'm sure there were others who were praying for Shawn. This time we are going to pray together and see Bill through this thing. I might not be able to say anything to him now, but one day I will."

They both knelt down and prayed for Bill, and even for the soul of Jane.

* * * * *

As Bill walked out the door Monday morning, DJ looked at Maggie, "I know we have a lot of things to do today, but please let's spend some time reading this morning."

"Oh DJ, you mean you want me to read don't you?"

"Why of course, we can read one of C. S. Lewis' books, and you can do all the voices again. That makes the story more interesting, Maggie."

As they walked toward Bill's office, Maggie asked DJ if he ever thought they might be able to share the truth about themselves with Bill. "I don't know Maggie; if you remember it was only because Sally had reached such a low point that we were able to share with her."

"I hope Bill doesn't reach that point Maggie."

DJ had chosen C. S. Lewis' book, *The Screwtape Letters,* to read.

"Why do you want to read that one?"

"I don't know, but I think it's something we need to hear again. So lets read it first."

It took some doing to get it off the book shelf. Luckily, it was on the bottom shelf, so with a little planning, they were able to get it out. "We'll put it on top of these other books until we're through with it. That way, if Bill was sees it, he would just think he must have left it there."

Maggie looked at DJ, "You mean, you don't think he will ask us why we didn't put it back when we were through reading it?"

They both giggled as they sat the book up against the bottom shelf. Maggie was lying with her paws up against the book. "Now, let me see how we are going to do this," she said. Then she began reading in a high, shrill voice, "My dear Wormwood."

DJ sat down. He was already into the story. There was something in this book they needed to hear, or to be reminded of, he was certain. He just loved the way Maggie made the stories come alive by doing all the different voices.

Maggie glanced over at DJ. She could tell he was already into the story, and to just see the expression on his face made it all worthwhile. She would read to him for the rest of her life. If the truth be known, she had always loved DJ and over the years, they had grown closer together. Maggie didn't even want to think about what life might be like without her DJ.

* * * * *

Bill walked into the office and Tracie was already at her desk working. She didn't say much to him that morning. Her heart was still full from the night before. She and Earl had moved closer in their own lives last night. It took a lot for him to open up and tell Tracie about the guilt he felt and she knew it. Bill was on the top of their prayer list, but right now, her thoughts were on home.

Jarrod brought a pile of papers to Bill's desk and set them down, "Glad to have you back, and oh, I'm suppose to tell you that these need to be ready by the end of the week."

Bill looked at the papers, and asked "Just when do I get to sleep?"

Jarrod said as he was walking out, "I think Joe said you were supposed to have caught up on your sleep while you were off."

Bill picked one paper up to start proofreading. He was halfway through with it when the phone on his desk rang. "Paper," he answered with a sharp tone in his voice.

"Well, well, I can tell someone isn't having a good first day back at work." Jane knew she needed to fix her mistake from the night before and she didn't want to wait too long about doing it.

"Oh, I think they have saved every article for me to read and some of them have to be ready by tomorrow. I'll have to stay up late tonight just to get that done."

"That answers my next question,"

"What do you mean, Jane?"

"Well, I was going to ask if you wanted to go out and get a bite to eat, but I guess not." Just then it hit her, "but maybe I can pick something up and come over there. We can eat together and then you can get to work. I will help you by doing some of your housework. Oh, Bill, that will be so much fun."

Bill thought about it for a second, then said, "Sure, that's a great idea, but I am going to have to work, so don't get mad at me if I can't spend time with you."

"Bill, I'm not a little girl. I can help you with your house work and you can get your papers read. I think it will be just the greatest thing."

"Ok, then come over a little after six and we'll get started."

Jane knew she was going to have to get to Bill's house earlier then six, so she called him right back, "Honey, could I use your outside key again? I'll get over there before you get home. That way I can get started with my work. I'll already have the food so as soon as you get home, we'll eat and you can get back to work. I'll finish up with my work, then I'll leave you to finish yours."

"Ok, that sounds like a good idea." Bill hung up the phone, but he didn't have time to really think about Jane going over to his house to work. If he had, he might have remembered she never liked housework and she paid someone to clean her own house.

As Jane drove up in Bill's driveway, DJ and Maggie heard her, so they put the book on top of some other books and went and laid down. Imagine their surprise when Jane walked in using Bill's key again. She had some papers and pictures in her hand.. Jane set them down as she poured herself a drink. DJ walked by and saw the pictures and he had enough time to read some of what was written there. He looked at Maggie with a funny look, but he wouldn't leave the room. Jane picked up the phone and dialed the number to the bank, "Yes, may I speak to a Mrs. Louise Hayes please? Yes, I'll hold." She waited for a minute and then she heard a voice on the other end of the phone.

"This is Louise Hayes. How may I help you?"

With a voice which would have sent a cold chill down anyone's back, Jane said, "I think I'm the one who's going to help you."

"Pardon me," Louise had no way of knowing how this day was going to turn out. She didn't know by answering her phone that day, her life was going to be dragged through the mud. "Excuse me, but I'm afraid you must have the wrong person."

"This is Louise Hayes, who before she was married, worked as a prostitute in another town and let's see, you even lost a child. Did I leave anything out honey?"

"That was a long time ago," you could hear the tears in Louise's voice, and she had to talk very low so no one would hear her. "Who are you and why are you doing this to me?"

"The *who* is not important, and neither is the why. All you need to know is that I will show this information to your husband and your boss if you don't do what I ask." Louise was silent for a moment, "What do you what me to do?"

As Jane told her what she wanted, DJ and Maggie just sat there not knowing what to do or think. Never had they seen such evil in one person, but now they knew what she wanted with Bill, and that she was out to hurt him in the worst way possible. Louise told Jane she could give her Bill account numbers, but Jane would need his password. She indicated she did not know if anyone could get that information.

"There are laws, you know, and the bank isn't going to leave that kind of information lying around," said Louise.

"No, I'm sure they're not, which is why you are going to have to break into the bank's main files and get the information for me."

"But I could go to jail for the rest of my life."

"Shame, isn't it honey," Jane was trying to sound so sickly sweet; just as she was about to remind her she would drag her life through the mud. "Yes, it's sure a shame. Why, I mean, what do you think your husband's family will think of their daughter-in-law when they find out you used to sell your body, and think how the other parents will react toward your little girl. That's right you do have a little girl now, don't you?"

Louise sounded as if all her life had left her body, "Give me some time. I need some time to see what I am going to have to do to get the information for you."

Jane had a cruel smirk on her face as she said, "I'll call you next Monday."

Chapter Eleven

Count Down

Jane thought she had everything planned out so carefully there couldn't be a mistake. If it hadn't been for the fact, there were a pair of ears listening to every word she spoke, she just might have gotten away with it all. However, the best laid plans never turn out the way we think they will.

DJ and Maggie noticed how Jane used Bill's phone, which might not seem strange, if it weren't for the fact she had a cell-phone and Jane hated using a regular line phone. So of course, DJ and Maggie watched her to see if they could pick up on anything, but Jane never gave away her plan. DJ did come up with an idea one night while they were praying over the matter. He asked Maggie if she thought they could tape Jane's phone conversations. "Yes, I know Bill has some tapes which are already open, so we could use one of them. Also, he has the sound system in his room with a tape recorder built right in, so yes I do. Why?"

"Well, here is what we are going to have to do and it will be tricky. We can't get caught, or it's all over. Every day when Bill leaves, we will put a tape in the recorder and if Jane goes in there to use the phone, we will turn it on."

"DJ, think about that for a moment. Do you think she is going to wait and watch us turn the tape recorder on?"

"No silly, as soon as she comes over, one of us will go in there and turn it on and as soon as she leaves we will turn it off."

"But, Bill listens to music every night while he is going to sleep."

"Which is why I said it was going to be tricky. If it were easy love, we wouldn't be able to catch her in whatever she is planning."

There were a few times when they came close to getting caught by Bill. Once, DJ had to run like someone was at the door, while Maggie got the tape out. (If you are asking yourself how a dog could do that, well with their mouth of course. The tapes were dropped in with the tape part being on the bottom, so they never got their month on the tape itself, just the case.) But remember, it did take them a few seconds to do it, so there were those times when Bill almost caught them. Once, Maggie had just put his tape of music back in and had to pick up the other one and hide under the bed until Bill fell asleep. DJ was so worried she was going to get caught, but Maggie was very good at moving quietly, so she never woke Bill up. Another time, when Jane was there she called the man who was getting the information for her and she called from Bill's bedroom. They got it all on tape. So, the day they got her on tape talking with Louise, they knew they had her. That time, after Jane left Bill's house, Maggie said, "We have to get Bill to listen to this tape now DJ."

"No, not yet. Let's give her more rope to hang herself with. Besides, we are going to have to figure out some way to help Louise also."

Maggie put her head down when DJ said her name. "What is it Maggie?"

"Oh DJ, how could she do that to herself?"

"My love, sin can make people do some of the craziest things. Later they will regret having done them. But Louise's mistake was in not telling her husband the truth about her past. You can never build a lasting relationship on lies, Maggie, and Louise is going to have to face up to her past before all of this is over."

Maggie knew DJ was right, but she didn't see any way things were ever going to turn out right for Louise. This could very well be the thing she had feared all along.

* * * * *

Wednesday morning Paula called Bill just after he arrived at work "I'm calling to tell you again, how much I enjoyed our trip to the mountains, and to ask you if you could bring DJ and Maggie to the nursing home this afternoon? I have missed seeing them and everyone has been asking me ever since I got back when their next visit is going to be."

Bill thought for a moment, his mind was in conflict; he was more confused than ever, "Wait just a second and let me look and see what my day looks like. I'll be right back." He put the phone down and moved a lot of papers around on his desk, trying to make it sound as if he was looking over the work for the day. A very large part of him wanted to see Paula again, but then there was Jane and she was making him feel like he had taken advantage of her. Bill picked the phone back up, but his voice couldn't hide the truth, "Today isn't going to be a good day for me, Paula, maybe next week."

"Bill, I'll leave and not be here if that's the problem. I know you have a girlfriend, and maybe I shouldn't have gone with you to the mountains, but remember you asked me to go."

"I know I did, and no, your not the problem Paula, it's me. It's not you, it's me." "Bill, is there anything I can do to help?"

Bill thought to himself, "Don't be so beautiful, and stop making me feel so comfortable every time I'm with you." To her he said, "No, Paula, there is nothing you can do, but thank you anyway. Tell you what, I'll try to get them out there by 4:30 this afternoon if that's not to late."

"Oh no, and I will have everyone ready for their visit. And Bill, thank you for bringing them."

Bill had not seen Jane since Monday night and every time he called her there was no answer. "Well, maybe she had to go out of town and just didn't have time to call me. I'll bet it was her friend. That's it; she went to see her friend who just lost her husband." However, Jane knew each time Bill called her cell-phone, but she didn't answer. She was too busy making plans to have him take up her time.

While Bill was cleaning off his desk getting ready to leave for the day, Tracie walked over to his desk, "Bill, I know this is none of my business, and please don't get mad at me, but I think you would be a lot better off with Paula than Jane. Now, that's all I am going to say, but a woman has an intuition about these things and I just hope you will listen to me about this."

Tracie turned and walked away. She knew if Earl had any idea what she had just done he would blow his top. He was so afraid of that woman coming after his business, but Tracie had to do something. To sit by and watch Bill being thrown to the lions was unmerciful. There was something about the way she said that to Bill which troubled him. It was as if she knew something, but wasn't going to tell him, and he knew her well enough to know Tracie wasn't going to tell him until she was good and ready.

When Bill pulled into the driveway of the nursing home, he saw Paula getting into her car to leave. He got out and ran over to her car before she left, "Hey now, wait a minute, DJ and Maggie want to see you too. Why, they were so excited when I told them we were coming here today. They will not understand why you left without speaking to them."

Paula had such a large lump in her throat, "Ok, I'll come over and speak to them."

As she walked over to the car, Bill asked her if everything was all right, "I didn't do something to hurt you, did I, Paula. If I did, I am truly sorry."

Paula thought to herself, "Why are you being so kind? Why can't you be cold and mean? That way I could walk away so easily, but no, you are killing me on the inside." Her audible reply was, "Bill, I'm all right. I didn't want to cause you any conflict, that's all."

DJ and Maggie both gathered around Paula and did their very best to show her all the love they could. DJ even licked her on the face when she bent down to pat him on the head. "Hey there fellow," she said as she reached out and picked him up in her arms. "Oh, I have missed you too, little fellow."

Maggie was standing there, just waiting to be patted, "Oh girl, you know I haven't forgotten you," Paula told her.

As they walked down the hall, Bill looked over at Paula. "Thank you for staying," he told her.

Paula said in a very low voice, "I wanted to stay Bill."

Bill put his arm through hers as they walked down the hall. DJ and Maggie beat them into the large room. Everyone calling for them to come and see them first could be heard from one end of the hall to the other. "Sounds like we have another hit on our hands, Paula."

But Paula was deep in thought and never heard Bill. She was wondering what it would be like to be able to openly tell him how much she loved him and how much she needed him.

"Did you hear me? I think we have another hit on our hands."

"Yeah," she replied, "but then again, I think we could stay out and just send in DJ and Maggie and everyone would be ok with it." Paula thought, "How long will I be able to hold this together? How long will I be able to hold my tongue and not say something to Bill about how I feel?"

* * * * *

Thursday morning Bill's phone rang just as he sat down at his desk. "Hello, this is Bill."

"Did you miss me, Darling?"

"Jane, where have you been? I have called your phone and you never answered me at all. And you didn't return any of my calls. Why?"

"I was out of town on some business, but I'm back now and I'm all yours, so when and where do you want to go out? Tomorrow night?"

"I don't care, you pick a place, and it will be fine with me."

"Ok, then pick me up around 6:00 and I'll tell you then where you are taking me." Bill laughed, "Ok, it's a date then." As he hung the phone up, the words of Tracie ran through his mind. Should he ask her? No, she wouldn't say anything, because if she were going to tell him anything, she would have the day she gave him the friendly advice. Bill was in early that day and no one was even there yet. "How did Jane know I was here already?" he wondered to himself.

While he sat at his desk wondering how she knew he was already in the office, she drove away from the side street where she had been watching him. She was just counting the days now. It won't be long until I can get my hands on his money. Jane had done this so many times she was starting to get a little too overconfident.

Maggie saw that in her, and told DJ it would work to their advantage. Overconfident people always make mistakes and Jane was making her share of them now. By trying to throw any evidence off of herself, she had placed herself right in the middle of the fireball. One thing DJ and Maggie were not able to do was to sit around doing nothing, while she pulled off her little scheme. They had made a promise to Sally to look after Bill and they were not about to fail now.

The one thing Jane had lost sight of was the power of love. Pure love was driving the guardians now. The love they had for Sally, plus the love they had for Bill kept them on guard. They were already making their plans for Monday when Jane showed up to use Bill's phone again.

Jane went into the bedroom. DJ just had time to push the recorder switch on and hide under the bed before Jane entered the room. She dialed the number and waited for an answer. The voice on the other end said, "Good morning, First Home Trust Bank, this is Louise Hayes speaking. May I help you?"

Jane was already smiling, "Why yes dear, you can. Remember, if I can get your extension number without asking anyone inside the bank, then I can find out more about you than you would possibly ever want me too, so I hope you haven't forgotten Monday morning I will call you again. And please, don't make me angry."

Louise was crying softly now, "Please leave me alone. I have never done anything to you. I don't even know who you are, so why are you picking on me?"

"Because you are the one with the most to loose, honey. You are the one hiding from your past. Be sure of one thing, dear. There is nothing you can do that I will not find out about and even if you try to leave town and go somewhere else to start over, well, I'll find you and I will ruin you."

Louise was so afraid, "I don't know if I will be able to get the information you want. There are too many safety checks in this system. If I try to just go in there and get the information the whole system will shut down and it will tag my computer as the one trying to gain access."

"Now listen here to me you little slut. I'll see to it everyone in this town knows who you are. Maybe you can go back into your old line of work, since you won't have a job at the bank anymore."

Louise knew she had no way out of this. She was always so afraid of her past catching up with her and now it looked as if those days were here. "I'll need his password. If you can get me his password, then I'll be able to get you the information you want."

At first Jane wasn't going to hear it, "No, you will have to get it without any help from me."

As calmly as anyone could under such pressure, Louise spoke and said, "Then you had best send your information to my husband and boss, because without the password there isn't going to be any deal."

Jane knew Louise was telling the truth. One thing she knew was when someone had their back against a wall, they would do whatever they had to do, to find a way out if there was one. Otherwise, they would go through with the deal. And since Louise was so calm, Jane knew she was on the up and up. "Ok, sweetie. I'll call you as soon as I have the password, but if you try to leave town or to double cross me… well… just know, I have someone watching you at all times."

Jane hung up the phone and walked out of Bill's house. Maggie took the tape out and they sat there in silence, not knowing what to say. Never before had they seen such evil in one person.

Finally DJ spoke, "Maggie?"

"Yes love."

"We must be very careful here, because if she finds out about us, that woman would kill both of us to get what she wants."

"I know love, I'm afraid of that, too."

They both knew Jane was the most evil person they had ever run across, and they knew even better now, Bill was in very serious danger. They even talked about telling him about themselves, but that still wouldn't help Louise and DJ was determined to do something to help her as well.

"How could we sleep at night, Maggie, if we left her to take the fall for all of this?" DJ questioned. "We are going to have to get more on tape, then get Bill to listen to it."

Maggie's greatest fear was something might happen to DJ. She knew he would get in the way to keep anything from happening to her. Maggie just laid down and tried to go to sleep, but she was afraid the dream she had been having would come back. The one were DJ was killed, leaving her all alone in the world.

* * * * *

Rev. Ron was moving into the new parsonage. He was going to like this move and the members from the church he was leaving had accepted it as God's will for him, so they chipped in and helped him move. It was a wonderful day as they unloaded the U-HAUL truck. Members from both churches were working together. After the truck was unloaded Ron prayed with both groups, they stood and held hands while he prayed. He thanked God for the church where he had been ministering and for this new door which had opened to him. Ron asked for God to bless both churches and to be with the new pastor who was following him. While he prayed, something inside of him told him he needed to pray for Bill and it had to be today. After lunch everyone left the parsonage, old friends saying their goodbyes and the new members telling him if he needed anything whom to call.

"Pastor, we will come by and check on you and Kathy later, but right now we know ya'll need to rest and unpack," one of the church members said.

As everyone drove off, Ron got the keys to the church. "Oh Ron, you can put your office together later, let's lie down and rest," Kathy suggested.

"It's Bill, honey, I need to pray for him and now."

"What do you mean you need to pray for him now?"

"While I was praying with the people, the Lord laid Bill on my heart. I must pray for him today, now and not put it off."

"Have you talked with him dear?"

"No, but now is not the time to call, I'll pray first, then I'll call him."

Ron entered the sanctuary. It was quite inside, and the presence of God was there. As he went to his knees at the altar, he knew this was where he would spend a lot of his time. This was where real ministry was born, not in some backroom making deals over coffee. He was beginning to see the church of today had lost sight of real ministry and the source from which it came.

* * * * *

Steve Godwin drove by as they were unloading the U-HAUL. It made him so mad that Ron was moving into the church he wanted. The bishop had taken away his Area Rep. position as well. All his career troubles, he blamed on Ron. Why did he have to stick his nose where it didn't belong anyway? As far as Steve was concerned, Tom Dixon was getting what he deserved. Why did Ron have to go to the bishop and stick his nose into his business. Well, let him move into his church and parsonage, but mark my words, the day will come when he would make Ron pay for what he did. Steve didn't care if it took years to get even, he was going to make Ron pay. Steve was a man so blinded by sin he couldn't realize he had done anything wrong. All he saw was that things didn't turn out the way he wanted, therefore, someone had to be at fault.

* * * * *

Friday evening when Bill arrived at Jane's house to pick her up, she was ready and waiting for him. She had dressed once more to draw his mind away from anything which would make him think she wasn't falling in love with him. Jane knew she had to be very careful and not have a lackadaisical attitude toward Bill or he might smell a rat, and then it would all be over. Jane opened the door as soon as Bill rang the doorbell and stepped out and kissed him as hard as she could. She was trying to take his breathe away with her kiss, and from the way he stepped back she was pretty sure she had.

"Boy, if that's what I get when you come back home, maybe I should send you away more often."

"No sir, I missed you so badly it will be a long time before I leave town again." Bill's head was spinning. Again, he wasn't sure about his feelings, maybe Paula was just a good friend and he was confusing his feelings of friendship. Yes, that had to be it. Before he could say anything to Jane, she kissed him again. It was another long kiss, which was meant to sweep Bill off of his feet. When Jane pulled away she looked into his eyes with such hunger, Bill almost gave in right then and there. Luckily, Jane didn't want to play things that far this time, she already had the night planned. All she needed was time to work her magic on him.

As they got into the car, Jane asked Bill, "Where do you want to go tonight?"

Bill replied, "I thought you were going to pick a place, or didn't we agree on that?"

"Yes, but I decided to let you chose the place where we would eat, after all you are the man of the house, so to speak. If we are ever going to see how far this relationship is going, then it's time I step back and let you make the decisions."

This really took Bill by surprise. He had never thought he would see the day Jane let any man make the decisions. It made him feel even more like this was the right choice. Jane had to be the right one for him. Just look how things were turning out. She was allowing him to step into the place a man longs to stand in, the head of the household.

Jane saw the look in Bill's eyes and she knew she had him right were she wanted him. "Bill darling,"

"Yes dear, what is it?"

"Well, I was going to talk with the people at First Home Trust Bank, but you know they always want you to come up with a password for your account and I have never been good at that. Could you help me?"

"Sure how many letters do you want in your password?"

"No honey, I mean well, do you use a name or just numbers? What's your password dear?"

"What? You want my password?"

"No, I don't want *it*, but, I thought you might tell me so it could give me some idea of how to create one."

"Jane, a password can be anything from a group of numbers like your date of birth, or even your cat's date of birth?"

"I don't have a cat. Why won't you help me? It's not like I'm asking you to sign over your account to me or anything like that, I just wanted an idea."

"That's what I'm trying to do, give you an idea of what a password can be."

They were still sitting in Bill's car in front of Jane's house, and Jane was getting madder by the minute. Why was he being so hardheaded? All she wanted was his password. "So, what you're telling me is you don't trust me. Is that it, your afraid I might steal a few dollars from your checking account? Oh, here it comes. Boy, I should have known this day was coming. You can take the woman to bed, but don't trust her with anything. Now how is that for a lasting relationship?"

Bill was trying to help Jane with what he thought was her problem. What he didn't realize was she really did want his password. "Jane, please try to understand. If we were already married, I would have no trouble letting you have my password, but we're not yet, so I don't think it would be the right thing to do."

In a fit of rage, Jane pulled out her account book and said, "Here is my password and my account numbers. See, I'm not afraid you might steal from me, but it seems to me I am the only one who shares that kind of faith and trust." With that, Jane got out of the car and slammed the door as hard as she could. "And to think, I was even thinking about trying to get you to stay with me tonight. Oh, I know that's the wrong thing to say to Mister Prefect here, but, I guess that makes me the worst person in the world, doesn't it?" Jane turned to walk away and Bill got out of the car. Jane turned around so fast it took Bill by surprise. She just held up her hand and said, "No, don't you come near me, and stay away from me, do you hear me, just stay away from me!"

As she walked away Bill, said, "Jane, I'm sorry, please forgive me, let's talk." Without turning around she said, "Call me tomorrow I'm just too hurt to talk with you right now."

* * * * *

Bill drove home wondering how things got so out of hand. He wasn't saying he didn't trust Jane, but it just didn't make good sense to give your password to someone you're not married to. When he arrived home, he went on line and checked his bank account, then he changed his password on his savings account. He didn't know why he was doing it, but something inside of him told him to.

DJ and Maggie could tell Bill was troubled about something, but they didn't know what. Bill got a cup of coffee and went out onto the back deck to sit down. DJ and Maggie followed him outside. "I guess you two need to go out too, so let just stay out here for awhile." While Bill was drinking his second cup of coffee, his phone rang. Bill got up but you could tell he wasn't too happy about answering the phone. "If she starts again with me…."

"Hello, Bill. Am I calling you at a bad time?" Paula's voice sounded so clear and free from accusation, Bill sighed with relief.

"No, not at all, I'm just outside drinking coffee with the dogs."

Paula laughed, "You scared me for a minute. I thought you were angry at me or something."

"It might be the 'or something,' but it has nothing to do with you, Paula, I can promise you that. What are you up tonight?"

"I thought about going to the coffee shop and getting some coffee, and I wanted to see if you wanted to go along."

"I have a better idea, why don't you come over here. You know I'm in a coffee club, so I truly have the very best coffee in town anyway."

"That sounds great, I'll be right over."

* * * * *

Jane called her friend, Lisa Ainsworth, "I just put him through the ringer. I had him telling me he was sorry and asking me to forgive him."

Lisa broke out laughing, "Stop it. I can't stand much more of this. So, tell me did you get his password?"

"Not yet, but I will have it by the end of the week."

"What!! You didn't take advantage of the situation? Jane, he would have given it to you tonight. Girl, now he will have time to cool off and rethink it."

"No, what he is going to do is cry himself to sleep thinking he has lost me, so the next time I ask him for his help, he might even give me the account numbers as well."

They both started laughing, "You are one bad woman. I would hate to be some little woman, thinking my man was safe with you out there looking for someone to take advantage of."

"Oh honey, I just take their money. If they want someone to take advantage of them, the fair will be in town next month. They can let someone read their palm." They started laughing again. Jane just knew Bill was at home sitting there worrying over the fact she didn't want to have anything to do with him right now, or maybe for ever. She thought she had played it out just right. He never knew it was all just a set up. Later that night, she walked out of her house as a car drove up. It was the young man she had met on Lisa's boat, "Where do you want to go?"

"Anywhere that is away from here. I don't want anyone seeing us together, at least not yet."

* * * * *

Bill opened his door, "Hello Paula, come on in. We're out on the back deck. I know DJ and Maggie will be glad to see you."

After Paula left, Bill was even more confused. He had spent an enjoyable evening just drinking coffee with this beautiful woman, and not one time did she blow her top at him or try to get him to do something he didn't want to do, or put him on a guilt trip. No, it was just an evening of tranquil peace. Bill had almost forgotten what that could mean to a relationship. He had forgotten about the times he had spent with his wife doing just what he and Paula had done; nothing but drink coffee and talk about what was going on in their daily lives. And the peck on the cheek she had given him as she left was a pleasant surprise.

Paula sensed there was something troubling Bill, but she knew it wasn't her place to ask. For Paula the situation was also confusing. She could tell Bill liked her, and it seemed he wasn't too crazy about this Jane woman anymore, so why was he holding on to her?

Bill looked at DJ and Maggie as he turned off the lights, "I surely wish I had it as easy as you two. I mean, you know who your mate is. It was chosen for you. What's so hard about that?"

Maggie looked at DJ, and then looked up at Bill, as if to say, "You don't know everything, mister."

Bill looked at Maggie, then he said, "I swear there are times when I think you know everything that comes out of my mouth."

Maggie picked her head up and looked away from Bill, then she started walking out of the room. She made a blowing noise and looked at DJ, as if to say, "Are you coming with me?"

DJ looked at Bill and with his head down as he walked out of the room. You could tell he thought, "Boy, have you messed up this time."

Bill stood watching them walk out of the room, and said, "All right, I'm sorry. I didn't mean it. I don't even know what came over me."

DJ wagged his tail, but he kept on walking. Bill walked into his bedroom, talking to himself, "Now I can't even get along with my dogs."

They listened for sounds indicating he was asleep before they started talking to each other. "Keep your voice down, Maggie."

"I am, but did you know Paula was coming over here tonight?"

"No, but I do think it gives us something to hope for."

"How? Bill is still holding on to Jane."

"I know, but look here, he is also reaching out to Paula as well. He doesn't even know what he truly feels right now, because the enemy has his emotions so muddled."

"DJ, how long are we going to have to wait before we let Bill hear the tapes?"

"I'm not sure, but it shouldn't take too much longer, love. We need to be very careful, things could very easily blow up in our face if we push it too hard. Jane is going to have to say enough on the tape, so we catch her with her hand in the cookie jar." Maggie giggled a little, "You and your cookies, DJ."

"No, I'm not talking about real cookies, girl. I was using the term."

"I know, but I just can't help thinking about the time when Sally gave you that big cookie to eat. It was peanut butter if I remember precisely and you ate the whole thing by yourself."

"Well, it was my cookie. Sally gave it to me, didn't she?"

"Yes, but I would have given you a bite of mine."

"I'm sorry, Maggie. You know how I am when it comes to cookies and those kinds of things. I just can't control myself." They both giggled and lay back down to sleep. It had been a long day and tomorrow was going to be another busy day for them.

Chapter Twelve

A New Slant

Jane woke up Saturday morning with her young man lying by her side. He was still asleep. Doubtless he couldn't handle his drinking as well as she could, but then most men couldn't. As Jane laid there, she tried to come up with a good plan to get Bill to give her his password. As much as she hated to admit it, Lisa might have been right; the other night could just as easily have been the right time to make her move. Now she was going to have to come up with something which would keep him from any suspicion she was up to no good. Her mind was in a fog from the night of drinking, but as she laid there, she realized she had her work cut out for her. All because she took too much for granted, she had allowed her over confidence to make her careless and now she was going to have to take greater care so as not to tip her hand. Little did Jane know it really didn't matter if she was careful or not, wheels were moving to bring her life of reckless living to an end. There are times when it seems like evil always gets away with its plans, but what most fail to see, is that time will one day run out and then judgment will fall upon the guilty.

* * * * *

Bill was still lying in his bed. He had slept a little, but he woke up early that morning and couldn't go back to sleep. He could hear DJ and Maggie sleeping on the floor at the foot of his bed. He knew Sally let them sleep in her bed, but he wasn't going to let dogs sleep with him. The floor was just fine for them. They hadn't been asleep long when Bill woke up. He just lay there thinking about Paula, and then about Jane. He didn't know why it seemed so clear when he was with one or the other. However, when they were not around, he just couldn't seem to think straight. Maybe a cup of coffee would help him get awake better, or better yet, maybe he could go back to sleep. Bill rolled over and was finally able to worry himself to sleep.

* * * * *

Paula was still sitting in her chair in deep thought. "What had she been thinking? Why had she reached out and kissed Bill good-bye? Yes, it was only on the cheek, but he had a girlfriend, and besides, she had never done anything like that before. What kind of girl did he think she was now?" she wondered.

Oh, if her mother knew about this, it would be the end of life as we know it. How did it happen? Let's see, we were standing in the doorway and yes, for some reason beyond her, Paula just leaned over and kissed him on the cheek. And the look on his face… was it one of shock or surprise? Could it have been one of disgust? He must think I'm the cheapest thing alive. I'll call him later and try to explain it to him. Yeah, I didn't have a clue what I was doing, then he'll think I'm crazy. Won't that be just wonderful, Paula, the crazy woman. If only

Paula had known, that one act was going to help keep Bill from falling totally under Jane's spell. It's always strange how one act of love from a pure motive can help set a mind back into straight thinking, even when everything else or even someone else is trying to lead it down a wrong path.

* * * * *

As Jane was driving home, she was thinking about how she could approach Bill again about his password. Maybe he would bring it up again out of guilt, or she might even be able to help from that perspective. She could go over to his house, crying and tell him how she knew he really didn't love her. First she had to go home and get fixed up. When Jane walked into her house, she saw the light blinking on her phone. "Let's see, who left me a message."

"Jane dear." It was the friend who had brought Paula's friend to the restaurant the night she made-out with Bill in front of everyone. "Hello Jane dear, I went by Bill's house last night like you asked me to, and you wouldn't believe whom I saw walking into his house."

Bill was jerked out of a sound sleep by the banging on his front door. "All right, all right, I'm coming. Gee whiz, I have a doorbell, can't you ring it?" Bill had no idea who was banging on his door. He opened it to a woman who was mad and ready for war. "Where is she?" Jane raged as she pushed right pass him.

"Where's who?" Bill still wasn't awake yet, but he was getting there fast.

"You know! That little slut who works at the nursing home! She was here last night, a friend of mine drove by heading home and she was surprised to see the woman walking into your house. And I was embarrassed when she left me a nice little message telling me how my boyfriend had his little whore over here all night while I was crying my eyes out because of you."

"Now wait a minute. Paula is just a friend and she didn't stay all night."

"So, you admit you slept with her then? Boy doesn't that say a lot, you can't or won't sleep with me, but bring that little slut over and you can't wait to jump into bed."

Bill reached out and grabbed Jane by both of her arms. "Now wait a minute, I did not sleep with anyone last night. Paula came over for a cup of coffee, that's all. She was my sister's friend, for goodness sake. All we did was sit out on the back deck and drink coffee and talk."

"Sure, and I'm the tooth fairy. Admit it! You went to bed with her didn't you?"

"No, Jane, I didn't and you are just going to have to trust me on that."

"How can I trust you when the first time my back is turned you have another woman over at your house."

Bill stood there not really knowing what else to say, so he just stood there in silence.

Jane was getting more furious as the seconds ticked by. It was too bad Bill didn't have a friend who happened to drive by Jane's house when she drove off with her young fellow last night, or someone who happened to see her getting in early this morning. Strange how she could honestly be so mad when she was the only one who was guilty. But then again, Jane knew how to play her hand well, and right now she was putting on the performance of her life. Jane just burst into tears, "So tell me, was I that bad in bed? I must have been for you to go out looking for someone else. Is that why you came up with this I can't sleep with you crap? You thought I was pathetic in bed, didn't you?" "No Jane, in fact you were very good in bed. I didn't sleep with anyone and I still can't sleep with anyone, not until I'm married to them. Please try and understand that. Bill had tears in his eyes. Jane knew she had pushed him about as far as she could on that point, so now for the next item.

* * * * *

Paula had fallen asleep sitting in the chair. She didn't sleep long though, and when she awoke, she was thinking about the time she met Sally. It was the seminar where the dogs were teaching nursing home administrators how important dogs could be in helping the elderly. Paula remember how well DJ and Maggie worked with Sally. In fact, everyone there was talking about how well they obeyed, even before she spoke the command. Yes, she remembered that's why she went looking for Sally after the demonstration. She wanted to find out where Sally had DJ and Maggie trained.

Paula sat there just letting her mind grow quite. She could see the backroom, she was walking through all the other dogs she stopped and talked with a lady and patted her Labrador retriever. It was a yellow one, she remembered, because the lady said no dog had ever beaten her dogs until today, but DJ and Maggie worked circles around her dog. In fact, the Labrador looked a little confused by the way DJ and Maggie were doing their jobs without Sally saying hardly a word to them. That's what the lady couldn't understand; how she got them to remember how to do all they did without ever telling them what to do. She looked at Paula and remarked she had never seen anything like it anywhere. I remember leaving her and walking farther back, I passed more dogs, but I didn't stop to talk with anymore owners, because I wanted to meet Sally before she left. I came around a corner and there she was bending over patting DJ and Maggie on the head. Then she started talking to them, nothing strange about that, but then, what happened next, DJ, he.... The phone rang, Paula jumped and everything was gone again. She snatched up the receiver, "Hello!"

* * * * *

Bill was still standing in the middle of his living room. Jane was still crying, she knew with Bill, this was her best weapon. "So... I guess that's why you didn't want to help me the other night. You're planning on dumping me right?"

Bill's mind was spinning. He walked toward the kitchen. "Where are you going?" Jane asked, crying even harder.

"I'm going to make us some coffee. I need a cup and I think you could use one as well. Come on in here. Let's sit down and talk. We don't have to yell at each other, do we?" He didn't know why he was saying that, because Jane was the only one who was yelling. Maybe it would help her feel better if he took most of the blame.

Jane felt like she had Bill right were she wanted him. Lisa should have been here to see her performance this morning. She would have seen how to recover from a mistake for sure.

DJ and Maggie were standing there, not knowing what to do. They knew this was all an act on Jane's part. They knew Bill had a good heart and he was going to allow himself to be pulled into her trap if he wasn't careful, but right now there wasn't anything they could do about it but watch. And watch they did. They stayed in the background, but they didn't let Jane out of their sight, and she was so busy playing Bill she didn't even notice them. That's how most people go through life, never noticing the things which are really important until it's too late.

Bill made them coffee and Jane sat there wiping her eyes. She was still crying, but not as hard. "All I ever wanted was to find a man I could love and who would love me, and I thought I had found him," she looked up at Bill with a pitiful expression on her face. "But I guess I was wrong."

"There it was, the arrow hit its mark. Bill broke down now and started to cry uncontrollably, "Jane I'm so sorry, I didn't know you felt that way about me. I thought you weren't interested in me at times to be truthful."

Jane moved up closer to him, she held him in her arms while he cried. "I know I don't show my feelings like I would like to, but I have to blame that on my father. He never showed his feelings, and didn't like it when we did. But Bill, believe me, you are all I ever think about."

Maggie had enough. She walked out and went into the other room. DJ would have to stay there on guard. She couldn't stomach much more, and she was just about ready take matters into her control, which is not what guardians are supposed to do.

DJ did stay. He knew why Maggie walked out. Her feelings tended to be deep, which could be useful at times, but there were times like these when it got in the way of their job. It didn't matter though. He loved her anyway, and couldn't imagine what life would be like without her.

* * * * *

Ron was sitting in his office studying for his Sunday message. He had Bill on his heart the last few days. Maybe he would call him later and ask him to come to church. Tomorrow, after all, he was at his new church and he would like for Bill to be there. They would have him over to eat after the service, and then he could talk with Bill. Ron knew he missed an opportunity to help Bill the last time he had come over, maybe he could make it up to him now.

Ron picked up the phone, "Dear, remind me later to call Bill and ask him over tomorrow, ok?"

Kathy liked the new phone system in this church. She like the fact Ron was more like his old self, and he was more peaceful now. He was back in the will of God, where before he wasn't. It really doesn't matter what happens in your life, if you are out of His will, everything will be out of place. Ron had found his place again, and he wasn't going to let anything ever lure him away. Kathy had something she needed to tell Ron, but was waiting for the right time. It seemed miracles still happen.

* * * * *

Jane left that day with Bill's old password. He told her it was an old one but maybe it would help her. She started to get mad until she realized it was a birthday. Now all she had to do was to figure out another birthday which was important to him, then she would have his password. It would mean she would have to go through his house while he was at work but that never stopped her before. Jane was already making plans for Monday. She figured just as soon as Bill left for work she was going to go into his house and start looking around. She would have to be very careful because if he even thought someone had been in his house, he might change his password again. One thing Jane knew about men was, they are creatures of habit. He would use another date for his password. All she had to do was to find it. Somewhere in his house was the key and she wasn't going to stop until it was hers.

Bill was sitting in his chair when the phone rang, "Hello. Yes. I would love to have lunch with ya'll tomorrow, and tell Ron I'm looking forward to hearing him preach in his new church. Yes, I'll see ya'll tomorrow."

* * * * *

Ron usually didn't wear a robe his first Sunday, but this was a much larger church and he wanted to make a good impression on his new congregation, so he wore his new robe. The service was going just as he had hoped. Everything was just perfect, the singing was exceptional, he felt as if this was going to be the best day of his ministry. As he entered the pulpit, Ron did something he rarely did; he asked if anyone had a word of thanksgiving they would like to give before he started his sermon.

One little old lady stood and gave thanks to the Lord for their new pastor. Ron graciously thanked her. Another member stood and thanked the Lord for the rain they had received a few days earlier. "Yes," Ron said, "we are all thankful for God's abundant blessings. Is there anyone else?"

Kathy sat there wondering if she should, then a young man jumped up and said "I found a job, praise the Lord."

Ron was smiling. "This is wonderful," he thought.

A young girl stood up, her eyes filled with tears, "I thought about running away from home because I thought my parents didn't love me, but last night we talked and now I know they love me, and I'm not going anywhere."

Ron said, "Praise the Lord for that."

Kathy stood up, "Well maybe I should say a word of thanks." Ron knew what she was going to say. Kathy was going to thank everyone for all the kindness they had shown them. She stood there for a moment, "I don't know how to say this." Everyone grew quite. What was going on? What was troubling her? What was she going to say? What sin was she going to expose? "I found out three weeks ago, even after the doctors said it would never happen, folks, I'm pregnant."

Ron burst out crying as he gave out a loud "Praise God."

People jumped up from their seats and the women ran to Kathy while the men ran to congratulate Ron. Bill stood back and just watched it all in total amazement. Never had he seen anything like this. He knew this had to be one of the best things he had witnessed in a long time.

Ron never preached his sermon that Sunday, but no one cared. They were all excited about the miracle in their midst. When they sat down for lunch later, Ron asked Bill if he would mind giving thanks. Bill bowed his head and for the first time in a long time he prayed a prayer of thanksgiving, "O Father. We thank you today for such good friends and for the wonderful news they shared with everyone today. Truly it demonstrates your loving care for your servants Ron and Kathy. And I know you are going to bless their work here as you blessed their labor in Ron's previous pastorate. Also, Lord, I would like to thank you for their friendship to me. I know there were times I treated Ron with such contempt and cruelty and yet he never treated me in like fashion, instead, he always showed me Your love. It's because of his witness, I'm standing here today. Thank you for what he has meant in my life and for his prayers for me over the years, Amen."

Bill looked up to see Ron and Kathy both with tears running down their faces. Ron looked at Bill and said, "Thank you, Bill."

* * * * *

Bill got home late Sunday afternoon. DJ and Maggie were both worrying over him, but as he let them outside he said "Hey, ya'll guess what?"

They both stopped and looked at him. "Ron and Kathy are going to have a baby." Then he started laughing out loud, "My goodness, here I go talking to my dogs as if they can understand every word I am saying."

DJ had already gone out to the back of the yard, he was behind a tree when Maggie got to him. "DJ, did you hear the good news about Pastor Ron and his wife?"

"Of course I heard Maggie, I'm not deaf, but you had better hold it down or Bill will hear you. Remember he is not deaf either."

DJ was so happy for them, as was Maggie. However, such good news also brought pain to her. She could never let DJ know, but it hurt because she would never know what it was like to be a mother. She had chosen to be with DJ and she was happy with her life with him. She looked at him as he was walking around the yard. He was everything she could ever want. She only hoped he knew how much she really loved him.

Maggie walked back up to the deck where Bill was sitting, drinking coffee. She was hoping he would call Paula and tell her the good news. That way she could hear more of the details.

DJ watched her walk up the stairs. His heart went out to her. He knew, he could see the pain even when Maggie thought she had it masked so well. "Why did I make on over it so?" he thought. "Oh, Maggie, I'm so sorry love, you'll never know how I wish we could have pups, but please know my love for you will live on even after I am gone." He walked up to the back deck to join Maggie.

Bill was still sipping his coffee and looking out over the yard. They sat looking at him. He looked down at them and said, "Well, I might as well go all the way and make a fool out of myself. Listen to what else happened today."

* * * * *

Monday morning Bill got up earlier than most Monday's and dressed for work. "I guess I'll go in and get started early today. That way maybe we can sit out on the deck for a while this afternoon."

As soon as he walked out the door, DJ said in a low voice, "Go quickly and put the tape in the recorder. She will be here any minute."

Maggie looked at DJ, "Not this early."

"Maggie, go now before she comes," DJ spoke sternly and emphatically.

With that Maggie ran into the bedroom and just about the time she got the tape in and the door shut on the tape recorder, Jane walked in the front door of the house. She knew she was going to have to be very careful. So she looked in one drawer of his desk at a time. She knew it could take weeks of searching using this method, but she was determined to find it sooner or later.

DJ was standing against the wall, out of sight, but he could still see Jane and hear everything she was saying. How he wished Bill would walk back in and catch her looking through his stuff like this, boy she'd be out then.

Just about that time he heard the front door open, and Bill walked back down the hall. Now, by God, she was out. DJ ran to meet Bill and try to get him to come into his office. What he didn't see, but Maggie did, was that Jane ran into Bill's bedroom and undressed as quickly as she could and got into his bed. Bill walked into his bedroom, with DJ barking as loud as he could.

"Ok DJ, I see you, but I forgot my papers, and your treats aren't in my office."

As he walked into his bedroom, a shocked look covered his face. There was Jane in his bed, under the covers, with her clothes lying on the floor.

"Well, I came over here looking for you and when I couldn't find you, I thought I would sleep in your bed, so when you went to bed tonight it would smell like me. I wanted you to think about me all night." Bill just stood there, not knowing what to say. "Ok," Jane said, "I know I used the key which is only for emergencies, but for me, darling, this was one. You see, I couldn't sleep all night. I was thinking about you."

Bill walked over to the bed and kissed her on the lips, "Then have a good sleep dear, but I have to get this work done or Joe will have a running fit. Will you be here when I get home?"

Jane pressed up close to Bill, "If you want me to, and I can stay just like this?"

"I wish you could, Jane, but you know I can't, but do stay, please."

"I'll be here when you get home and I'll behave myself, I promise." She reached up and kissed Bill one more time. She held on to him as if her life would leave if he left, but the whole time she was kissing him she was thinking to herself, "Get out, so I can get back to looking!"

She stood and watched him drive away, and as soon as he was out of sight, Jane dressed and went toward Bill's office, but the door was locked. "Now why did he lock this door? Does he think something is going on? Is he suspicious about something?" Maggie was behind a door laughing to herself. Bill's office had a lock you pushed in to lock, so while Bill was in his bedroom talking with Jane, Maggie stood up on her back legs leaned on the door and pushed the lock in. DJ stood against the door so it wouldn't shut while Maggie was locking it. Then Maggie pushed the door so it would close and ran out before she was locked in. DJ stood behind her laughing to himself as well, he knew Maggie's idea was going to work and he just loved it.

Jane was so mad she ran out to her car and drove off. Maggie was looking out the window, and said, "I don't care how you leave honey, just leave."

DJ was rolling he was laughing so hard, "Whoever said one evil woman was smarter than two guardians?"

Jane drove down the street, "I guess I'll have to go back there for dinner tonight now, and I wanted to spend time with my new young friend so badly." Jane was speaking about her young lover she met on Lisa's boat. He was only for her amusement. When she was through with him, he would be tossed aside.

* * * * *

DJ and Maggie were both wondering what Jane was looking for. She was going through all the drawers in Bill's desk. "She's looking for something Maggie, but I can't for the life of me figure out what it is."

"Neither can I," Maggie looked so perplexed, "if we knew what it was she was looking for, then we could hide it so she would never find it, DJ."

"Well, we don't know, so let's keep our ears open while she is here tonight."

"Do you really think she will be coming back tonight, DJ?"

"Yes Maggie," DJ was a little short when he answered her.

She put her head down, "I didn't mean to anger you."

"I'm sorry Maggie, I don't have a clue what she is looking for or how it is going to help her get Bill's money. I am so afraid she will pull this off before we even know what she has done."

"I don't think that is going to happen, love. Think for a moment, she is using his phone, so we will always be here when she comes over, and we are taping her conversions on the phone. There isn't anyway she is going to get by us, besides, I know there is no one smarter than you, so how can she pull this off without our knowing it?"

DJ walked over to Maggie and licked her on the face. "You always know what I need don't you?" Theirs was a love which had grown so deep one always knew what the other one needed at just the right time.

* * * * *

When Bill arrived at work he was running to get to his desk. He wanted to get through the day as fast as he could. He was becoming so blind, he no longer even doubted Jane. It was as if she were gaining complete control over him.

Tracie walked over to his desk, "Bill, Joe came in looking for you."

"Oh great, I wonder what he wants now. I work here long hours. I take work home, what more does he want from me?"

Joe opened the door to his office. "Bill, can you come in here for a minute?"

"Sure Joe. Just let me put this file away and I'll be right there."

Tracie leaned over and said, "Remember, keep your head about you."

Bill walked into Joe's office. It wasn't much to look at. It was plain but sufficient. Bill remembered the office he had back at the University. His wife helped him decorate and it was the talk of the campus for months.

"Sit down, Bill. I know you are wondering why I called you in here today. I have been meaning to for some time now. Well, let me just get to the point. You have changed over the last several months. I mean, you haven't been coming in with a hang-over or smelling like booze, so I am going to give you a raise. I know it's way past time, and I just want to tell you how glad I am you are working here with us." Joe stood up and held out his hand.

Bill stood up and shook Joe's hand, "Thank you, Joe. You never know how much this means to me." Bill walked back to his desk with a strange look on his face.

Tracie hurried over to him, "What happened? He didn't fire you did he?"

"No. Matter of fact, he gave me a raise and said how glad he was to have me working here."

Tracie leaned over and whispered to Bill, "Was he drunk? I mean, Joe has never said anything nice to anyone that I know anything about, and I have been here for years."

* * * * *

Paula's day wasn't going quite so well. She had two employees call in sick. There was trouble with one of the stoves in the kitchen, which meant lunch was going to have to reshuffled. It was going to take her being in the kitchen all morning to help. Paula looked at Mrs. Blackstone, "Let me run to my office for just one minute and I'll be right back."

Paula walked into her office, "Why of all days did this have to happen?" She had not been getting much sleep lately, and Bill hasn't called either. Why is he still running after that slutty woman? Paula had never faced it before like she was now… she loved Bill, but how was she going to let him know it?

Mrs. Blackstone was working as hard as she could in the kitchen. One of the employees asked if she wanted someone to go down to Paula's office and see if she was through there. "No dear, she's there, but let her be for a moment. She has a lot on her right now, and we need to be helpful to her." Mrs. Blackstone could see Paula was in love. Anyone could who had two good eyes. Mrs. Blackstone wondered if Paula knew she was in love. She remembered how it was when her husband was in love with another young woman. They had just met and she knew he was the one for her, but all she could do was pray and hold on to God in faith. "Oh God, help Paula to hold on to you during this time of testing, and let her faith come out shining bright as gold."

* * * * *

Ron was over at his office early that Monday morning. He had so much to be thankful for. He thought how things could have turned out so differently, but God in His mercy had taken Ron through the arduous situation he had been in with Steve and had landed him in a new church and now he and Kathy had a child on its way. Yes, Ron knelt at the altar, giving God thanks for all He had done for them.

Kathy was sitting in the kitchen drinking her cup of coffee and reading her scripture reading for the day, when she stopped and looked out the kitchen window. Today was such a beautiful day, when Ron came back over from his office she was going to ask him if he wanted to drive to the store with her. He needed a new shirt and some pants to go with them. Of course she wasn't going to tell him that's the reason for his going with her. Kathy smiled thinking it would be such fun to see him making a fool of himself over this child. She chuckled a little, "Lord you know I would rather have a little girl, but I know Ron would just burst with pride over a son, so give us a son. You know Ron's a good man and he will always do what he knows is right. Even when he gets off the right path, he'll always come back to you and get right back where he belongs."

Kathy sat there for the longest time just day dreaming about how it was going to be with the arrival of their child. Never would she take this blessing lightly, for it was one they had long ago given up. However, in God's timing it came, and now they both could see what a blessing God's timing really was.

Ron was sitting in his office now, with his Bible in hand. Reading the scripture was a daily routine, one he wasn't going to give up for anyone. *"That the genuineness of your faith, being much more precious than gold that perishes, though it is tested by fire."* Yes, he knew what that meant. Maybe the Lord was speaking to him about a message for this church. We all have our times of testing, and it's so our faith will come out like shining like gold. He reached for a piece of paper and started to jot down some ideas. Yes, this might be just what the Lord wanted him to preach this coming Sunday morning.

* * * * *

Bill arrived home early that Monday evening. He was half expecting Jane to be there and when she wasn't, he didn't know what to think. "I wonder if she is coming back tonight." He walked to his office, but the door was locked. "Now, how did that happen?" He went to the bedroom and got the key out of a drawer by his bed.

DJ was following him, watching everything he did. "What is it boy, do you have to go out? Wait just a minute and I'll let you and Maggie outside. Boy, I wonder where Jane is or if she is even coming back."

Bill couldn't help feeling something was amiss when he walked into his office. Even though everything was in it's right place, it was the feeling you get when you just know someone has been in your room. He was walking over to the first drawer Jane had opened, one she hadn't had time to put back in order when the doorbell rang. Bill jumped up and walked into the living room.

When he opened the door, Jane reached out and kissed him. She was afraid he had already found the drawer out of place. Jane knew how Bill kept everything in it's own place, even in his desk drawers, so she was trying to cover up any suspicion he might have toward her.

"Hello there," Bill said after the long kiss. "I was getting ready to call you and see if you were still planning on being here tonight."

"Why Bill Thomas, how could you think I wouldn't show up to spend time with you. You know I would rather spend time with you than do anything else."

Maggie was standing behind a doorway where DJ was, "Oh boy, I think I'm about to lose lunch."

DJ turned around and said, "Shush, Maggie, they will hear you. Now keep it down."

"That's the problem DJ. If I have to listen to any more of her lies, I don't think I can."

DJ stepped back and chuckled a little himself, "If we get caught, its all your fault, Maggie."

With that, they both ran into the back bedroom where they could be alone for a minute. There they could try to get their composure before they went back out in front of Bill and Jane. Bill was walking back into the kitchen when DJ heard him say, "You won't believe what I found today when I arrived home?"

"What did you find dear?" Jane was a little nervous, but you couldn't tell it by the look on her face.

"My office door was locked, and from the inside. I don't remember locking it. I don't understand how it got locked."

For just one moment Jane was about to get on the defensive, and then she realized Bill was not accusing, but was merely making a statement. "I don't know. I didn't go near your office, so I wasn't aware it was locked. How did you get in?"

"Oh, I keep a key in the drawer by the bed. In fact, I keep all my extra keys there. I know it's not the safest place to keep them, but then again, if someone breaks in here they must be smart enough to know how to find my extra keys."

Jane sat there feeling like a complete fool. She was lying by the keys all the time. Why didn't she look in that drawer? Well now she knew where to look if the door should ever be locked again.

DJ was standing in the doorway of the kitchen and his heart fell within him. Bill was telling the enemy everything. Didn't he ever read the story about Samson and Delilah? DJ felt like running up to Bill and saying, "Hello, there is Delilah, if you didn't know it and she is out to get you Samson." Maggie walked up behind DJ. She didn't know what they could do now; it seemed as if Bill was working against them as well.

* * * * *

After Bill had gone to bed, DJ and Maggie got together in the living room. "DJ, what are we going to do now, he has told her everything she needs to know?"

"Not everything Maggie. She is still looking for something. All he did was stop us from locking her out of his office, which means we are going to have to be more careful now and keep a closer eye on her."

"But how will we know when she finds whatever she is looking for?"

"Besides, it's like you said, she is using his phone and, Maggie, Jane will have to call someone to gloat over her victory, and we'll get it on tape."

Maggie said in a low voice, "DJ we had better start our time of worship before it gets too late." Then they started to sing the old songs, as usual, those God's people and guardians have been singing for centuries. Maggie remembered how she used to love to sing with Sally. If only Sally were here, she could reach Bill and talk some sense into him. DJ knew Jane would be back tomorrow, and with each day she was getting closer to the thing she was searching for. They would have to be at their very best if they had any hopes of stopping her.

"Oh, Creator," DJ prayed, "Help us to see what it is we're suppose to do here. How do we stop this evil woman? How can we help the woman at the bank as well?" "Amen," Maggie said, "let's find a way to help her DJ. You're right, we should. It's the right thing to do."

* * * * *

Jane didn't get there as early Tuesday morning as she did the day before. There wasn't going to be any more mishaps. She was going to be sure Bill was not going to walk back in on her.

DJ and Maggie were both ready for Jane. Just as soon as she walked into the house, DJ took up following her at a safe distance. Jane went back to Bill's office and started looking through each drawer. Her only problem was, he had five filing drawers, and each was full of papers and letters. Jane looked for hours and still nothing. She knew she couldn't stay there much longer, so she went into Bill's bedroom and set on Bill's bed. She reached over and picked up the phone, little did she know Maggie had been in there all along waiting to see if she ventured back into the bedroom. Maggie had pushed the button on the recorder and was under the bed hiding.

Jane called the bank and when Louise answered, Jane said, "I just wanted to remind you as soon as I have the right password, you are still going to have to fulfill your part, or try and explain to your husband about your past."

Louise was angry, and you could hear it in her voice, though she never raised it when she talked with Jane. "I read some strange lady was killed in a car accident and I was hoping it was you."

Jane laughed, "Don't get your hopes up, sweetie. I'm not going anywhere, and I will get the information soon enough. So don't forget our little deal, or should I send a picture to your husband now?"

Louise was silent for a moment, she felt anger and fear, and a sense of helplessness. She was trapped and there wasn't anyway out of this nightmare.

Jane said, "I'm waiting for an answer, and I don't like to be kept waiting. Do you hear me you little tramp?"

Louise was crying now, she was trying to hold on to every ounce of control she had left, but it was slipping away fast. Finally she said, "I can't talk now, my boss is coming down the hallway. Call me when you have something." She hung the phone up and cried. Her boss wasn't coming down the hallway. Almost everyone was out to lunch, but it worked, it got her off the phone with that horrible woman.

Jane put the receiver down, and she smiled, "She is afraid and that is what I want… to keep her afraid. That way, she will do what I ask, when I ask it. I think I might mail her a copy of a police report I have on her, that ought to do the trick." With that, Jane went back to looking, but left an hour later.

As she drove off, Maggie was upset. "DJ, we need to do something very risky, but I feel it might just help us out in the long run."

"What is more risky than what we are already doing my love?"

"Let's call the bank and talk with Louise."

* * * * *

Paula's day was a little better, but that was not her real problem yesterday. She had days before when they were shorthand and she had handled it just fine, but this was different. Now everything inside of her was turning flips, she was happy and then sad. She so wanted to call Bill, but he hadn't called her in days now, so maybe she was getting a message from him. Maybe he was telling her to back off that, he truly loves this woman, Jane. If that was the case, she would be better off just backing off and walking away. There was just one hitch, she was in love with the man and she didn't know what to do about it. Paula had always read her Bible to start the morning off, and it seemed now every time she picked it up, all she heard was to stand still and wait on God. With tears running down her face, she looked up and asked, "How long do I wait, how long do I do nothing but sit here wondering if he is ever going to come around or end up married to that woman?"

There was a light tap on her door. “Yes, who is it?“ She was trying to wipe her face before anyone saw her. Mrs. Blackstone walked in and took one look at Paula.

“Oh dearest, you have it bad.”

Paula tried to speak and say she didn’t know what Mrs. Blackstone was talking about, but instead, she just set there and cried.

“Now, now dear. It’s going to be all right. Mrs. Blackstone moved over to sit down beside Paula and put her arms around her. I know what you’re going through. I went through it once myself years ago.”

“So tell me,” Paula asked, “does it get any better, I mean will he ever wake up?”

“All in God’s good time dear, all in God’s good time. I have wanted to talk with you for some time now, but never felt like it was the right time, and this morning before I came in to work, it was as if the Lord spoke right to my heart and said, “Now Blackstone, you march in there and talk with that young girl. She needs someone who understands and who can comfort her. So here I am, not much I know, but I’m all the Master has at His disposal here, I guess.”

Paula hugged Mrs. Blackstone. “No, your just what I need right now. I need someone to talk to and I have asked the Lord to send me someone. Thank you for coming.”

They sat in Paula’s office for almost an hour talking, with Mrs. Blackstone telling Paula all about her experience, and how she had to wait it out in faith, while her husband ran after another woman. “You love them dear, but it doesn’t mean they are always using the head God put on their shoulders. Men can do just like us. They can get so caught up in their own emotions they forget what real love is and run after the shadow of love. It’s not real, but to a heart that is chasing it, it looks real enough. Have faith girl, God hasn’t given up yet. Would He have sent me in here today if it was hopeless? No, it's never hopeless as long as we can pray, and wait for His timing."

* * * * *

Maggie had picked the receiver up with her mouth and set it down on the table, "Now all I have to do is to push redial, DJ, and it should call the same number."

"What are you going to say to her, 'Hi, I'm Bill Thomas' dog and I just wanted to talk with you about the mess you're in.'"

"No, of course not. I'm not sure yet, I was going to go with it and let my heart lead me, DJ."

So, he pushed the button for redial. Louise answered her phone again, but before she could say anything, Maggie spoke, using Sally's voice, "My dear, I'm calling you because I know you're in a pickle and you need help."

"Who are you and how do you know anything about me?" Louise was getting tired of feeling like she was on the outside looking in.

"I know that woman calls you and when she is through with you; you're torn apart on the inside with fear and uncertainty, but she wants to hurt someone we love very much."

"Then why are you coming to me? If you know what you say you do, then you know she is going to make me help her hurt Bill Thomas."

"I know dear, but if we turn over everything we have now, it might cause you as much trouble as her, if not more. Therefore, we are going to wait and get more on her and you're going to help."

Louise was shaken now, how could she ever do anything? "She has information about me you are unaware of."

"No love, we know about that too. You should have told your husband long ago. You should have trusted his love, dearest. But enough about that right now. All I wanted to do was to call you and let you know you're not alone. I'm here and I am going to walk with you through this whole nightmare."

Was this a ray of hope; was there really someone out there who did care about her? "But why are you helping me? You don't know me, not really."

"Maybe not, but I know you have carried enough shame over your past, and I'm not going to let that woman hurt you either. No, together we're going to shut the door in her face and send her off to jail."

"You can't. She'll send the information to my husband."

"Louise, I think you need to face the fact she will do that anyway. This woman is so evil. And she is out to hurt everyone she can, and she will do everything she can to try to cover her tracks."

"I don't even know her name. I'm not sure who she is."

Maggie laughed, "Well in time, I'll tell you her name, but not now. You might use it before it's the right time. We'll help you through this and in the end, your marriage will be stronger, you'll just have to trust me on that."

"Well, could you at least tell me your name? I need to know someone by name is out there."

"I can't tell you my real name, for now, just call me Sally."

Hearing that, DJ ears perked up. He was shaking his head, "No," but Maggie turned and looked the other way. She knew it made him mad when she did that. DJ wondered why Sally's name of all names?

Maggie said to Louise, "Let me just say this. I'll keep you in my prayers, and Louise, think about going to church this Sunday. There is a church close to you and they just got a new pastor, a Rev. Ron Wilton, I believe."

DJ just couldn't believe his ears. "Why didn't she just say and oh yes; by the way I'm a dog?"

When Maggie hung up the receiver, DJ was standing there looking at her. "Ok, I did what I said I was going to do and you said you thought it was a good idea."

"Yes, the part about helping the girl. But to tell her you were Sally and sending her to Rev. Ron's church, Maggie, you are putting us in harms way here."

Maggie put her head down for a moment, then she looked up at DJ, "My mother told me once, guardians sometimes have to take great risks to do their job, and if this is one of those risks," she moved closer over to DJ, "lets take it together. Believe in me DJ, as I have believed in you in the past."

He put his head over on her, "You know I'm with you and we're in this thing together." DJ looked into Maggie's eyes, "I have always believed in you, my love, and I always will.

Chapter Thirteen

Persistence Isn't Always Good

Joe Rushing sat in his chair until late that Tuesday night. He was given to working late and spending little time with his own family. If the truth were known, Joe had a problem, one he had been able to keep hidden from his fellow workers, however, not from his wife or kids. Joe did drink heavy at times. He might go weeks without taking a drink, then he would stay at the office late and drink, or go home to a backroom where he sat and watched TV and drink until he passed out. The next day he would always have some excuse for not showing up at work. Of course his reason for drinking always had to do with the paper. Joe knew if it weren't for Bill Thomas, he would have lost his job long ago. It was Bill's insight which had put the paper back on track. Now, the articles were well written and sales were up.

Joe looked out the window. It was late. As he took another drink, he remembered there had been a time in his life when he was one of the best paper men in the state, but now he was just hanging on to past glories. He sat there and thought about Bill Thomas. He had heard Bill was going back to church, which caused him concern. What if Bill decided to go back to teaching. That concern was one reason Joe had been drinking so much lately. Oh God, what am I going to do if Bill goes back to the University to teach? How will I be able to keep my job? Joe had never been a religious man, nor did he ever give it much thought, however, after watching Bill pull himself out of the pit he was in, he had to admit it had been on his mind. He had overheard what church Bill was attending. Maybe he would show up and do an article on the new pastor. Let's see, Rev. Ron Wilton was his name. That way, no one would know why he was there and if he went back he could always say he just liked what he heard, nothing more. He took another drink. I wonder if my wife will go with me or should I go alone?

Joe sat back in his chair and put his bottle down on his desk. Maybe it was time he stopped hiding from the truth and faced it head on. He could have done more with his life but instead he got into a rut. He became comfortable with doing as little as he had to, and when the day came he stopped getting the awards for his writing, his job opened up to run the paper. He had an opportunely to get back into his game, but once again he just settled down with his normal lackadaisical self and did no more than was required of him.

How did I get like this, and how do I change after all these years? Can I reach back and find that something which will help me change my life? Can I reach out and make things right with my family after all these years of neglect? It was late and the room just had one small light burning, but for the first time in a long while Joe was beginning to see things a lot clearer.

* * * * *

Bill was sitting in his office at home. He still had a feeling things weren't right, as if someone had been in there. Who could have gone through his house? Jane knew where the key was, but if she came over, he knew she wouldn't go through his things. Or maybe… she did seem to want his password. No, how could he even think such a thing. Jane had showed her true feelings to him the day she came over crying. She did love him. Besides, no one knows about the money he had put away. He couldn't touch it, he wouldn't touch it. He tried not to even think about it, but then it would come to his mind at times like a bad dream. Why did he even keep it since it made him feel the way it did? Maybe he should just give it all away and be done with it. But he knew what Sally and Rachel both would say to him, "Bill put that money to good use. Help somebody with it." Yet every time he thought about touching it he felt sick inside. No, it was better to leave it where it was for now. One day he would know what to do with it, and then everything would fall into place.

* * * * *

Paula lay in her bed trying to go to sleep. She had a very hard day, not so much because of her job, but more because of her heart. She had finally admitted to herself that she was in love with Bill Thomas, thanks to the help of Mrs. Blackstone. However, that opened a larger door of trouble for her, because now she wanted to tell Bill how she felt. But there was that woman whom everyone knew was no good for him. At least she saw it in other's eyes when they were together. Why couldn't he see it? Why was Bill being so blind to what was under his very nose?

Then a troublesome thought hit her. Was he sleeping with her? Were they living together in secret? No, how could she even think that about Bill? Paula knew Bill Thomas, and she knew he would never sleep with a woman who wasn't his wife. What was it then that kept him tied to her? She wasn't trying to be vain, but she knew she looked as good as that woman, maybe even a little better. "Oh God, why do I have to go through this now? Why couldn't he just make up his mind and choose me?"

Paula was going to learn the secret to any lasting relationship is honesty. She was also going to have to learn how to forgive. Which was something she thought she knew how to do, but this path had only just begun and there were more bumps in the road ahead of her.

* * * * *

The Rev. Marshall Wiggins was staying up late again tonight. He had already read the New Testament through in five different translations, and he was growing more each day in his faith. He was reading books by men like E. M. Bounds work on prayer and faith. He was also reading the works of some of the early church fathers. Everything he had once made fun of, he was now studying, and with the help of the Holy Spirit, he was finding out how foolish he had been. His members were so thankful for their 'new pastor.'

Marshall had not left that church, instead, he stayed. But, he wasn't the same man as before. Now when he stood in the pulpit he trembled, for only now did he understand the great responsibility he had as he stood before the congregation to preach God's Word. No Sunday passed without one of his members walking up to him and telling him how much this change has meant to them as a church.

"Preacher," one old fellow told him, "I'm glad you found yourself, and better yet, I'm glad the Lord got hold of you."

Marshall was walking in the church with the lights off now praying, "Yes Lord, thank you for getting hold of me, and for stopping me in my tracks. I might not be climbing far up the ladder in the world's view of things, but, I know I am walking with you and that is far better than anything I was seeking before."

Marshall's wife was at home waiting for him to finish at the office. These days were better days for her. God had answered her prayers after all these years. The man she married was finally back home again.

* * * * *

Jane was making plans to go out of town for a few days. All the looking around Bill's house was starting to get next to her. She needed to let her hair down and have some fun, and her friend Lisa wanted her to come down on her boat and party for a few days.

"Jane dear, there will be men here and all you can drink. You know if I'm throwing a party there is going to be plenty of alcohol. Please come and let's have some fun, then you can get back to snooping around Bill's house. My goodness girl, you're going to dry up if you don't get out and get drunk and have some fun."

Lisa knew it wouldn't take much to get Jane to leave Bill for a few days. She sat there on her boat wondering if she could find out what Jane was looking for and maybe beat her to the prize. It did sound like such fun, and it would teach Jane a lesson. She should never have let him off the hook when she had him in her bed. That woman is going soft on me, so maybe I should teach her a lesson. It just might wake her up to the hard realities of life. There was one thing Jane and Lisa both knew about each other and that was, they couldn't trust each other as far as they could throw each other. Their friendship was based simply upon the fact not many people wanted to have a lot to do with either one of them. Once good people got to know them, it was over. There weren't many friendships in their lives, so all they had was each other. It was a sad picture of what humanity can do to themselves when they put their own greed ahead of everything else. They end up alone, without any true friends.

* * * * *

By Friday afternoon Jane was once again on Lisa Ainsworth boat. They had spent the last two days there. It was one party after another with a long line of men always coming aboard Lisa's boat, looking for fun and a good time. They were watching the sun go down when Jane asked Lisa if she ever got tired of all the parties and the drinking.

"Girl, have you gone crazy? How could anyone ever get tired of having fun? You see, that is why I told you to come down here for a few days. You are so wrapped up with that guy, Bill, you are forgetting what it's like to have fun. I sure hope he has a lot of money and you're able to get it, or this is all going to be one big waste of time for you, girl."

Jane took a drink, and then she looked over at Lisa, "Is a couple of million dollars worth it to you?" Lisa sat up and looked at Jane. This was the biggest catch she had ever gone after, and it would put her 'up there' as far as money goes. Jane laughed, then Lisa laughed along with her.

"Maybe I should take him off your hands, Jane."

"Oh, just you go ahead and try. I'm telling you this guy is so old fashioned he doesn't believe you should sleep with someone unless you are married."

"But, I thought you said ya'll slept together."

"Only one night. I did and we did, and it has been eating at him ever since. I have used it every chance I get."

Lisa laughed again, "Ok, ok, I can see you're not in over your head, but do hurry up on this one. I would like to take my boat to another port soon."

Jane looked at Lisa very intently, "You already have someone else in your sights don't you?"

Lisa smiled such an evil smile, one that was dripping with sweetness, like honey dripping fresh from a newly pulled piece of honeycomb. "Why dear, you know I don't like for my bank account to get too low, and the way we've or should I say, I have been partying, it doesn't take long. I have met this really nice older gentleman online. He has no children, and his wife died about two years ago. He is so lonely, and I have already been to see him once." She looked over at Jane with that glimmer in her eyes which told her Lisa wasn't telling all the truth, "or maybe twice," she finished.

They both laughed out loud, "My god girl. You won't do. How do you find them so quickly?"

"Oh honey, don't you know? I believe in the power of the internet. I just love technology." The evil of their laughter would make any caring person tremble at the very sound of their rejoicing. Such evil has taken place time and again, ever since the fall of mankind. Evil gathers together to rejoice over its plots to destroy the life of God's people.

* * * * *

Bill was sitting at home wondering why Jane had to leave town so suddenly. She never seemed to feel the need to give him any explanation about where she was going or why, yet she always wanted him to give her every detail of his actions. There were just so many things that made him feel uneasy in this relationship. But Bill was still blind to the power she had over him. Jane had so masterfully used his own guilt against him, Bill was no loner able to see things clearly. Bill, being a normal man, was getting lonely though, and he wanted someone to talk with. He reached over and picked up the phone and started dialing the number.

"Yes, this is Bill. I know you know it's me, and I'm sorry I haven't called before now. Do you think you would like to go to the Café

Florentine? I'll pick you up in about twenty minutes, then? Ok, we can just meet there if that's what you want to do." Bill hung up thinking, "Paula wasn't being herself. But then again, he hadn't called her and she knew he had a girlfriend, so why should she be jumping with joy to hear from him? Why should she even meet with him at all?"

Bill began wondering if maybe he had made a big mistake. "No, I can't start thinking like that, it always gets me into trouble. Jane made her feelings plain to me. She just doesn't know how to show her feelings right now. In time she'll come around. I just know it."

DJ sat there listening to Bill go on and on about Jane, till he was at the point where Maggie was the last time Jane was over, he was about to lose his lunch. Why did Bill allow himself to be blinded by Jane? DJ knew Jane was using his own guilt against him, and he was praying Jane would show more of her hand before it was too late.

* * * * *

Paula was getting dressed to meet with Bill. She wasn't very excited about meeting him tonight. She had cried all she wanted to over him, and he wasn't showing any signs of turning loose of Jane. So why was he calling her? Was he just trying to cause her more pain?

As Paula drove to the Café Florentine, she was playing it over in her mind. She was going to tell him as long as he had his girlfriend, she didn't think they needed to meet like this anymore. She asked herself, "I wonder what my mother would say if she knew I was meeting with a man who is involved with another woman. No, tonight is the very last time we are going to meet." Tears started to fill her eyes as the words came to her mind, "No, I can't start crying now. I'm tired of crying over Bill Thomas."

Paula walked into the café. Bill was already sitting at a table when she got there. As she approached the table something happened in her heart. She looked into his eyes and saw a man who was torn apart on the inside. Paula didn't know all that was going on in Bill's life, but that brief look told her to wait, now was not the time to break things off for good with Bill. He was hurting in ways even he didn't understand, nor was he aware of everything happening around him. No, he was going to need her help later on, and even if he never fell in love with her, she could be the friend he would need one day. Bill stood up and pulled out a chair for her, "Please sit down, and I'll get you some coffee."

Time spent over coffee. It wasn't much, but it was those times which brought normality back to Bill's life, and it was those times which were keeping him from falling beyond any hope of recovery. Paula wouldn't know till later that her very actions now, just being a friend were what would reach him in his greatest hour of need.

As Bill drove home from the café, he felt better about his life. There was still doubt about Jane hanging over him. Was she the one after all?"

DJ and Maggie were waiting up for Bill. As soon as he walked in, they were walking around him as if to say, "Well, how did it go with Paula tonight?"

Bill laughed at them, "Why, you two are just about as nosey as any two little old ladies I have ever seen. We just drank coffee and talked, that's all." But it was the sound in his voice which spoke volumes to them. They knew he was in a better frame of mind. It was times like these they had been praying for, and they were seeing their prayers answered.

* * * * *

Early Sunday evening Jane rolled back into town. She called Bill from her cell phone to see if he wanted to take her out to eat. When Bill picked up the phone Jane said, "Bill darling, I am back in town. My weeping friend is much better now, so how about you taking me out to eat tonight." He started to answer her, but before he did, Jane said, "On second thought, I'm going to take you out tonight. It's on me tonight, so you can't refuse me or you might break my heart." Bill softened a bit, and willingly gave in to her request. "Good I'll drive by in about ten minutes, so be ready."

Bill put the phone down and changed clothes. DJ and Maggie both knew who was on the phone with him and they didn't like it one bit. Jane drove up in the driveway and blew her horn, Bill looked at them and said, "I'll be back in a little while. My ride's here, I guess."

Maggie watched as they drove away. "DJ, we have to do something soon, or she is going to win this battle."

"I know Maggie, but I don't know what to do, and no, before you ask again, we're not going to tell Bill about ourselves, that's not an option right now."

"You mean to tell me you're going to just sit here and do nothing while that...., I can't even think of a name to call her that I wouldn't have to repent over."

"Well then don't, Maggie. We have to keep our heads about us while everyone else is losing theirs. I know this is hard for you, and yes, it's hard for me too, but we have to find some way to help Bill, Louise, and whomever else she may be trying to hurt. Also, Maggie my love, if we can find a way, we must help Jane as well."

At that, Maggie jumped up and said, "You help her. I'll help the others."

DJ followed her to the door heading into the den. "Maggie, please listen to me for just a moment."

Maggie turned around and said, "I promised Sally, I would look after Bill, not the snake who was trying to harm him. I can't talk about it now DJ, I need my space right now."

DJ stood there and watched her walk away from him into the other room. He knew Maggie's heart, and he knew she would come around sooner or later about Jane, but he also knew it was her pain talking right now. Maggie loved Sally deeply and she still missed her. This wasn't easy for her to go through, and DJ knew he was going to have to be patience with Maggie.

* * * * *

When Bill got into Jane's car, he noticed she wasn't all decked out as she usually was. "I know, I'm not dressed up to go out, but hey, you might as well see me as I really am, right? I mean if this thing keeps going the way I hope it is going, you're going to be seeing me every morning waking up without any makeup on, so, I'm giving you a trial run to see how you can handle the real me."

Bill laughed. How delightful! She was going to let her hair down and be herself around him. He thought to himself, "See, all it takes is just a little time and Jane is going to show you who she really is." Little did he know this was all a plan she had laid out months ago, and she was right on schedule, all she needed was his password and this little merry-go-round ride would be over for her. Jane knew how to build a man's hope that she was finally relaxing and beginning to be herself, when all the time she was setting the net for the final catch. "Where are we going to eat this time?"

Jane looked at Bill. She knew how to play him and tonight was going to be a masterpiece. "There is a little kitchen a little farther down the road."

"Yes, I know it," Bill said, "I didn't think you would ever eat in a place like that." "See, you don't know everything about me, now do you?"

They pulled in and Bill was delighted with surprise. The place was called the Country Kitchen, and all they served was home cooked meals. Jane got out before Bill and walked around and opened his door for him. "Hey, wait a minute. I'm supposed to do this for you."

"No sir, tonight I show you how lucky I am to have you in my life." She reached out and kissed him. It was a kiss which blinded his eyes to everything going on around him. He should have known by the way the people acted toward them, they had never seen Jane before. This was all an act, but it was very effective and Jane knew she was back in the driver's seat.

When they got back to Bill's house, Jane said, "Let me say good night outside. I don't think I should come in tonight, dear."

"Why? I can make us some coffee and we can sit and talk for a while." Jane grabbed Bill and kissed him. She kissed him so hard Bill thought he was going to lose his breath for a moment.

Jane pushed away, "Bill, I want you so bad right now if I came in I know I would end up begging you to let me stay. I'm too proud to beg, but that is what you have reduced me to, a beggar. So please, let me go before I can't." Bill kissed her once more and told her how much he loved her, but she was right, they should end the evening, if things were going to get out of hand.

Bill walked in on cloud nine, "Boy, I didn't know she cared for me like that." While Jane drove away dialing Lisa's number, "Yeah, he took it hook, line and all, baby. I got this fish on the hook good now." Jane was laughing as she drove down the street. She was going to his house tomorrow and now, she was going to find something.

* * * * *

Ron was concerned for Bill. He looked troubled the last time they were together, but he didn't have a chance to talk with him about it.

Maybe he could see Bill one day this week. Ron turned the lights off in his office. He prayed as he left, "Lord, I know we talked about Bill earlier tonight, but please keep your hand upon him." One thing Ron knew was, one should never procrastinate about something important. However, he had this new church, and now Kathy was going to have a baby, and he had to go to the doctor every time she went. Ron was so taken up with becoming a father he was forgetting his Father's business. Bill was a man in need, Ron used to know that, but we tend to forget where people really are in their lives. Ron had seen some changes in Bill's life, but Bill still needed Ron to be there. He wasn't ready to fly solo yet.

* * * * *

Bill had been very persistent about going after Jane ever since the first day she walked into his office, and now it looked as if his persistence had paid off. He had what he thought he wanted, but in fact he was going to end up finding out what he really wanted was right there all the time. He had seen hints of it, but then the darkness would blind his eyes again so he wasn't able to act upon what he knew was right. No, Bill Thomas would never have gone for a woman like Jane when he was younger, but then he had gone through a terribly dark time in his life. He was so lonely when Jane walked into his life. She entered at the right time to knock him off his feet. Sally could have reached him, but her voice was being muffled in his heart now. He no longer thought about her. His days passed without so much as a notice of her being gone. The power of sin to blind a person's heart has yet to be fully discovered, but the day would come when Bill would look back and see its powerful influence in his own life. Persistence is a good thing if we are going after that which will add fruitful years to our life, but it can be just as deadly as any poison if we are running after sin. Bill knew not what path his feet were on, but he was soon to find out.

* * * * *

That night as they met in the other side of the house, Maggie was deeply troubled over the way Bill came waltzing in as if he had found the love of his life. "DJ, I'm so afraid. If we can't stop her, Bill is going to get hurt badly, and all because we didn't tell him who we are."

DJ looked at Maggie, "No my love, Bill is going to get hurt because he stopped his ears to the voice of reason, to the voice of love, and he allowed lust to speak in his ear. He hasn't listened to his heart even though his own heart has been trying to speak to him." DJ looked at Maggie with tears in his eyes, "There's a storm coming Maggie. Bill's life is in danger and I'm not sure anymore if we can stop it from happening."

Maggie put her head down and cried. Her heart was breaking in two. DJ went up beside her, "Listen to me, love. We are not giving up yet. The evil one hasn't won this battle yet and I will die fighting for Bill." Maggie put her head over on DJ. He was the love of her life, and she knew he meant every word he said, but if something happened to Bill, what would happen to them? Would she lose DJ as well. It was all too much for her right now. She shut her eyes and went to sleep. DJ sat there while she slept. He prayed about tomorrow and what it would bring.

Chapter Fourteen

The Coming Storm

The next day DJ knew Bill would be going to work early. Bill liked to start his Mondays early these days,. As soon as he was out the door, DJ looked over at Maggie and said, "We have a lot of work to do before the enemy comes here."

They went into Bill's bedroom and put the tape in the recorder. Then DJ sat Maggie down and told her his plan. It was daring and very risky, but Maggie liked it from the very beginning. "Oh DJ, when did you come up with this wonderful plan?"

"Last night after you fell asleep. I was asking the Creator to open my understanding so we would know how to stop this evil plot against Bill. I also asked for a way to help Louise and after I prayed, I just lay down very still and listened to see what He would speak to my heart. And this is was what came to me, so if you don't think it will work now's the time to speak up."

"My dear, you have found the answer to our dilemma, let's do it."

"No Maggie, I didn't find it. It was given to me."

Maggie smiled at DJ and walked over and pushed him with her body, "You silly boy, you. You know what I meant."

"I know, but let's make the call before she gets here."

They ran into Bill's bedroom and took the phone off the receiver, Maggie called the number she had watched Jane dial. When Louise answered the phone, Maggie said using Sally's voice again, "My dear, we have a plan. It's risky and daring, but it's one that will help everyone and maybe keep you out of trouble as well. Are you in or not?"

Louise said, "I don't know who you are, but if it will keep me out of jail, count me in."

Maggie very quickly went over the plan with Louise. "My God, this is brilliant. It just might work. How much time do I have before she calls?"

"I don't know dear, so you get busy and for goodness sakes don't let on that you are up to something. This woman is evil and she will stop at nothing, so play it as if you were totally under her control."

"I will, and Sally, thank you again for all your help."

"Oh sweetie, it wasn't just me. I have a wonderful fellow who is helping me. We're in this thing together, and he came up with this plan, with God's help of course. Now you get busy and we'll be in touch."

* * * * *

Jane wasn't in a hurry that Monday morning. It occurred to her after she dropped Bill off at his house, where she could find his password. She remembered where she saw the file which was labeled 'birth certificates and papers.' It had to be there. All she had to do was call the tramp and give her dates until they found the right one, then the tramp would have to transfer the money into Jane's account. When Jane walked into Bill's house, DJ and Maggie were ready for her. They didn't bark at her, but DJ just sat there as she walked pass him. Jane was so caught up with her own self importance she didn't even notice the dogs were acting a little strange. She went straight to Bill's office and opened the file drawer. "Here it is, now let me go into his bedroom. I don't know why he doesn't have a phone in his office. Men, you can't count on them to do anything right."

Maggie looked at DJ with a glance that said, "Do you remember where we hid the phone?"

Jane sat on the side of the bed and dialed the number again. Louise answered. Before she could say good morning, Jane spouted out, "Save the good morning crap for someone who cares. I have some numbers here, so let's get to work and you had better not screw this up, or else your husband is going to receive some pictures in the mail, do you understand?"

"Yes, I understand. Give me the numbers and let me get you out of my life."

Jane called out the first date, but it wasn't the one, then she called out another one, still no go. That was the dead wife and daughter's birthdays. If it wasn't theirs whose could it be. Evil does have its moments. Just then, DJ walked where he could see what she was doing. "I know, she opened the file again; here is his dog's birthday, 5/23/1999." Louise was silent for a moment. Jane said, "Well, what's happening? Is the account opening or not?"

"Oh yes, it's the password all right and I'm in his account now. So, what do you want me to do?"

"Take all his savings and put them into this account," she ordered as she read out her own account number.

"You mean all seven million dollars?"

Jane's mouth dropped open, then she laughed, "Boy did I hit it big with this one! Yes, I mean all seven million dollars."

"Well," Louise said, "there is going to be a problem with that, and you might want to hear me out before I go any farther with this."

"Now you listen to me you little…"

"Lady, I've had just about all the name calling from you I'm going to take. If I transfer this large amount right now, it will be red flagged and the bank will immediately shut your account down and freeze both of your accounts until they can reach Bill and ask him if he's sure he wants to transfer all of his savings into your account."

"Why didn't you tell me this before now?" Jane spouted, "I can't be this close to it and not touch it! If you don't come up with something soon, I'll mail your husband the pictures."

"All right, here's what I can do, but it's going to cost you."

"I knew it you hadn't changed, how much of this money do you want?"

"None, but I do want all the information you have on me, and I want it ***all***! Do you understand ***me*** now?"

Jane smiled to herself, "Sure honey, whatever you want."

"Now, what can you do?"

"Simple, Bill has another account that he transfers money into whenever he goes out of town, so what I am going to do is to have some of this money transferred now and the rest will be transferred later today. But, it will not be transferred into your account until I get the information from you."

What do you mean?"

"I mean, I can go to the library and use their computer and start a program that will finish the transfer. That way you will have your money and if you want to you can have a bank somewhere else make a transfer from your account tonight. I will set it up so that when it's through, everything will be deleted. That way no one will ever find out where his money went. The bank will have to replace it and you'll be long gone, hopefully forever. But if you don't give me *every bit* of information, I won't make it to the library and they will see where you tried to tap into his account. Now do we have a deal?"

I should have known when you deal with a little slut you should always be careful, they double cross you every time. Yes, we have a deal, but when and where do we meet." Louise said, "Call this number at 7:00 tonight and I'll tell you where to meet me. Bring what I want."

Jane put the receiver down, "I need to go and call my offshore bank to get ready to make a transfer tonight and then have my plane tickets ready to go out of the country for a few months. Why not a year?" she laughed. "Seven million dollars! Wow! I'm going to sit back and take it easy for a long time. Lisa, beat this deal if you can!"

DJ watched Jane drive away, "Ok Maggie, leave the tape in there now."

"But DJ, Bill always plays his tapes while he goes to sleep."

"And tonight he is going to hear something different. Rewind it and just get ready."

* * * * *

Paula sat in her office. She hadn't slept much the night before. She had spent most of the night lying in bed praying, when suddenly a peace came over her as if to tell her it wouldn't be long now and everything was about to burst lose. She was sitting there, staring into space, when Mrs. Blackstone walked in.

"Paula I need to ask you about lunch today. Some of the things I had planned to cook didn't come in with our order, so would it be all right if I changed it to this menu instead? Then taking a good look directly at Paula, she exclaimed, "My dear, what is it, you look as if you have seen a ghost? Don't tell me my husband lied to me when he said I looked beautiful to him this morning."

Paula looked up with tears running down her face, "It's almost over. Don't ask me how I know, but soon everything is going to be all right."

Mrs. Blackstone sat down and reached across the desk. She took Paula's hands and together they thanked God for letting Paula know what was coming next in her life. Then they prayed for Bill, "O Lord, watch out for him during this dangerous time and take care of him."

Paula looked up at Mrs. Blackstone, "Do you think Bill's in danger?"

* * * * *

Rev Ron was at the hospital when all of a sudden he felt strongly in his spirit he needed to pray for Bill, and that he couldn't put it off. He hurried home and as he walked through the kitchen he told Kathy, "Nothing for lunch, and hold all my calls."

"Ron, what is it,?"

"It's Bill, darling, I have to pray."

"What's going on?"

Ron stopped and turned toward her. His expression shook Kathy all the way to her soul. "I don't know, but if we don't pray, we might lose Bill for good this time."

Tears filled her eyes, Kathy reached over and took the phone off the hook. "Voice mail will have to answer, I'm in this thing with you 'till the end."

Together they sat down at the table and started praying for Bill Thomas. Little did they know, across town two other warriors were praying as well. Bill didn't know it, but at that moment his soul was being lifted up to heaven by a group of people and two guardians who loved him. It's the power of love that makes prayer so strong and powerful, nothing is as powerful as love, for God is love.

* * * * *

Joe had sat in Ron's church that Sunday morning and the message hit him right between the eyes. He saw where he had thrown his life away, but now he was going to do something about it. While Ron was closing the service, Joe bowed his head and asked Christ to come into his heart and make him a better man. There was a peace that flowed through him he had never felt, and with it an assurance his life was getting back on track. He felt like being the newspaper man he started out to be so many years ago.

"Bill," he yelled out, "I want to see you in my office, please."

Bill rose from his desk. When he walked into Joe's office, he was shocked to hear Joe say, "I'm going to help you out and take some of the load off of you. I'll read over half the articles from now on, and I am going to write my own article every week. It's something I have always wanted to do, but just never got around to it. Well, it's about time, don't you think?"

Bill looked carefully at Joe. He saw a different man before him, "Joe, what's happened to you? You're different somehow."

Joe had tears in his eyes when he told Bill about the church service yesterday. Bill said, "Man, I miss one service and look what I missed."

Joe laughed, "Well, don't take this the wrong way, but I'm glad you weren't there. I might not have stayed if you had been."

"I understand, Joe, and I don't take it the wrong way. Matter of fact, I totally understand."

Together they laughed and everyone out in the outer office couldn't believe what happened next. Joe walked around his desk and gave Bill a great big bear hug. Tracie said, "If I didn't have my real teeth, they would be on the floor right now."

When Bill walked out, Joe looked at all the staff and said, "Who said it was a coffee break? We have a paper to get out, so everyone back to work." Bill laughed, this was the man he always knew Joe could be, and maybe his days were numbered here after all.

* * * * *

When Bill got home that Monday afternoon, he called Jane to see if she wanted to go out and get a bite to eat, her phone was disconnected. He called her cell phone, "Boy, am I going to have fun picking at her about forgetting to pay her phone bill;" but her cell phone had also been disconnected. Bill got into his car and drove over to her house, and there in the front yard was a 'For Sale' sign. He called the realtor, but it was late and no one was in the office.

"What's going on here?" Bill thought. "What has happened to Jane? Where is she?"

He drove back home not knowing where to look or whom to call. He walked into his office and picked up the phone to call one of her friends. Then he realized he didn't know any of her friends. In fact, he didn't know who she hung around with when she wasn't with him. For the first time, it was beginning to sink in that the woman he thought was being so open to him had, in fact, kept him in the dark about her life and who she really was. He opened his file drawer and the first thing he noticed was things were not in order. He pulled out the one file which was sticking up a little. It was marked 'birth certificates and papers.' "My God, what has happened right under my nose. How can I stop this?" Bill got on his computer and logged into his account at the bank. When he checked everything, it showed where Jane had tried to transfer some of his funds. The security system had kicked in and rerouted the transfers to his other account and then back into his regular saving accounts.

Bill called the bank security officer and asked if they had noticed anything happening to his account. "Yes sir and we were ready to call you. We have already contracted the police and they are looking for Jane Hendricks now. Just as soon as we know anything, sir, we'll let you know what we find out."

* * * * *

Jane had called the number from her new prepaid cell phone and she was now sitting in her car by the library on a side street. There was a street light and she thought, "If this woman was so smart, she would want to meet in the dark where no one could see us."

About that time, Louise walked toward her car. She stood just inside the shadows, "Do you have the information I want?" Louise asked.

Jane held up a package, "Here is what you want sweetie, now come and get it."

"Throw it to me," Louise said.

Jane shook her head, "Baby, you have watched way too many spy movies." She cracked open her door and threw the package to her.

Louise picked it up and looked inside, "Now give me the rest of the information, or it's no deal."

"You little...."

Louise interrupted her in a very clear but determined voice, "I've already told you I am tired of you calling me names."

Jane started to open her door and get out, when Louise put her hand into her purse. Jane froze, "You brought a gun to use against me?"

"Remember." Louise said, "I used to walk the streets. How do you think I stayed alive all that time? It wasn't just my good looks. *Now,* the rest of the information or I walk away and all that's going to happen is nothing.. that's right, nothing at all. Your account is receiving all the money at one time. You will be shut down, and the authorities will know you were trying to steal Bill Thomas's money."

"And you will go down with me, just remember that sweetie," Jane snarled back at Louise.

"I would if I hadn't fixed it where it looks like you broke into our security system and withdrew his money all by yourself. Now, if I don't go and punch in some numbers soon, your going to go to jail, so what is it going to be?"

Jane cursed Louise and reached under her seat and pulled out another package, which she threw to Louise. Louise picked it up and started to walk away, "Hey, what about my money?"

"You can go home now, it's all taken care of. I had already programmed the computer to transfer the money anyway. Since you didn't know it, I played you and got everything you had on me."

"Why you little….."

Louise turned around with her hand in her purse, "Do you really want to make me angry, or do you want to go on your trip, you chose?"

Jane pulled away from the curb as fast as she dared, "I'll get that tramp for this, she hasn't seen the last of me yet."

Louise took out her cell phone and dialed the number to her husband's cell phone; "Sherman, could you meet me at the Café Florentine? We need to talk. There is something I need to tell you."

"This sound serious, what's it about, dear."

"About how I didn't tell you the truth when we first met, and now I think you need to hear it from me. Your mother is watching the baby. Please, meet me there in twenty minutes."

Sherman said, "I'm on my way now and honey, it doesn't matter, everything is going to be all right."

Twenty minutes later when Sherman walked in, Louise was already sitting over in a corner. He walked over to her and she said in a very low voice, "I have something here to show you, and then I am going to tell you all about my life, my real life. My father never worked in a bank. He died in jail for trying to rob a bank, and I was forced to walk the streets to have something to eat. Here are some pictures. I got them from someone today who was going to send them to you, so here they are."

Tears were flowing from his eyes, he looked at his wife and reached out and took her hand, "Louise, I know this must have been one of the hardest things you have ever done. I don't need to see those pictures. I'm just glad you finally felt like you could trust me enough to tell me the truth."

"But Sherman, I was a whore, do you understand that? What if your mother ever finds out? What will she think of me?"

Sherman, shook his head, "Have you been in this family this long and you don't realize how much everyone loves you?"

Then he pulled out an old letter. "This was sent to me by an old girlfriend who wanted to break us up when we were dating."

He handed it to Louise. It told all about her life, and yes in there was a picture of her on the street. "You knew all this time and you never said anything to me about it, why not?"

Sherman said, "I know we haven't been in church in a long time, and that's as much my fault as anyone's, but I still remember what the Bible says about love and forgiveness, and that our past is forgotten."

Louise started to cry, "That's what she said."

"Who?"

"The lady on the phone the other day. Oh Sherman, let me tell what I almost did trying to hide this from you."

They talked for hours. Louise finally realized, Sherman loved her for who she was now, and her past didn't matter to him. As they walked back to his truck, he opened the door.

"My car is over there I need to drive it home," Louise reasoned.

“I called my mom. And she is going to watch the baby tonight, and we’re going out and then to a hotel for the evening. It’s time we had some time alone, don’t you think?”

Louise jumped into Sherman’s arms, “What did I ever do to deserve you?”

“I think that should be the other way around, but let’s talk about it later. I already have us a room and I don’t want to be out all night do you?”

Louise smiled at this wonderful man. “All I want tonight is to be in your arms, nothing more.”

* * * * *

Jane had gotten to a place were she could check her bank account with her lap top. It was then and only then she realized she had been played for a fool. All of her accounts were frozen, and, records showed she had tried to remove money from Bill Thomas’s saving accounts. She knew the law would be looking for her, so she headed out toward the port where Lisa had her boat. “She’ll let me hide there until I can get out of the country.” When she got to the port, Lisa’s boat was gone. When she tried to call their contact man, his number was no longer in service. She was all alone and on the run without a penny to her name. What was she going to do? Before she could pull away from the dock, a police car was pulling up, with policeman jumping out and yelling for her to get out with her hands up into the air. She was handcuffed and put into the backseat of the police car. How did it all turn out this way? What went wrong with her plan?

* * * * *

By now, Bill had received a call from the police telling him they had picked up Jane. When he hung the phone up he was so upset. He became so angry. "Why did I ever believe anyone could be good? I should have known this was how it was going to turn out! Oh yeah, thank you God. Boy, I know you're getting a good laugh out of this. Bill ole boy, fell hard for the woman and she just about took him to the cleaners. I hate everything about this life. I wish I were dead."

He reached over and opened his drawer, but his gun was gone. "She took my gun, too? What else did that witch take from me.?"

"Nothing you didn't let her take, Bill."

He turned around and there sat DJ. "Who said that?"

"Bill, if you would listen to the tape in your recorder, it would help you to understand everything better. Jane was only able to go as far as she did because you opened the door to her."

Bill was just looking at DJ, "Now I know I have lost my mind. I'm sitting here talking with a dog."

"Don't you remember when Sally was passing away, how she talked to us? You told Frank it was the drugs they had been giving her, but Bill, she was speaking the truth. We told her about us because one night she came home so upset she was going to take a whole bottle of pills. That's when Maggie stopped her."

Maggie walked around the bed, "Hello Bill. I'm glad we can finally talk with you. Please don't be mad at us for not telling you sooner, but we had to wait until the time was right."

Bill got up and ran into his office. He took out a box and in it was a letter Sally gave him before she died. On the outside it read, *When DJ and Maggie pass away please read this.* Bill opened it and what he read was the same story they had just told him. Tears filled his eyes as he read about how God had changed her life, and that DJ and Maggie were the ones who pointed her to God's Son. *It's in Him that we find love Bill, not in this world or the things of this world, but only in God's Son.*

Bill was weeping as DJ and Maggie sat there. They didn't know Sally had ever given Bill a letter, nor had he ever mentioned it around them. "But I don't understand how all this can happen. I mean, you can talk and you understand things?"

"Yes, and we have many more gifts too. But, Bill you can't tell any one about us. That would cause us great harm."

"No, it would get me a free trip to the nut house that's what it would do."

They sat up the rest of the night talking and telling Bill all about their time with Sally. Bill was moved to tears many times during their talk. He finally began to realize how much they loved Sally, and how much they loved him. As the sun was coming up Bill asked DJ, "Now, what am I going to hear on that tape?"

"Oh yes, well, let me give you a rundown before we listen to it. You are going to hear the voice of Louise, who is the woman Jane was trying to blackmail to get your money."

"Wait a minute, the police said she did everything by herself."

"Oh yeah, well maybe I should start from the beginning."

After an hour Bill sat there laughing so hard, "How did you know what to tell that lady, DJ? I mean, that was a great idea."

"See Maggie," DJ said," I told you it was a great idea. We wanted to help her out of the mess she was in and to give her a chance to make things right with her husband." "Well, did she?" Bill asked.

"We don't know yet," Maggie said, "we were going to call her later today after you went to work and ask her."

Bill looked at his watch, "I'm late for work. There isn't anything I can do about it is there? So, let's go call her, shall we?"

Maggie looked at Bill, "My dear, I can change my voice to sound like a person, so I used Sally's voice." Bill stood there shocked. "I'm sorry

Bill, but I felt by using her voice, she was helping us help you, can you understand?"

Bill reached down and patted Maggie on the head. "Let's go girl and make the call, and it's all right. I know how much Sally loved you two. She would have gotten a kick out of this."

When Louise picked up the phone, Maggie said, "Well, how did it go with your husband last night, my dear?"

Bill sat there with tears running down his face as he heard Sally's voice coming from Maggie. "Oh Sally, it was wonderful just like you said it would be! Sherman knew all along. He was just waiting on me to tell him. I'm married to the most wonderful man, Sally."

"Well, my name isn't Sally, it's Maggie, but I just wanted to call you and see how things went with you dear."

"Please tell your friend he was such a great help to me. I would never have been able to have pull it off without his help. How did he know what to do?"

"Oh, he likes to read up on things and I'm sure he read it somewhere. All my love to you dear."

As Bill put the receiver down, he said, "You two are the most wonderful gifts any man could ever hope to have in his life. I just wish I knew what to do about Paula."

"I think I can help you with that Bill," DJ walked up and said, "Here's what you do."

Chapter Fifteen

A New Dawn

As Paula walked into her office, Mrs. Blackstone came running up to her. "Dear, did you hear the news this morning?"

"No, my TV is acting up, so I just got up and came on in to work. Why? What's happening that's so important?"

"Your Bill Thomas was almost taken for every penny he had last night, and yes it was by the other woman."

"What?" Paula was yelling it out before she even knew what she was doing, "She did what? How did they catch her?"

"Wait a minute, one question at the time please. It seemed she tried to go into the bank security system and transfer money from his account. The bank isn't saying how much, of course. They did catch her. It seems someone called in a tip on where to help find her. It was a woman's voice the news said, but Bill Thomas said he had no idea who it was. He was thankful for their help in bringing her to justice."

"I wonder where Bill is now?"

About that time Paula heard him say, "If you turn around you'll most likely find him, although, I wouldn't blame you for never speaking to him again."

Paula turned around and threw herself into his arms, "Bill are you all right? How did all this happen?"

"It happened primarily because I was being foolish and acting like a fool. I treated you badly and I hope you will allow me to try and make it up to you."

"Of course I will. You can have all the time you want."

"Well then, will you give me the rest of your life?"

"Paula's mouth fell open, "Bill don't tease with me like that."

Bill held her close, "Paula, I'm asking you to marry me. To forgive me for hurting you and for not realizing how I really felt about you. I allowed my guilt to blind me. So I might as well tell you now what I did. You see I…."

"Before he could say another word, Paula put her hand up to his mouth, "It's not important to me, dear. It's past, and that evil woman is out of our life forever."

Mrs. Blackstone stood there with tears running down her face. She wiped her face and said, "Well, it looks like we're going to have a wedding, so let me start planning now on how many we're going to feed."

"Oh no," Paula said, "I couldn't ask you to do all of that for me."

Mrs. Blackstone reached over and kissed Paula on the cheek. "It would be an honor if you would allow me to do it dear."

Paula was crying now. She hugged Mrs. Blackstone and said, "Yes, I would be honored to have you do all my planning."

All right then, let me get down to my office and get to work. How much time are we going have before the wedding?"

Paula looked at Bill. He took out his phone and called Ron. "Bro. Ron, how soon could you do a wedding? No, for me and Paula Welch. That soon? I'm sure it will be fine. I'll talk with Paula. Ok, write it in and we'll come by later to talk with you. Ok goodbye."

"Well?" asked Mrs. Blackstone.

"Three weeks," said Bill, "he can do it in three weeks."

"Oh jumping toad fogs, I had better run to the kitchen. Don't you worry about a thing dear, I'll take care of everything."

Bill looked at Paula, "There is one thing I must insist on, DJ and Maggie, they have to be at the wedding. I'll make it right with Ron, but they're the ones who brought us together, and I couldn't see having the wedding without them. Besides, it would be like having Sally there also."

Paula took his hand. "You know I love them, so it's all right with me."

* * * * *

The next three weeks went by so fast for Bill and Paula. Bill spent long hours talking with DJ and Maggie. They taught him some of their old hymns. He found many of the words came right out of the Psalms. Bill even discovered how much DJ loved the writings of C. S. Lewis. Bill and Maggie would take parts as they read the *Chronicles of Narnia*. Bill loved the way Maggie could mimic any voice she wanted. She made the white witch sound so evil, even Bill found himself hurrying to get home so they could enjoy the stories together.

One night Bill asked them when, or if ever, they were going to tell Paula about their ability to talk, and their being guardians. DJ sat down in front of Bill and said, "Maggie and I have talked about that in great detail and we decided to leave it entirely up to you. After all, she is going to be your wife, and even though we will be her guardian too, how much she knows about us, well, Bill, you're still the head of this household, and in this we submit to your decision."

Bill had tears in his eyes as DJ spoke. Here was this wonderful little creature who had not only helped reach his sister, but had saved him from losing everything he had, and told him how to fix things with Paula. Bill had to admit, he would never have been bold enough to ask her right out to marry him; not after all he had done. But DJ and Maggie both confirmed she was in love with him and was only waiting for him to realize the truth about Jane.

"I'm going to have to think about it. I'm not sure how to break this kind of news to her. I mean, how do you tell the woman you love, it was your dog who told you what to say to her after you had been a complete fool?"

"You know Bill, now is maybe the time you and I should have that guardian to man talk about the things you should never tell your wife."

Maggie laughed and said, "Oh no you don't. He is going to tell her everything, the only good marriage is one which is built upon the solid foundation of truth. DJ you have always been open and honest with me, so why would you tell Bill that?"

DJ was laughing by now, "See, I can also teach you how to get a rise out of your wife as well."

Bill laughed along with DJ and Maggie, "No, thanks. I think I can do that well enough on my own, thank you sir."

Maggie looked up at Bill and asked, "Have you given any thought to where you are going on your honeymoon, Bill?"

"I thought we would all go back to the mountains for two weeks."

Maggie's eyes brightened up. "You mean?"

"Yes," said Bill, "back to Whitworth Georgia. I plan on talking with Dr. Pittman about my old job."

"You mean your going to go back to teaching?" DJ asked.

"That is what I love doing the most, and it's time I stop running from it and put the past behind me."

DJ bowed his head for a moment. Maggie did the same. Then DJ said, "Oh Heavenly Creator, thank you for allowing us to see your plan fulfilled in Bill's life. Thank you for our small part in this great work of yours."

Bill reached down and picked DJ up and looked him right in the eyes, "It wasn't a small part, my friend. Ya'll reached out to me and kept me from throwing my life away. And now I'm about to marry the woman of my dreams. How can I ever thank you enough for all you both have done? Besides, look how you helped Sally, when my life was in the pit and I wasn't in any shape to reach out to her or be any help to her. So God put you two in her life. For that I will always be thankful to my heavenly Father, and yes I thank God every day for allowing you two in my life."

Maggie started singing an old hymn. DJ picked right up with her and Bill joined in also. It was the most wonderful experience he had ever had. Bill said later, "I can't remember when I have felt the presence of God so strongly. These last few weeks have changed my life. I now understand how important it is to have daily time with God in prayer and worship and yes, I am going to tell Paula. She needs to be a part of our worship time together as well."

Maggie smiled, "I knew you would see it that way. In fact, we both did. DJ said last night he believed you would tell her."

"But not until your married," DJ said.

"Why?" asked Bill.

"Well, ours is a secret which has been kept for centuries, and there is only a few times in our history guardians have told their charges about themselves, at least that's how the stories go."

"Would you, I mean could you, tell me some of your stories? I would love to hear them."

DJ looked over at Maggie, and for a minute they spoke in a very ancient language. Bill remembered hearing it before, but he had mistaken it for something else. Maggie looked at Bill, "You'll have to promise never to repeat what we tell you, and that may mean even to Paula. We will have to wait and see how she handles our ability to talk and understand more things. You know most humans can't accept the fact we have this ability, which is why we have to keep it a secret."

"I understand." said Bill, "but I think Paula is going to surprise you. There is something about her that is so wonderful. I can't wait until we are married."

"Patience, my friend." said DJ, "patience, that day is almost upon you. Then with a wink, he said, "and then your freedom will be gone."

Maggie walked over and pushed him with her body, "See what I have to put up with? It's a wonder we ever got anything done with all his foolishness."

Bill laughed and sat on the floor with them. "Now tell me some stories," he said. DJ took the lead, he sat in front of Bill and began to tell him about the guardians, their history, and how after the fall of man, the Creator sent the first pair of them out of the garden to help watch over man. There were many sad places in their history and Bill understood why they have kept their secret from man. In the past, when someone did find out, guardians were outright killed or tortured to death because mankind was afraid of them. It was late when they finished telling the first of their history.

Bill sat with tears running down his face, "Now I understand what a sacrifice you make every time you open up and trust someone with your secret."

"These may be modern times, Bill, but mankind is still given to great cruelty, which is why we must be very careful. Can you imagine what would happen to us if it got out we have the ability to talk and to reason? Why, by the time they got through with us they would have cut us into a thousand pieces."

"Not to worry," promised Bill. "No one will ever know, I promise you, and I know Paula will keep it to herself as well. She loves you both as much as I do."

DJ and Maggie walked over to Bill, "It's late now and you have so much to do tomorrow. Know this… our lives are now in your hands forever. It's only out of our deepest love for you that we told you about our gift."

Bill was crying again, "Sally was right when she told to me ya'll were the most wonderful thing that ever happened in her life."

Maggie shook her head, "No it's was finding God's love, Bill. That's always the most wonderful thing that can happen in the heart of a man or a woman. Our task is just to help you along the way."

That night as Bill got into bed, he reached down and picked up DJ and Maggie and placed them on the foot of his bed. "Now I understand why Sally said it was where you belonged. She was right. My sister was right."

Never had Bill slept so soundly. Was it because of the love he was experiencing, or the peace which came from knowing there were two there who would gladly give their lives for his? Only heaven knows such answers.

* * * * *

The day of the wedding came and everyone in the church was just as busy as bees. There were some folks wondering why Bill Thomas was going to have dogs at his wedding. Ron even had to admit it was the strangest request he had ever had anyone make. But after talking it over with the board, they decided to allow Bill's dogs to attend the wedding. Everyone was there from work. Even Joe took off to be there, and he was tickled to see Bill's dogs there. He took plenty of pictures for the paper. The church was packed. Every seat was filled. DJ and Maggie were sitting at the front of the church over to the side, of course, but they had a front row seat.

The time came for Bill to come out and stand in the front. Dr. Pittman was there as his best man. In fact, so many were there from Whitworth, the paper there wrote, *the town had packed up and moved to South Carolina for a wedding.*

The music began the wedding march and then Bill saw her. Paula was the most beautiful thing he had ever seen. She was wearing her white wedding dress, which was flowing behind her. There at her side was her father. He was as proud as any father could be. Her mother sat in the front pew, tears flowing freely.

Bill looked over at his new in-laws and realized he was becoming part of their family and the future was in the hands of God. He and Paula had already talked about the plans of going back to Whitworth. Her dad wanted Bill to move closer to where they lived and take a job at the paper there, but Paula told her dad she was going to follow Bill wherever he went, even if it was to the end of the earth.

Paula dad had nodded his head in agreement, "Yes, that is what you should do, darling. I'm just being a foolish old man, I guess."

Bill said, "No sir, just a loving father. But, I promise you I will take care of your little girl."

All these thoughts were going through his mind as Paula approached. Before he knew it, Paula was standing right there beside him. Rev. Ron looked so stunning standing there in his new robe. This was a very meaningful time for Ron as well. For here was a man, who at one time wanted nothing to do with him or the church, and now here he stood about to get married. Ron was fighting back tears himself. DJ and Maggie looked so proud sitting there, no one knew what they had planned, but they had their own surprise for Bill and Paula.

Ron started going through the service, each saying their vows to the other, then it came time to light the unity candle. It was here Bill found Paula had a beautiful voice as she sang a love song to him. Bill stood with tears streaming down his face as he looked into her eyes. Everyone could see the love she had for him. At that moment, Bill knew his life was going to be blessed by God's loving hand. It finally came down to the placing of the rings on each other's fingers. Finally, Ron said, "You may kiss the bride." Maggie leaned over against DJ and together they stood close by each other.

As Bill and Paula turned around, the recessional began. Bill and Paula began walking hand in hand down the aisle. It was then, DJ and Maggie pulled away from the person who was holding them and ran and jumped up with excitement down the aisle ahead of Bill and Paula. Rev. Ron broke out laughing as did the whole church. Bill and Paula were delighted with their little performance. Paula whispered to Bill, "How did you teach them to do that?"

"To be honest, I didn't know they were going to do it myself. There is more to these two then meets the eye."

At the reception, DJ and Maggie sat there behaving themselves. They had done what they wanted to do. They wanted to show everyone there they were as excited as everyone else about Bill and Paula getting married. It came time for Bill and Paula to leave. Someone asked who was going to take care of the dogs while they were away.

"No one," said Bill, "they're going with us."

Tracie said Bill, "I'll keep your dogs for you. You don't need to take them with you on your honeymoon."

Paula spoke up and as she put her arm through Bill's arm, she said, "If my husband said they're going, then they're going. Besides, I can't imagine leaving them behind, can you dear?"

"No, I can't, said Bill.

* * * * *

They had been driving about an hour when DJ started making a grunting sound. "Ok, ok," said Bill, "I'm going to tell her."

"Tell me what? Bill, what's going on with DJ?"

"This is going to be kind of hard to explain Paula, but it's something you need to know. I'm just not sure how to go about it."

"About what Bill? You're not making any sense to me right now, so please just tell me what's going on."

About that time DJ spoke up, "Oh for pete sake, Bill, just tell her we can talk and then we can get on explaining it to her."

Paula's mouth fell open. Maggie said, "Oh no, that's not a good sign. Bill you might want to call your shrink. I think she is going to blow." Maggie giggled as she said it.

Paula turned around and then as if coming out of a dream it all came back to her. "I remember now! That day Sally was helping with the seminar, I went back to talk with her and as I came around the corner I saw her talking to DJ. Then I saw his mouth moving as if he were answering her back. I don't know why I had such a hard time remembering it. I tried and it never seemed to come to me."

DJ spoke up and said, "The human mind can block things out when it doesn't understand, which is why it's so hard to get some humans to come to faith. They can't understand it, so they block it out. It's called unbelief, Paula. You couldn't believe what you saw, so you blocked it out. The enemy has been using the technique against people ever since the fall in the Garden of Eden. Unbelief can be a powerful force in a person's life. If one gives way to its full power, it will lead a soul down a very dark path."

"I know," Paula said. Then she looked at Bill, "Oh my God, I'm holding a conversion with my dog."

"Guardian, if you please," said DJ.

Bill was laughing by now. You should have seen the way I reacted when I found out."

"How long have you known?"

"I found out the day I found out the truth about Jane. These are the two who set her up, so not only did she not steal my money, but they helped a woman Jane was blackmailing. I told them they ought to be working for the FBI."

"No," said Maggie, "God has us right where we need to be, with you two."

For the next few hours they talked back and forth. Bill telling Paula what he knew with DJ and Maggie filling in the rest. By the time they arrived at Whitworth, Paula did understand one thing very clearly, this was never to be spoken of around anyone. "We take it with us to the grave," Bill said. "I owe them that much."

"I do too," Paula said, "because if it weren't for DJ and Maggie, we might not be here right now."

"Oh no, you wouldn't," Maggie blurted out.

"What do you mean?" Paula asked.

DJ looked at Maggie, "Now you've done it. They shouldn't have their first fight until we at least had this one."

"Wait a minute," Paula said, "there is nothing to fight over, is there Bill?"

Bill looked a bit sheepish said, "Well, I don't think so. I hope you see things my way when I tell you. You remember when I asked you to marry me, and I said I wanted DJ and Maggie to be at our wedding because they were the ones who brought us together?"

"Yes, how could I forget that day. You were so brave and sweet and you came to me, and it was all their idea. Is that what we're talking about here?"

"No, I wanted to ask you, I love you, but I was afraid you wouldn't ever speak to me again. DJ was the one who told me to go to you and ask you to marry me. He and Maggie both knew we loved each other, and all we needed was a little push."

Paula started laughing, she reached back and rubbed DJ and Maggie's head, "I can't believe this, but the best marriage counselor I know is a dog."

DJ grunted again, "Guardian, if you please."

By now Bill was laughing. Maggie was doing her voices. In a high screeching voice, she said, "Would you please send Mrs. Thomas in for her two o'clock appointment."

Bill was crying, he was laughing so hard. He reached out and took Paula by the hand and said, "What I did, I wanted to do. I was just afraid, and didn't know how to go about it. They helped me once again to find the strength to follow my heart."

Paula said, "Well, we might never be able to tell anyone about all of this, but I will always carry it in my heart. I owe the two you everything. You gave me the man I love."

* * * * *

The next two weeks went by far too fast for this newlywed couple. However, during their time in Whitworth, Bill was able to meet with Dr. Pittman, who informed him his job had been waiting on him the whole time he had been gone. "It's been hard, but every year I was able to find someone who was about ready to retire, and they would come and take the position for a year or two. Now, it is going to be good to have you back again, Bill. Paula will fit in just fine here in Whitworth."

"I have no doubt about that, Dr. Pittman. She has already made more friends in the last two weeks than I did in my first year here."

"Well, you have to remember, she does look slightly better than you do,"

Bill laughed, "Yes, I can say that is the whole truth."

Together they both had a good laugh over it, and Bill thought to himself, "Look what I have missed. But it was my wandering in the wilderness that brought Paula to me, so I guess I can't complain too much about it."

Dr. Pittman said, "Bill you're doing it again, your mind is off somewhere else. Oh my goodness man, you're on your honeymoon. Go spend time with your wife, because come this fall, you're mine again, and I'm going to work you harder than I ever did in the past."

Bill got up and held out his hand, "How can I thank you for holding my job, sir." "Just come back my son, and it will be thanks enough for me."

They hugged like two brothers, for that is what they are... brothers in faith... brothers in a common cause... to bring Christ's message of hope to the world.

* * * * *

The next few months at the paper went by as fast as their time in the mountains. Bill found out he didn't have to worry about the paper going under. Joe was writing some of the best articles he had ever read, and Tracie stepped up to her new job, as proofreader.

"I can't do your job," she told Bill.

"Yes you can. You have the education. All you need is the opportunity to prove it to yourself."

Paula cried many tears with her employees. They were all so glad to see her find the happiness she deserved, although, they were going to miss her more than they knew how to express with words.

Mrs. Blackstone walked into her office on Paula's last day there, "My dear I need you to come with me. We are having some trouble in the visiting room, with some of our guest, and I thought, well you're so good at handling people, would you please, this one last time, help this old woman out?'

Paula looked at Mrs. Blackstone. She knew she was going to handle her job just fine. Anyone who could put a wedding together in three weeks could do just about anything, in her opinion. "I honestly think you can handle it."

"Please dear."

Her voice was so pleading, Paula gave in and said, "All right, but now you can't call me when I'm gone." Laughing she said, "You hear me now, don't you?"

Mrs. Blackstone said, "Well maybe not for something like this, but to talk to an old friend."

Paula said, "Anytime, call me anytime."

As they walked into the Visitor Hall, where DJ and Maggie always went to meet with the elderly, the room was packed out. Bill was standing over against the wall with DJ and Maggie. There were many people there. There were family members who had visited there with their loved ones and had witnessed the love and care Paula gave to all the residents. There were even family members of folks who had passed away there during Paula's tenure.

As she walked into the room, everyone stood and began to applaud. The room was filled with the sound of hands thundering together as they clapped as hard as they could to show Paula how much she would always mean to them. Paula stood there speechless.

Bill walked over to her, "When they told me what they were going to do," he wiped away the tears from his eyes, "I thought it was the nicest way I had ever heard of people showing someone appreciation." As he kissed her he whispered, "And so did DJ and Maggie. We're all so proud of you."

Paula hugged Bill around the neck and kissed him one more time. Then as she stepped out to the middle of the room, she held up her hand. The clapping died down, and as Paula looked around she remembered all the families. Those whose loved ones died while staying there, and how she tried to do everything she could to make that time easier for them. Then there were all the employees, who had faithfully done their task everyday without complaining, just doing the work required to help the elderly and many of them doing it 'as unto the Lord.' "I didn't know when I came here years ago, this day would ever come. I thought at one time, I would live and work here my whole life, but God had other plans for me. He gave me a wonderful husband, and two special pets, as you very well know. They made everyone here so happy with their visits!"

Someone spoke out, "Can they stay behind?"

"No," Paula laughed, "I'm afraid they go with us. They will continue to give joy wherever they go, of that I am sure. And I will work in Whitworth, not at first, but later, maybe in a nursing home up there somewhere, if my husband doesn't mind."

Bill said, "Not at all dear. I think they will love you there, just as they did here." Paula spoke for ten more minutes, but it was all the many faces which moved her so. She knew she could leave there knowing she had done everything God had called her to do.

* * * * *

Ron had phoned and asked the couple to come by the church for a moment. When they arrived at the church Bill said, "There must be a meeting going on. Look at all the cars. Maybe we should call him later."

"No," Paula said, "Ron, said this was only going to take a minute. After all the trouble you gave him, you owe him that much Bill."

"I wished he had never told you about how I treated him the first years I was here. I wasn't myself, you know."

Paula took his arm in hers, "Well let's go in real fast and get out and head home. Remember we leave in the morning."

They walked through the doors and there was everyone who worked at the paper. Everyone in the church was there. The fellowship hall was packed. Bill's mouth fell open and Paula reached over and said, "When Ron told me about this, DJ and I thought it was a wonderful idea."

"You mean you knew about.. Your… oh no,"

"He and Maggie never let on."

"We need to talk with them when we get home." Bill held Paula close.

"Hey now," Ron called out, "ya'll come on in here and stop whispering to each other."

Kathy was sitting down. She had grown so much and the baby was due anytime now. She wasn't going to stand much.

Ron spoke first. "Friends we're here tonight to say farewell to Bill and Paula. They have enriched my life and I know many others here as well, so before I allow Bill to say a few words lets show him our appreciation. Everyone stood and the roar of the applause filled the fellowship hall. Bill stood there weeping openly. His heart had been healed from the time of his wilderness traveling. He had come home and he knew once more God is and was always a good and loving heavenly Father.

He held his hand up and as he spoke, he said, "I am so thankful to be here in this place with this group of people and with Ron and Kathy, whom I call my friends. It was their love that helped break down the wall I had allowed hate and bitterness to build in my heart. I know this church is blessed indeed to have them here serving Christ together with you. As long as I live, I will never forget what they did for me. Thank you so much for this wonderful night."

The people clapped again and this time Joe got up and asked if he could say something. "About a year ago, Bill came back after his sister's death with two dogs, and the next thing I know he started acting funny. He stopped drinking and he started showing up to work on time. Everyone was laughing. But in all honesty, I saw Bill Thomas let go of the hate and bitterness he spoke about, and it made me start thinking maybe there was something to this church stuff. So, I came and well, I found out there is something to it, and it's real."

Again the clapping with people standing. Then out of the back, a tall woman with clear hazel eyes. "I don't know where to began. All I know is that Bill Thomas helped me when no one else would have, and now for the first time in my life, I am living without being afraid of someone finding out about my past. After talking with Rev. Ron, I found out Christ had paid the price for my sins, my past has been washed away, and Sherman and I have never been happier in our married life. Mr. Thomas, I don't know who that lady was who called me on the phone. But I think she must know you, so somewhere you have some very good and dear friends who love you."

"Thank you," Bill said. He knew he needed to get the floor back before Louise Hayes said Maggie's name. "I am blessed," Bill said, "with a loving wife, and with a church family that I will always call home."

Everyone stood and Ron started singing, "*We are blessed, We are blessed.*" The food and fellowship was great. Ron walked up to Bill and hugged him around the neck, "I know you are going where God wants you, but please know I count you among my dearest friends and I am going to miss you terribly."

Bill and Paula stood at the back of the fellowship hall as everyone walked by to say their farewells. Kathy and Ron came up to them, both hugged them and said, "If there is ever anything we can do to help you two, please don't hesitate to ask."

"We won't, but" Bill said, "now, I am looking for you two to come up to the mountains to visit us. I will…"

"We won't take, no, for an answer," Paula chimed in.

As they lay in bed that night, Paula asked Bill if he thought it was always going to be like this. "What do you mean?"

"Well, you know, so wonderful."

"With you, my dear, it couldn't help but be anything but."

DJ and Maggie were lying on the floor by the bed, when Paula called his name. "Yes," DJ answered.

"Thank you and Maggie for helping to make tonight such a wonderful experience for the both of us."

"We didn't do anything. All we did was not tell either of you what we knew." "Exactly, and that made tonight such a wonderful time for us. Thank you both." Maggie moved over closer to DJ, "See love, everyone knows you have your moments."

Bill and Paula started laughing, then DJ and Maggie joined right in. "Ok, everyone," Bill said, "we have to get up early in the morning, the movers will be here at seven and we are leaving soon after them, so let's get some sleep."

Chapter Sixteen

The Unexpected

It was getting dark. Now light were flashing all around, the smell of gas and wreckage filled the air. Bill laid unconscious on the stretcher. Paula sat over by the ambulance holding a rag up to her head. "Just sit still," the ambulance driver told her, "we're going to get you two to the hospital in just a little bit, we're waiting for the helicopter to fly your husband out."

Paula tried to stand but she couldn't. "Now hold on lady. You need to sit here and be still."

"Where are our dogs? We had two dogs in the car with us! Where are they? Their names are DJ and Maggie, *please* look for them, I can't leave without them." As Paula tried to stand, she fell unconscious to the ground. The EMT said, "We can't wait! We need to get her to the hospital now! Two men in uniforms put Paula onto a stretcher, loaded her into an ambulance, and drove off with lights flashing and a loud, eerie siren screaming. Only a second or so later, the helicopter landed to pick Bill up and it took off with him.

Over in the cover of some bushes, DJ and Maggie stood watching everything unfold. "DJ, what are we going to do? Where are they taking them? Maybe we should go out and let them find us so when Bill and Paula get out of the hospital, they can come and take us home."

"And if they don't make it, then what, Maggie? We could be separated, or worse, they could put us down because no one wanted us."

Maggie was crying and shaking uncontrollably now, "Oh DJ, why did we detour and come this way?"

"Because Dr. Pittman asked Bill to stop and pick up some books for the university, and now the books are lost, and so are we."

"What are we going to do?" Maggie was so afraid, she had never been away from her owner before.

"We are going to go back into the city. If Bill and Paula pull through this, they will come looking for us."

"How will we live DJ? We don't know anything about living on the streets of a city."

"God will take care of us love, but that is where we must go. That is where we are being called to go."

So, broken hearted, the two little guardians turned away from the security of the home they had, to the streets of a city. However, even then they didn't know their steps were being guided, for in the city was a task, which needed their careful, loving touch.

Printed in the United States
142457LV00001B/197/P

9 781434 376633